PRAISE FOR
GODS OF THE GARDEN:

"This enlightening and engaging narrative allows its reader to gain a fresh perspective on human existence. With a steady tempo that glides effortlessly to the end, Robin Strong evokes varied emotions in the reader through the novel's characters and description. *Gods of the Garden* is a well-written and thought-provoking novel that will resonate well with young people figuring themselves out."

—Raya Darling, The Independent Book Review

"Two realities intertwine in this vibrant novel that will surely capture an audience. With powerful cinematic possibilities, *Gods of the Garden* features swift scene changes, teen torments, the mysteries of VR technology, and even a small sliver of romance. So compelling is Lucy's story that readers will eagerly await for the sequel."

— Barbara Bamberger, Feathered Quill

"Robin Strong poses interesting questions in this coming-of-age story. The characters are layered and complex as they face moral struggles. Lucy and Ian go through contrasting character arcs, making their dynamic all the more compelling to read."

—Pikasho Deka, Readers' Favorite

GODS

OF THE

GARDEN

ROBIN STRONG

Contact info: www.robinstrongbooks.com

Cover design: GetCovers
Author photo: That Maya Girl Photography

ISBN: 978-0-9862317-6-6 (hardcover) 978-0-9862317-7-3 (paperback) 978-09862317-8-0 (ebook)

Published in the United States, October 2022.

This book is dedicated to Ruth. With one simple phone call, you made a twelve-year-old kid believe she had something meaningful to say.

*"Power tends to corrupt,
and absolute power corrupts absolutely."*

JOHN EDWARD ACTON

IAN'S NOTES

TUESDAY, AUG. 2

IN THE BEGINNING, *there was only me.*

After months of tweaking and planning, I stood on the beach of a virtual world, feeling my lungs inhale the salty sea air for the first time. Every inch of sand under my feet, the humidity that kissed my skin, and the subtle scent of wildflowers that filled my nostrils were all created by my own hand.

It didn't matter that this reality was artificial. I had found a way to trick the brain into believing it was genuine. It felt as real as the world I lived in.

And also just as lonely.

CHAPTER 1
DEFINING MOMENTS

A SINGLE DECISION can define you, whether you like it or not. For as long as I can remember, I was the golden child. Lucy Fernández was a name on the honor roll, not detention slips. But after one impulsive decision in fourth grade, my perfect reputation was in danger of being ruined. And no matter how brief or justified the moment, I would spend the next eight years trying to prove that blip of rebellion was a fluke and not an identity.

At the time, I had no idea what I was about to do. All I remember was looking up from my tuna sandwich as Garrett Floyd—one of the most annoying kids at school—shoved the new kid to the ground.

The boy was so helpless. His wavy blonde hair was wild and free, but the expression on his face was tightly bound. With his shoulders tugged forward and his knees against his chest, he made himself small by pulling inward—a protective instinct, I'm sure. It was clear he had done this dance before.

Meanwhile, Garrett continued to taunt him. "Nice underwear! Couldn't your parents afford pants *without* holes in them?"

Everyone thought Garrett was an ass. There were probably things going on at home that would account for his bad behavior.

But back then, in my nine-year-old mind, he was the villain. And even though he didn't have any real friends, he had a gang of loyal followers who believed being on his side was safer than defying him.

The new kid had no one. It was his first day at school. His family had moved in across the street from me over the weekend. His tall, lanky body should have made him appear older than the rest of our class, but everything about his demeanor made him look younger. He was a tree that had grown too fast—the roots were too shallow. A quick breeze could blow him over with little effort. And in fourth grade, when we were all trying our best to stand out, there were plenty of winds trying to knock others down.

With every insult thrown the boy's way, the smaller he tried to make himself. It was like he wanted to disappear. As he moved to his knees, he awkwardly tugged on his faded blue sweats that seemed both too small and too big for his long, skinny legs. He twisted the fabric, trying to conceal the hole Garrett had so painfully exposed to the whole lunchroom.

It took only three seconds to see how powerless he was, and I couldn't stop myself from trying to save him.

"Leave him alone, you turd!"

I was surprised by the volume of my voice. It wasn't like me to yell. I was the girl who raised her hand in class—the one with perfect grades and dozens of awards on her bedroom shelf. I didn't participate in playground politics. Sure, I'd witnessed my fair share of recess scuffles in my five years at Paradise Elementary School. But I usually had no problem averting my eyes and pretending the injustices weren't there. Taking a stand was too messy—too disruptive. And that wasn't me.

Yet, here I was, inserting myself into the drama.

Garrett flipped around to see who dared question his authority as the class bully. "Or what?" He puffed his chest while his eyes zoned in on me. "I'm not afraid of some *girl*."

Wrong move, Garrett. There was always a little voice in my head, and it usually sounded like my mom. She was the one encouraging me to be my best. She also instilled a deep sense of justice within me. It makes sense—she is a lawyer, after all. Mom was a force you never dared fight. And for a brief moment, I felt strong like her. Before I knew what I was doing, the jarring push-back from Garrett's bulky body ricocheted through my arms as I knocked him over.

"Leave him alone, or I'll kick you so hard there will be a hole in *your* pants!"

I'll never forget the look on his face. Nobody dared stand up to Garrett—especially not a girl like me. Mouth ajar and eyes wide open, he considered his next move. Run or fight? Run or fight? I don't think I've ever been more relieved than when he stood up and walked away with a huff.

"Don't worry about him," I said as I helped the new kid off the ground. "Nobody likes Garrett. He's a jerk."

"Uh, thanks." He brushed some crumbs off his pants before straightening himself up. He towered over me.

"I'm Lucy," I said with a smile.

"Ian." He nodded carefully.

"Want to sit with me at lunch?"

Life is a frenzy of mistakes. It is the only way to learn, I guess. No matter how many times someone tells you a stove is hot, sometimes you have to feel for yourself. But in my house, mistakes were not okay. If Mom said the stove was hot, you believed her and stayed as far away from it as possible. Because of this, I often found myself in a mental tornado trying to determine the actions that would best live up to my mom's expectations.

That's why my impulsive decision to help Ian those many years ago was so surprising. I didn't think—only acted. Still, helping Ian never felt wrong. I'd like to think I'd do it again if given a chance. For the rest of elementary school, Ian and I ate lunch side by side. We played together at recess and after school. Ian wasn't just my neighbor—he was my best friend, my confidant. Standing up to Garrett forged a relationship that seemed unbreakable at the time.

Of course, Mom saw it differently. She got a phone call that same day from Principal Bona. Both Garrett and I were sent to her office to be reminded that violence was never okay. That only made matters worse. Mom disliked Garrett, and the idea of her daughter being lumped with him was too much. She was determined to make sure it never happened again. In her eyes, I had messed up—big time.

"I can't believe my little angel would do something so awful!" Mom's ruby lips pursed in disappointment. "You're lucky your dad is out of town."

As a pilot, my dad was often away. And maybe that is why she only said it when he was gone. The threat never carried any weight. Even if Dad were home, he was a teddy bear compared to her, and she knew it. He was her scapegoat—a way to soften some of her sharpness. Still, her disappointment pierced me. I'm sure she never intended to hurt me with her words. In her mind, she was carving me into the perfect daughter—a shining example. But a knife is a knife. You can't sculpt a masterpiece without making some deep cuts.

Despite the gnawing sensation in my gut at my mom's discontented scowl, I tried to hold my ground. The justice inside of me was stubborn. Even as a nine-year-old, I knew I had made the right call.

"But he was being bullied!" I stomped my foot and tried to lock my eyes on hers, but Mom's gaze was too powerful. With her authority hovering over me, my heroic moment sunk into a pit of shame. It had become a stain on my otherwise perfect record. I was marked. And every decision that came after that fateful moment was carefully calculated in an attempt to erase that original sin.

While Mom never stopped me from being friends with Ian, she kept her eyes on us. She liked that Ian was brilliant. She hoped that his knack for science and technology might round out my own academic skills. But his social awkwardness and lack of parental involvement proved too much of a risk. By the time I hit middle school, she had taken every opportunity to make sure I was hanging out with *the right crowd*—her words, not mine.

So over the years, Ian and I grew apart. By sixth grade, we ate at different lunch tables. Hanging out became increasingly infrequent. When we entered high school, any signs of our once strong bond were gone. What started as a firm friendship slowly strained into a distant acquaintance.

I had plenty of other friends, so I didn't mind much. But Ian wasn't so lucky. He faded into the background, trying to avoid the Garretts of the world as he fiddled with his gadgets at home. Nobody knew about his witty sense of humor or genius inventions. To everyone else, he was a gawky, acne-prone kid with a penchant for slacking off. But I knew the real Ian. And whenever I passed him in the hallway or bumped into him at the mailbox, his eyes would light up with a smile. Like me, he never forgot our time together. To him, I would always be the girl who gave him a chance when nobody else did.

And because of that, he loved me for a long time.

IAN'S NOTES
SUNDAY, AUG 7

Every time I take the VR headset off, my mind needs a solid ten seconds to reorient itself. I always feel a tiny bit dizzy coming back to my bedroom. What's fascinating, however, is that I don't have the same problem plugging into the program. The transition into the virtual world is always instant and euphoric, as if the mind knows my version of life is better than the real one.

CHAPTER 2
GREAT EXPECTATIONS

"A REPUTATION IS no small thing to sacrifice."

I rolled my eyes as I stared at the eggs on my plate. I had heard this speech a thousand times before. It was the first day of school—my senior year. And at seventeen years old, you'd think Mom would finally realize these lectures weren't necessary. I had followed the path she paved for me: Straight As, lots of friends, and a long list of extracurriculars. I had built a name for myself. But here we were, repeating the same old conversation.

"All I'm saying is people expect a lot from you, honey."

I ventured a glance toward Mom, but her intrusive gaze forced me to retreat back into my breakfast. "I know, Mom. Sheesh." My tone was a little sassier than I intended. But it was too late to take it back.

"Lucy Fernández, show some respect."

I hated it when she used my full name like that. I could always tell when she was angry as the subtle hints of a Spanish accent punctuated her words. Both my parents were children of immigrants. Dad loved infusing bits of his Mexican heritage into our home. Mom—not so much. Her childhood was marked with relentless teasing during school, enough to make her shed anything that made her unique. She perfected her English all on her own, working tirelessly to sound like the other kids at school. But when her emotions were near the surface, the small remnants of another life poked through.

Mom opened the blinds, filling the kitchen with a warm glow. "College applications are due soon. Are you giving up on the plan? On MIT?"

I scraped the last bit of food off my plate, trying to breathe quietly. "That's not what I said. Please stop twisting my words."

The whirring of the coffee machine stopped. Mom waltzed across the kitchen and poured herself a cup. She sipped while her eyes slowly scanned me. "Is that what you're wearing today?"

"What's wrong with it?" I asked, admiring my faded green t-shirt and favorite pair of jeans. It was comfortable and no-nonsense—my ideal outfit. Gulping the final swig of orange juice, I begged the clock to tick faster. As usual, there was plenty of time to spare.

Her eyebrows lifted as she shrugged, revealing the judgment in her eyes. "I was just wondering. I always loved wearing something new on the first day of school."

I took a bite of toast, suddenly self-conscious about my clothes. My mom—the lawyer with the unbeatable track record —was the very image of success. Her salon-styled hair, perfectly red lips, and black power suit muted my simple ponytail and makeup-free complexion.

Mom took another sip of coffee, returning to the matter at hand. "All I'm saying is if MIT is the goal, I think TechEd is non-negotiable."

I tapped my fork against the plate and took a deep breath. "And all I said was *maybe* I didn't need to do TechEd this year. Maybe I've done enough. My GPA, test scores—isn't it enough?"

Mom's expression dropped as if she finally recognized my frustration. She walked over and placed her hand on my shoulder. "You have done a lot, sweetie. I'm proud of you, but I thought you'd be eager to redeem yourself after last year."

"Redeem myself?" I scoffed. "Come on, Mom. I was the first junior ever to win the regional competition, and I came in third place at State. I didn't fail."

"Of course not. But third place doesn't get you to Nationals. The TechEd Tournament is one of the most prestigious STEM competitions, but the big schools don't care unless you compete at the national level."

I vividly remembered the heavy disappointment that lingered long after reading the judges' comments at the Arizona Finals last year: *Flawless research. Impressive presentation. Technology is lacking.*

I got up and rinsed my plate before putting it in the dishwasher. Lacking. Always lacking. My cheeks got hot. Thinking about last year's competition made me all twisted inside. Of course, I couldn't let my mom see that. I needed to keep my emotions in check. But I was mad. And the worst part was that I wasn't sure if I was angry at my mom for always downplaying my accomplishments or myself for tripping at the finish line.

"I'd like to compete again. I would." I slumped back into my chair. "But I haven't been able to think of a good idea. And I'd feel so stupid if I came up short again."

Mom walked over and smoothed back a misplaced hair on my head. "You are anything but stupid, hun. Put your mind to it, and you'll think of something brilliant."

Of course, a brilliant idea would solve my problems. But no matter how hard I tried, I kept coming up short. The competition was stiff. And as much as I hated admitting it, I wasn't sure I had the talent the tournament required. All of my success came from hard work and knowing how to play the game that is high school. I may have been above average in intelligence, but I wasn't anything remarkable.

Mom tapped her watch. "Oh, I gotta run!" She kissed me on the forehead. "Have a great first day. This is your year!"

I leaned back in my chair. My thoughts drifted as I gently fiddled with the small sunflower charm around my neck—a gift from my abuela for my quinceañera. I'd give anything to talk to her right now. Compared to my mother's torrid storm of perfection, Abuelita was like a ray of sunshine. Ever since she passed away last year, I found myself wishing I could spend one more afternoon in her garden. I pressed my thumb against the golden flower, trying to siphon some of Lita's warmth from my memories of her.

Meanwhile, my mom's words played on repeat. *Are you giving up on the plan? On MIT?* Mom was right. MIT had been my dream since I was ten. And the TechEd Tournament was the surest path there. It would be the last of a long line of accomplishments. But when your whole life is built on achievement, it is easy to wonder what would happen if you didn't win the final one. For all the awards and recognition attached to my name, I was terrified that none of it mattered if I didn't earn this final prize. MIT was more than the college of my choice. It was my salvation.

Or at least I hoped it was.

"Almost forgot my keys!" Mom rushed back into the kitchen. She stopped, squeezing my shoulder. "Chin up, girl. As I said, you've built yourself an impressive reputation. You've got this. Everyone loves you."

Sure, Mom, everyone loves me. Everyone, it seemed, except me.

"Hey, Luce!"

Across the street, Ian was leaving his house. I couldn't even remember the last time we talked. While he was still as tall as ever, he had put on some weight since we last spoke, making his thin frame not quite as fragile.

I smiled and waved. "Hey, Ian!"

His eyes lit up as he threw back his shaggy blonde hair from his face. I stopped and waited for him to cross the street. It was a tiny sprint, but he was already out of breath when he reached me.

"Senior year," he said, nearly gasping. "Crazy, huh?"

"Very weird." With a long sigh, I tried to fill the awkward silence. "So, how was your summer? I haven't seen you around much." I tried to sound sincere, even though I was responsible for the lack of connection over the years.

"Good," Ian said, shoving his hands into his pockets. "Been working on something cool—something big."

I nudged him in the ribs. "That sounds secretive. You're not causing any trouble, are you?"

He blushed. "Who me? *Never.*"

"Oh yeah? What about the summer after fifth grade when you took apart your parents' computer to build your own? Or eighth grade when you hacked the school's PA system, and the principal couldn't figure out who was advertising free hugs in the teacher's lounge during morning announcements?"

"Ha! I forgot about that," Ian said with a laugh. He seemed pleased that I had remembered these little antics of his. Of course, nobody else was privy to his harmless pranks because Ian wasn't just smart enough to pull it off—he was smart enough to get away with it. I guess it was one of the few perks of being practically invisible.

As we neared the school, I instinctively slowed my pace, hoping to avoid being seen with Ian. "So, tell me about this secret project."

"Not a secret," Ian said. "I was actually hoping to show it to you." He flashed his trademark grin, and I was surprised how much I had missed it. I could see a crowd of students outside the school. I stopped and faced Ian, turning my back toward them.

"Why don't you come by after school," he said.

"Come by?" I was surprised by his invitation. It had been years since I had been inside Ian's house. "Uh, sure... Yeah. Why not?" I wasn't trying to sound hesitant, but I couldn't help myself. As much as I respected Ian, most people would think it was weird if I was hanging out with him. Besides, I had too many other things to do, like finding a winning idea for TechEd.

Ian could read my reluctance. "No pressure. I know you're busy. But I think you might like it. It won't take long, promise."

I smiled, trying not to blow him off without committing myself to anything.

Ian could tell we needed a subject change. "So, what classes do you have this semester? Any good ones?"

"Hopefully," I said, thankful for the segue. "First period I have AP English with Chavis—who I've heard is hilarious. Then AP Computer Science, AP Calc, and AP Chemistry with Gunn."

Ian interrupted. "Sheesh. Your schedule is making me sad. Ever heard of going easy senior year?"

I ignored him. "After lunch, I have Lit Mag..."

"That's right, Madam Editor!" Ian gave a slight bow.

I laughed. "Why, thank you. After that, I have AP Spanish, and then..." I pulled out my schedule to remind me of my last class. "Ah, yes, Cultural Anthropology."

"With Howell?" Ian perked up.

"Yeah. Have you had her before?"

"Nope, but guess who also has Howell for seventh." Ian's voice was giddy.

I tried to match his enthusiasm but failed. "No way! After, like, what? Five years? We finally have a class together." I'm not sure why the news bothered me. I didn't hate Ian. For a couple of years, he was my best friend. But even though I still cared about him, people expected me to be a certain way—hang out with certain people. And I know how bad that sounds. The guilt was piling on thick, and my suffocating conscience told me to treat Ian like the good person he was. "I've heard Howell's class is *hard*," I finally said.

"Eh, I wouldn't worry too much about it. All the teachers love you. They probably have a shrine of you inside the teacher's lounge. Besides, you're like the smartest person at school. Well, except for me," Ian joked.

I laughed. But it was true. While I was Orchard High's star student, Ian was the real prodigy. He was everything I wanted to be: Innovative, gifted—*brilliant*. Had Ian applied himself even a little, I had no doubt colleges would be knocking on his door, paying him to attend. But he didn't put in the work. He was barely passing his classes. Like me, Ian had a reputation. Unlike me, it wasn't great.

"But seriously," Ian said. "Don't stress about Howell's class. You've got this. MIT, baby!"

I couldn't believe he remembered. The first time I learned about MIT was in fifth grade. I was utterly mesmerized after watching a video on YouTube about their robotics lab. Unfortunately, science and math were my most challenging subjects, but I didn't care. Since I was ten, I had wanted to attend that school, and Ian always believed I would make it. Hearing him cheer me on again made me realize it might be time to polish our rusty friendship. It was our senior year, after all. Football season, Fall Ball, yearbook signing—every milestone would be the last.

We stopped in front of the school. Ian pointed to a growing group of kids behind us who were waving at me. Ian shrugged. "I don't want to keep you from your friends. But the invitation stands. I'd love you to come over and see what I've been working on." He cocked his head back as if to say *goodbye*. "Have a great year, Luce." He quietly ducked away to his first class.

His invitation sparked my curiosity. It had been years since he shared one of his projects with me, which made me think whatever he was working on had to be big. I wondered if spending more time with Ian would make his genius rub off on me. And considering how hopeless I felt about TechEd, I was willing to do almost anything to feel even a little extraordinary.

IAN'S NOTES
MONDAY, AUG. 15

Hundreds of thousands of lines of code were necessary to get the details right. I crafted the texture of the rocks, shaped the patterns of the winds, and mimicked the sweet taste of fruit on the trees. All that work created a virtual reality that perfectly matched the one outside my window.

But I can't quite get the people right. Even after trying several algorithms, the results are always disappointing. The people come off as robotic and predictable.

Of course, I'll keep at it. Because if I can master artificial intelligence the way I've conquered the environment, there won't be much to tempt me from ever leaving this new world.

CHAPTER 3
IAN'S WORLD

LUCY FERNÁNDEZ FOREVER CHANGED ME.

The day she pushed Garrett Floyd was the first time someone stood up for me. Me—the awkward kid with no friends. My parents didn't have much money when I was younger. With so many mouths to feed, I guess it made sense that a new pair of pants would be low on the priority list. Hell, *I* was low on their priority list. Still, had I known there was a hole in the butt of those dusty blue sweats, I would have worn something else. Things might have turned out differently. Probably not.

Lucy's act of bravery didn't change my social status. I was never destined for popularity or teachers' praise. But a tiny seed of self-worth took root when she pulled me off the ground. She laughed at my jokes and marveled at my geeky ideas, making me visible for the first time.

Even as the years went on and our friendship faded, buried deep inside me was a belief that if Lucy Fernández had been my friend, there had to be something special about me. And while that fact wasn't enough to motivate me to try harder at school or worry about wearing the right kind of clothes—it fed my ego enough. So I kept doing things that made me stand out, even if nobody else noticed. Because with the right idea, Lucy would.

I was confident *The Garden* would grab her attention. And I patiently waited, hoping she'd be curious enough to check it out. Because if she did, she might never want to leave.

"Jane! Can you turn your stupid music down?" I shouted from my desk.

My house was perpetually loud. I tried to block the jarring bass pulsating from my sister's room before her tiny seven-year-old voice yelled back.

"I'm practicing for dance class, Ian!"

Not to be outdone by my sister's repetitive pop mix, my little brother Blake joined the discord with an epic tantrum right when Izzie began banging on the piano downstairs. Even with my oldest two brothers gone for college, my four younger siblings were hell-bent on ensuring I never had a quiet moment.

Pulling down on my noise-canceling headphones, I peered through the window toward Lucy's house. As an only child, she never had to battle the assaulting noises of dueling siblings as they vied for attention. My brothers and sisters were young enough to think that the louder they were, the more my parents would notice them. It didn't work that way. I remember lashing out as a kid, hoping Mom and Dad would see me. All they ever did was send me to my room. So, I hunkered into the solitude, working to create a better escape from the tumultuous world around me.

Finally, the music stopped—just in time for me to hear Mom knocking on my door.

"Come in," I said. My eyes were glued to my monitor as the door creaked open. School had only been out for an hour, but I was knee-deep in programming mode. "What do you need, Mom? I'm kinda busy."

"Too busy to share your secrets?"

I froze at the sound of Lucy's voice. I swiveled around as she nervously stood in the doorway.

"Luce! You came!"

Jumping to my feet, I could tell my excitement was disarming as she stepped back. I tried to rein in my enthusiasm, which was easy once I remembered where I was—the house of chaos. My messy room served as a "stay out" sign. Scattered on the floor were mini screwdrivers, a can of compressed air, and a small soldering kit. Crumbs, empty soda cans, and piles of notes cluttered my desk. The closet door was slightly ajar, showcasing cables, tools, and gadgets. I was a damn slob.

Lucy smiled weakly, twiddling the charm of her necklace between her finger and thumb. She was clearly uncomfortable, which made me more anxious. I needed to get my shit together. I wasn't about to waste this opportunity acting like a loser.

Picking up a black VR headset charging near my bed, I smiled. "Are you ready?" She nodded, and I walked over and placed the goggles on her head, adjusting the straps until it was snug.

"I'm not really a VR person," Lucy said as if regretting her decision to come over.

"Trust me. It is not what you think." I pressed a small, dime-sized disk behind her ear.

She flinched. "Ouch. What was that?"

"Sorry, the sting goes away fast. Promise."

"Wait, what are you doing to me?"

"Nothing dangerous, I swear." I plopped back down on my chair, peeking over my shoulder every two seconds. Lucy nervously crossed her arms. With every second, she grew more despondent, but I tried to ignore it as my heart raced on. "Ready?"

She shrugged. "Yeah, I guess."

I turned back to my computer. After a quick *tap, tap, tap* of the keyboard, I spun around as Lucy's body went motionless. I pushed my chair out of the way, reached for my second VR headset, and strapped in. There was no way I was going to let her experience this moment without me.

It must have been the hundredth time I had plugged into my virtual world. I didn't care. The beach and lush vegetation behind it always took my breath away. A vibrant, orange sky contrasted the ocean's blue horizon. The sound of seagulls drifted overhead while gentle waves swept across the sand. The only thing more beautiful than the world surrounding me was the sight of Lucy, silhouetted against the setting sun.

"Welcome to *The Garden*," I said as I walked up to her.

Lucy turned around, stunned. "Ian? Is that you?"

"Freaky, right?" I laughed as her eyes scanned my avatar. I still sounded like me, but instead of my gangly body and ruddy skin, I had programmed myself as a perfect ten. Chiseled jawline, broad shoulders, and toned muscles that pressed against my white t-shirt and jeans gave me an almost super-hero quality. I smiled at Lucy. "In here, you can be whatever you want."

With a sly smile, Lucy eyed me up and down. The hair on my arms raised as my stomach flip-flopped. I had waited years for her to look at me like that. But as soon as Lucy realized she was gawking, she turned back toward the ocean. "You look... *fine*." She laughed, shaking her head. "So when can I create my alter-ego?"

"Like you need one," I said quietly. Lucy turned back as if she didn't quite hear me. I cleared my throat, hoping she didn't. "You can create your own avatar if you want, but I already programmed a pretty accurate representation of you."

She glanced down at her body. Brown shoulder-length hair,

olive skin, her faded jeans. I even remembered to add the sunflower necklace she wore every day. Her eyes locked back on mine. "Wow, you're right. It's me." The tone of her voice caught me off guard. It suddenly occurred to me how creepy her pre-made avatar might come across—an obvious sign of my obsession. *Idiot.*

"So, what do you think?" I asked as I gestured to our surroundings, hoping to move on.

"I—" Lucy paused, drinking in the world around her as her posture relaxed. "I think this is incredible, Ian." She pointed toward a set of rugged cliffs in the distance. "Is that a waterfall? And the grove of trees behind it? Stunning." She turned toward the other end of the beach, where giant boulders stood tall against the rising tide. "I mean, I can't even believe it."

Lucy was gushing, and I was in heaven.

"I've worn VR goggles before," she said. "But this is different. I am utterly transported. It's all so... *real.* I smell the salty air and feel the humidity on my skin. Every sense inside my body is engaged." She knelt and grabbed a fistful of sand before letting it fall between her fingertips. "How is this working? This shouldn't be possible. Am I even in your room anymore?"

"You're still in sunny Arizona with me. Promise. Remember that small disk behind your ear? The one that came with a little pinch when I attached it?"

"A little pinch!" Lucy chuckled, rubbing the back of her neck. "I thought you were poking me with a hundred tiny needles."

"Well," I said, "I call it the Reality Amplifier. I've been working on it for a couple of years. It sends a signal that triggers the sensory parts of the brain, mimicking all your senses. You can smell and feel things that you normally couldn't in a typical VR setup. Pretty cool, right?"

"Uh, *extremely* cool," Lucy said emphatically. She turned

around and pointed past the sand dunes in the distance. "What's back there? Is that a garden?"

"Yep. Trees and grass and flowers for miles past the dunes."

Lucy perked up. Her reaction made me so damn happy, as I could tell the experience hypnotized her. My world was addictive —dangerously enticing. "I want to see it all," she said, ready to run. She stopped herself. "Wait. How close am I to your bed? Am I going to hit a wall?" Her spine stiffened, and her hands moved toward her head before she disappeared.

"Luce, wait!" I took off my headset.

A familiar rush of vertigo hit me as I reoriented to my bedroom. Lucy was bracing herself against my desk. "Whoa, trippy," she said.

I helped her back to her feet. "Yeah, I should have warned you. The transition back can be rough. You get used to it after a while, but the first time can be a little shocking."

Lucy rubbed her eyes and took a deep breath. "Sorry for the quick exit. I got so nervous I was going to run into something."

"No worries. I understand," I said. "But with my setup, you can walk, run, and dance inside the program without the real world ever getting in the way."

Her eyes sparkled. "How?"

"The Reality Amplifier."

Lucy chuckled. "Pinchy."

I laughed. "Well, all body movements begin in the brain, right? Before you take a step, the mind has to process where you want to go, the forces you intend to apply, and other neuromuscular triggers that let you interact with the world." I took a deep breath, hoping I wasn't losing her. "Pinchy taps into the brain and high-jacks those intentions. It takes over, giving you the sensation of using your body while simultaneously stopping the motor reflexes from taking action."

"Ian, you're a genius." Lucy gently punched my arm.

I gestured for her to put the headset back on. "Want to go back?" She smiled, and we both plugged in.

The change was instantaneous. Lucy and I stood silent as the waves crashed against the shore. I rolled up my pants and walked toward the edge of the sand. I sat down, letting the incoming tide gently lap my toes. Lucy joined me. "Why did you build this?" she said quietly. "What do you plan on doing with it?"

I shrugged. "I wanted a space that made me happy. Somewhere quiet and safe. Something that was mine." Lucy's eyes were stuck on me, and I swear my smile would permanently freeze my face. I turned back and gestured toward the garden beyond the dunes. "I've planned to create an actual civilization over there—a little village of sorts."

Her eyes lit up. "With people?"

"I mean, sorta. More like artificial intelligence in digitized human form, but yeah."

"What for?"

"I don't know, exactly." I wiped the sweat from my hands on my pants. "It can be lonely in here. I thought adding some artificial life to the mix would be fun. However, the simulated people thing is challenging. So, for now, it is just me. Well, me and now you."

Lucy shook her head. "You do realize most kids our age can't go around making their own worlds, right?"

I smiled as I laid back, tucking my arms under my head. I wanted to look chill—to make her think I was cool like her friends at school. Neither of us believed it. But it didn't matter. My world pleased Lucy, so I was good.

Finally, she broke the silence. "How do you do it?"

I sat up, trying to interpret the tone of her voice. "Do what? Code the world? Or are you asking about the Reality Amplifier?"

"No, I mean..." With a heaviness in her voice, Lucy sighed. "How did you come up with the idea? I've been busting my brains all summer trying to develop something for the TechEd Tournament and have nothing to show for it. And here you are, tinkering in your room and creating a masterpiece. How do you do it?"

I turned to face her. "The TechEd Tournament—the national STEM competition you won last year, right?"

Lucy shook her head. "Wrong. I didn't win."

"Oh? I thought you did."

"I won Regionals but then choked at State, coming in third."

I laughed. "Yeah, you're right. Third place is *so horrible.*" My sarcasm struck a chord as Lucy blinked back tears.

"Third place sucks when it means you don't move on to Nationals," she said. "If I want to get into MIT, I need to make it to Nationals. And *that* means I need a project that will blow the judges away. But unlike you, brilliant ideas don't come easily."

I didn't know how to respond.

"Sorry. Didn't mean to dump this on you. I'm just a little jealous of your mind," she said with a half-smile.

My eyes bounced between Lucy and the horizon. I opened my mouth every couple of seconds, trying to find something profound to say. With a soft sigh, I finally got straight to the point. "Then make this your project."

"Make what?" She raised her eyebrows. "This VR world? Are you crazy?"

Ouch.

She read my face and quickly backtracked. "What I mean is —this is *your* thing. I'm guessing you've spent hundreds of hours working on it."

"Thousands." I smiled.

She chuckled. "Right. *Thousands* of hours. Which is why I can't pretend your project is mine."

Shit. I wasn't suggesting that. "I didn't think you'd do it alone." A lump hit my throat. "I thought we could do it together."

"Together?"

"Yeah, together." The panicked expression on Lucy's face made my heart pick up its pace. I didn't want to scare her away, but how great would it be if we worked together? I summoned my most persuasive voice. "With my tech and your scholastic brilliance, we could use this virtual program for the competition. We could be partners." Waiting for Lucy's response felt like an eternity. Finally, her hands moved toward her head, and she disappeared.

I followed her lead and took off my headset, bracing myself as I grounded back into reality. Apparently, Lucy thought this conversation needed to happen in the real world. She sat down on my bed. "I'm not sure, Ian."

"Why?" I placed my VR goggles on my desk. "Weren't you just telling me you need a big idea? A big *tech* idea for the competition? You don't think this is big enough?"

"No. What you've built is incredible—*truly* amazing." She placed a hand on my knee, and my heart raced.

"So, what's the problem?"

Lucy stood up. "Well, for starters, the projects are supposed to have an educational element. What you've built is a lovely escape from reality, but I don't see how it is relevant to the focus of the competition."

I furrowed my brow. "That's where you'd come in. Think of this world as a blank canvas for you to build something educational. I have no doubt you could do it. And together we can program it inside *The Garden*. We'd be teammates."

Lucy bit her lip, clearly holding back her thoughts. She sighed as she sat back down next to me. "Do you even want to compete? It is a lot of work. Plenty of paperwork, rules, deadlines—"

"—expectations?" I said.

"Yeah, lots of expectations."

"And let me guess." My voice lowered as her hidden truth became apparent. "You don't think I'll follow through. You're worried I'll ruin your perfect reputation."

"No." Lucy froze. "I'm sorry if you took it that way. But, come on, you don't have the best record. You're barely on track to graduate. This project will require a lot of time and work, especially considering how soon Regionals are."

I walked over to my desk and powered down my laptop before shutting the lid. My slumped shoulders pulled me into my chair. "You're right. Of course, you're right. When it comes to school, I don't prioritize things the way you do. I guess I don't see why it matters. But tell me, truthfully, something else is holding you back."

Lucy stood up and sighed. "I'm not sure this is something I want to do with someone else. I want to prove that I can do this on my own, you know?"

It felt like a half-truth.

"On your own or not with me?" I asked. Lucy closed her eyes, wiping away a single tear. I was gutted. "I get it, Luce. You've got an image to uphold, and I don't fit in with the picture you've created."

That's when the tears flowed. "I'm sorry," she said. "Everyone thinks I have my act together. The truth is, I'm losing control. Mom expects me to win TechEd. My dreams all hang on it. But I already have a million balls in the air—and I'm juggling to keep them up. I'm worried about who I'll disappoint if I drop any." She grabbed the box of tissues off my nightstand and blew her nose. "Most days, I don't even like my life."

I'm not a touchy-feely kind of guy. I don't like most people. But I loved Lucy, and I hated seeing her like this. "You've got a great life, Luce. You're amazing. Everyone thinks so."

"I don't," she said softly.

"Well..." I sighed. "If you didn't care so much about what other people think, you'd probably like your life a little better."

Lucy's expression hardened. The tears stopped immediately, leaving behind red, puffy eyes. "What did you say?"

Dammit, why couldn't I keep my mouth shut?

"Come on, Luce. You're the most impressive person I know, but sometimes you worry too much about other people's opinions. It can't be a great way to live."

"But slacking off and being a loner is?" She bit her lip as if she regretted the words, but they had already wounded me.

"No," I said quietly. "It isn't. I guess we both need a little help, which is all I want to do—help. I guess the real question is: Are you willing to trust me with your reputation?"

My noisy house muted into a deafening silence for the first time in forever. Sure, Jane was blasting music two rooms down, and Mom was yelling at Chad to set the table, but I couldn't hear any of it. My entire future hung on Lucy's response.

"Can I think about it?" Lucy said quietly.

Deflated, I hung my head. "Sure." I put on my headphones and opened my laptop. "Let's talk later. I got some things to do."

A part of me knew working together was a big ask. People would talk if she teamed up with the school freak. But I also knew what I was offering with *The Garden*. I was giving her my world, my *everything*. It was a surefire win. And Lucy would do practically anything to reach her dream of MIT.

Anything, apparently, except work with me.

MESSAGE FROM DAD

Mijita! I know it's late, but I wanted to see how your first day of school went. Can't believe you're a senior!

Thanks, Dad. It was okay. Weird meet up with Ian. I'll tell you more about that on Friday.

Oh, wow! I haven't heard Ian's name in a while. Anyway, I had a layover in Boston and thought about you. It won't be long until I'm flying there to see you at MIT next year!

Assuming they accept me. Let's not get ahead of ourselves.

Stop it. Since when do you not achieve whatever you put your mind to? Mom says you're going to crush it at TechEd this year.

Well, if Mom says so...

CHAPTER 4
THE ASSIGNMENT

AT LUNCH THE NEXT DAY, I sat with my friends at my go-to table. Ian was alone in the far corner of the lunchroom—just like every other day for the past three years. But it never bothered me until today. Guilt pricked me as I tried to stay focused on the surrounding conversation. The high energy of my group contrasted with Ian's defeated solitude.

Are you willing to trust me with your reputation?

Ian's words from yesterday repeated in my mind. I kept picturing his hurt expression when I confessed my concerns about working with him. I hated that I didn't jump at his offer, but how could I? The TechEd Tournament was the key to getting into MIT. It had always been my plan to compete alone.

But *why* was that the plan? I hated admitting Ian was right, but I *was* worried about what people would think of me if I teamed up with him. What if he didn't follow through—or worse—what if he *did*? If Ian suddenly stepped up his game and people realized he was the real winner, what did that make me? The thought demons were in full force as I questioned everything—my skills, sanity, integrity.

"Earth to Lucy!"

Jake Wittingham waved his hand right in front of my face. Jake was Orchard High's most eligible senior. He was a walking stereotype: Football captain, student body officer, and teenage heartthrob. Last year he always ate lunch with the most popular seniors, which was impressive for a junior. He took a seat at my table for the second day in a row. A few of my friends figured it was a sign that we had finally peaked.

I snapped out of my daze and caught Jake's eyes. "Jake! Sorry, I guess I zoned out for a minute. Lots on my mind."

"Were you staring at Ian Gibson? You're not secretly crushing on him, are you? Because you can definitely do better." The whole table laughed. His teasing was innocent enough, but that didn't stop my cheeks from turning red.

I laughed politely. "No, I wasn't looking at anyone—or anything in particular. I was thinking about a project I'm working on." As a horrible liar, I always tried to sneak by with half-truths.

"Project? For what?" Jake tossed a couple of chips in his mouth. He leaned back in his chair while keeping his focus on me. "Is this about that STEM thing you did last year? What's it called? Techno Something?"

"The TechEd Tournament," I said, surprised Jake was aware of it. "Yeah, I've got to submit my application by next week, and I'm still working out the details."

"Nah, that can't be it. You're always a million steps ahead of things. I think this is about Ian." He winked, clearly making a joke. Little did he know how spot-on he was. "Were you with him yesterday before school? Are you two friends?"

I straightened up like I was in an interview. "He lives across the street from me. We ran into each other on the way to school." I thought about the strange coincidence of bumping into Ian yesterday. He rarely walked to school.

Jake leaned forward as if turning the interview into a journalistic report. "Ian was in my chemistry class last year. Freaky genius type, right? I mean, he slept through half the lectures, but when he was awake? Jeez. The dude would say things that went over Mr. Freeman's head." Jake glanced over at Ian and paused. "But you gotta admit—he's *weird.*"

I quietly laughed to myself. "I've known Ian for a long time, but we haven't talked in years. He is a little unconventional. I'll give you that. But he's a nice guy." I peeked at Ian from the corner of my eye, wishing I could talk to him.

"If you say so." Jake smiled.

I knew Jake had a little crush on me. He had asked me out several times over the last two years, and I was always caught off guard when he did. Other girls would love his attention, but I wasn't interested in dating the way other teenagers were. My studies came first. Sometimes I wondered what was wrong with me because boys were often the last thing on my mind.

For the rest of lunch, I tried to ignore Ian and stayed focused on the conversations happening at my table. Jake reminded me of the upcoming football game and invited me to the post-game party. I asked about his classes and what teachers he liked. A couple of kids at the table interrupted with some first day of school stories—being in the wrong classroom, teachers wildly mispronouncing names—that sort of thing. I listened, thinking about my first day and epic meltdown at Ian's house, which sent my thoughts right back to TechEd.

I'm sure I wasn't giving Ian enough credit. What if his VR thing was my ticket to Nationals? Even if we weren't that close anymore, after eight years of living next door, couldn't I trust him? But as much as I didn't want to admit what was holding me back, Ian had hit the nail on the head yesterday. I didn't want to work with him.

"... and then Coach Barnes told me my problem was how I was catching the ball. Crazy, right?" Jake waited eagerly for a response.

Focus, Lucy. "Uh, wow. That's totally crazy," I said, trying to sound believable. I snuck another glance at Ian again. His blue eyes stared back at me. We both looked away.

"Alright, everyone, the first day of school is usually a massive waste of time—reading policies and taking attendance," Ms. Howell said as she walked row by row, handing out a hefty document. "But now that we're on day two, let's dive into the semester project."

Even though she had only been teaching at Orchard High for two years, Ms. Howell had garnered a fierce reputation. She was strict but good. The graduating seniors who survived her class with a decent grade said it nearly killed them, but it was worth the experience.

"Cultural anthropology is more than the study of cultures," Ms. Howell continued, making her way back to the front of the classroom. "It's a discipline that helps you better understand others. It challenges you to step out of your bubble and take another person's perspective. As the world gets more complex and connected, you need a lens to view it with the proper context and tools."

I anxiously took notes, trying not to be too distracted by the empty seat where Ian had sat the day before. I'm sure his absence had nothing to do with what happened yesterday. Right?

Meanwhile, Ms. Howell's sentences continued to fire like bullets, forceful and direct. I scribbled in my notebook, getting every word on paper. Ian plopped down in the seat next to me.

"Hi," I mouthed silently, looking for any sign of retribution. Ian barely acknowledged me and instead picked up the five-page document on his desk and casually flipped through it. I turned my attention back toward Ms. Howell, determined to start class on the right foot. This thing with Ian couldn't distract me. I needed to focus.

"Mr. Gibson, thank you for finally joining us," Ms. Howell said. "I assume whatever kept you from arriving on time won't be a problem again?"

"Of course, ma'am," Ian said dutifully.

After a long-winded, thirty-minute lecture, Ms. Howell finally paused and surveyed the class. "A lot of you will struggle," she said bluntly. "But that is part of the fun, right?" A few students squeaked out an awkward laugh. The rest of the class quietly moaned. "Okay," Ms. Howell continued. "Please look at the handout on your desk."

I finally picked up the document and glanced at Ian. "I'm sorry," I said quietly.

He sighed as his expression melted. "Me, too," he whispered.

That small exchange was enough to relax my nerves a little.

"As you'll see from the handout," Ms. Howell said, "your big project for the semester is to create a fictional culture. You'll be working in teams of two."

I glanced at the other students in the class, trying to size up a potential partner. I knew almost everyone, but I wasn't close to any of them. What about Zarine Rashid? She had always lingered around my group of friends. She was a little quiet but bright and on top of things. Then I caught Ian looking at me. He raised his eyebrows as if asking me to team up with him. Suddenly, I was back in the storm from yesterday. I wanted to give Ian a chance, but he showed up late to class on the second day of school. I was right to think working with him was a liability.

Ms. Howell continued. "You will be creating an artifact to illustrate the culture you've created. Past groups have created short documentaries. Others have made comic books. One group even made a 3D map and model of their culture." She turned on the projector and clicked through a handful of slides showcasing projects from previous semesters.

I perked up. An idea was budding.

"Along with your artifact," Ms. Howell said, "you and your partner will give a detailed presentation on your civilization. As you'll read in the handout, you'll need to cover language, rituals, and government."

The idea fully blossomed, and I reluctantly released the thought of working with Zarine. So much for a safe partnership. My adrenaline spiked as I contemplated what I was about to do. Jumping headfirst into this scheme would either launch me into my dreams or destroy everything I had worked for. I couldn't tell if I was excited or ready to throw up, but there was no turning back once the solution hit me.

I smiled at Ian. "This is it," I said with quiet intensity as I pointed to the whiteboard. Ian shook his head and shrugged—he clearly didn't see the vision that was now propelling me forward. There were only five minutes left in class. I pulled out my notebook and scribbled some notes. As soon as the final bell rang, I hopped out of my chair and motioned Ian to follow me. He gathered his things, intrigued by my strange behavior, and chased after me as I left the building.

"What are you doing?" Ian said as he sped up to match my pace. "What's with the secret ninja moves? Who are you hiding from?"

"Nobody. I want to talk." I cut across the lawn and headed toward a covered picnic table. Ian followed me, occasionally looking over his shoulder. By the time he reached me, he was out of breath.

"I've got it," I said, unable to hide the smile on my face.

"Got what? The crazies?"

I ignored his sarcasm and held up the handout from Ms. Howell's class. "This is the answer."

"To what? World peace? The cure for cancer? I have no clue what's going on." Ian tried to sound annoyed, but he was pleased I was talking to him.

I took a deep breath and pointed to the document again. "Ms.

Howell's assignment—the fictional culture—we can build it inside *The Garden*."

Ian stopped for a minute. He grabbed the paper from my hands and read through the overview again.

"Wait," he said slowly. "So, you're suggesting we use my project—my *baby*—for a silly school assignment? Luce, I was offering it as a way to win TechEd. Not to suck up to some teacher."

"Hear me out," I said. "You were already planning to add people to *The Garden*. So let's do it for this assignment. We can create the civilization inside your virtual world."

"We?" Ian interrupted.

I started pacing. "But there is more. As Ms. Howell discussed anthropology's importance, I realized that this assignment is the perfect setup for the TechEd Tournament. So we can use *The Garden* for the class project *and* as a winning idea for the competition. Get it?"

"What do you mean?" Ian asked.

"The whole idea of using VR to help students better understand cultural anthropology is a huge opportunity. Think what someone could learn about government, human behavior, or relationships through this kind of technology—*that* is the educational focus we need to make *The Garden* a real contender for TechEd."

Ian's face lit up. "We?" he said again.

I smiled back. "Yes, Ian. *We*." The momentum inside of me faltered as lingering fears snagged my attention. "There's just one thing. You have to promise you'll follow through. Too much is riding on this for you to slack off. That means coming to class on time, too. I don't want Ms. Howell grading us with any bias against you. Fair?"

"Totally fair." Ian's genuine excitement bolstered me up. "Let's set the rules."

"Rules? I don't think—" But before I could finish, Ian had

already sat down and grabbed a notebook from my backpack. With a quick click of his pen, he began writing.

"Rule #1: Get to class on time." Ian smiled.

I nodded my head as I sat down next to him. "Okay, yeah. Rule #2: Establish and stick to the project schedule." Ian continued to scribble out the words as I spoke. "Rule #3: We both need to sign off on any major updates or changes."

"Rule #4," Ian said. "Always have snacks."

I laughed. "Good rule."

Ian added an exclamation mark at the end of Rule #4 and underlined it twice. With a smile as wide as his face, his blue eyes locked onto mine. "I promise, Luce. I won't let you down." There was a tenderness to his voice that quieted all my fears.

I packed the notebook in my bag and sighed. "I hope I haven't let *you* down. Are you okay working with me?"

Ian pulled back. "What do you mean? I was the one who wanted to work together in the first place, remember? I'm in. One hundred percent."

I closed my eyes, swallowing my pride. With a sharp inhale, I dared to speak the scary truth. "You could win this thing on your own. You're smarter than me and have already built an impressive piece of technology. I'm not sure what I can add."

"Are you kidding?" Ian said. "You found a perfect educational angle in less than a day. Plus, you realized we could combine it with the anthropology assignment. That means less work for me!"

We both laughed.

"Besides," Ian said, "you understand the ins and outs—how to craft a presentation, abide by the rules, and suck up to the judges. I'd never make it out of my bedroom without you." He leaned over and put his hands on my shoulders. "Lucy Fernández. This project needs *both* of us to succeed. And if you're serious about trusting me, I think we'll nail it. So, what do you say? Partners?" Ian reached out his hand. I grabbed it, giving it a hearty shake.

"Partners."

For the first time in a while, I felt good. There was momentum and clarity. And more than anything, there was Ian. As much as I resisted working with him, I was relieved not to do this thing alone. We had come full circle, only this time, his brilliance was saving my ass.

I put on my backpack. "So... What's next?"

Ian grabbed his things and smiled. "The fun part."

CHAPTER 5
IAN'S REDEMPTION

WHEN LUCY SHOOK my hand outside Orchard High and said we were partners, it was a defining moment.

"Your place or mine?" I asked as we neared our homes after school that day.

Lucy chuckled and scrunched her nose as she thought it over. "It looks like my mom is home from work." She pointed to the shiny black BMW in front of her house. "She often brings home treats after a big win. Wanna check it out?"

"I'm glad you're taking Rule #4 seriously." The smile on my face would not leave. There was no way to hide my emotions. I was thrilled to be partnered with Lucy. I needed her. And if we spent enough time together, she'd realize how much she needed me, too.

"Your place it is," I said. "After you, milady."

I bent over with a flourish of my hand and an exaggerated bow. I've never been great with social interactions, but Lucy always put me at ease. She curtsied in return before bee-lining across the front lawn towards her house.

"Mom!" she yelled. "You home?"

I closed the front door and followed her toward the kitchen.

Lucy dropped her backpack on the dining room table as her eyes honed in on a pink bakery box. "Ooh! Delilah's Desserts. Jackpot!" The pristine packaging stood on the counter like a fancy gift waiting to be opened. I peered over Lucy's shoulder, not realizing I was practically breathing down her neck. But I couldn't help myself. I wanted to be near her.

Inside the box was a dazzling assortment of eclairs, lemon bars, Florentines, and cupcakes. Lucy shot me a wide grin. "What do you want?"

I scanned the room like a thief, afraid of getting caught. As easy as I felt around Lucy, I felt equally uncomfortable around her mom. "Are you sure we can eat these? Should we ask your mom first?"

Lucy laughed and rolled her eyes. "Dude, are you scared of my mom?"

"Uh, absolutely." I laughed. "She's intense!"

Lucy rolled her eyes, but she knew I was right. Putting down the box, she walked toward the bottom of the stairs. "Hey, Mom! Are these pastries up for grabs?"

"Go ahead!" A voice yelled from above.

With an I-told-you-so smirk, Lucy eyed me. I thought she was so cute when she was snarky. "Now, what would you like, sir?"

My eyes grew big as I scanned the desserts. I was a sucker for sweets. I carefully pulled out a lemon bar and took a big bite. "Damn, that's good."

Lucy grabbed a mini devil's food cake. As we sat at the table, she pulled out the same notebook in which I had scribbled our rules. She wrote *The Garden Project* across the top of the second page in her neatest handwriting. Oh, great, another list. I let her ruminate on her notes while I focused on my dessert. Lucy got straight to business.

"First, we must establish a timeline and figure out our to-do list." There was a pause in her voice and shock in her eyes as I practically made out with my lemon bar. She snapped. "Hey, pay attention!"

"But this isn't the fun part," I said with a moan.

She gave me the sternest look—one she probably learned from her mom. "You want to win? We need a plan."

"You and your plans. Have you ever tried winging it?" I licked a bit of lemon curd from my fingers.

Lucy took a deep breath, trying to stay pleasant. "There's a lot of moving pieces. We need to register for the regional competition, ask a teacher to be our advisor, figure out what research we'll need to do, plan a killer presentation—"

I interrupted. "—and code an entire civilization that looks and acts real before we integrate it into a complex VR program." I didn't want to rain on her parade, but the truth is none of the administrative stuff mattered if the coding wasn't perfect.

"Right, that." Lucy's enthusiasm deflated.

"How about this?" I said, trying to be helpful. "You focus on the research, presentation, and contest stuff. I'll start on the coding. We're both going to need help from each other as we go, but let's stick to what we know best."

"Sure," she replied, clearly a little bummed. "But promise you'll show me the code and explain what you're doing as you go, okay? I want to come out of this a better programmer."

"Sure thing, nerd." With a smirk, I took another bite of pastry. I'm not sure why Lucy was getting so worked up over this division of labor. I was happy to do the hard tech stuff, confident she'd nail everything else. Still, she hated giving up so much control. I stared at the shortbread crumbs on the table, wishing my lemon bar was still there. "That was so good. Can I have another?"

"Hey, you two!" Mrs. Fernández marched into the room with arms wide open. She loved making an entrance. "There better be an eclair left for me." She smiled as she made her way to the box of pastries.

"Oh, were those yours?" I said, trying to be clever.

"Ha, ha." Lucy's mom smiled a little too big to be authentic. I'm sure her dramatic flair helped her in the courtroom, but in real life, it was off-putting. "Hello, Ian. We've missed seeing you." The words didn't sound believable. Mrs. Fernández was the main reason my friendship with Lucy died, and I hadn't forgiven her. She walked over to the table, looking down over Lucy's shoulders. "What are you guys working on?"

Lucy quickly closed her notebook with an almost protective instinct. "Oh, nothing," she said, looking at her mom. "A school project." She began stuffing things back in her backpack with a forced smile before shooting me a panicked glance. "Should we head to your house, Ian? We got lots of coding to do."

Mrs. Fernández scanned Lucy up and down before facing me with questioning eyes. "A school project, huh? For what class?"

Lucy cleared her throat. "Cultural Anthropology. We're supposed to create a fictional culture and do a presentation on it."

"That sounds interesting. So how does coding fit into it?" Her mom had on her lawyer's face as she tried to piece the facts together. Lucy shifted in her chair. Her mom took note. Man, I'd hate to be the criminal sitting across from Mrs. Fernández in a courtroom.

Lucy continued. "Well, we're creating a computer-generated model of sorts for the project. Like a digital culture. Should be cool."

I interjected. "Come on, Luce. You're leaving out the best part!" I wasn't sure what Lucy was trying to hide. But with her mom's big expectations for TechEd, I figured telling her about our project was a surefire way to ease her worries.

"What's that?" Mrs. Fernández quickly turned her attention to me. Luce shot me an alarmed look, subtly shaking her head. Like a perfect idiot, I had no idea what she was trying to communicate.

"We're teaming up for the TechEd Tournament!" I exclaimed.

Lucy's head dropped. Her mom tried to hide her disappointment, but I saw it. I don't know what I did wrong, but I was the guilty party based on both women's expressions. I stared across the table at Lucy's cupcake, wishing I could burrow inside it.

"Oh, really?" Mrs. Fernández's forced smile was turning more rigid. As she turned back to Lucy, her expression melted into a frown. If she was trying to hide it from me, she did a horrible job.

I reached over and grabbed Lucy's cupcake and started peeling back the paper liner. The awkwardness was killing me, and I was desperate for a distraction. Too bad I never took a bite because my mouth was the one getting me in trouble. "Yeah, we can knock out our anthro project while also preparing for the competition—a whole two birds with one stone thing. It was all Lucy's idea."

Mrs. Fernández slowly walked toward the hallway. "Lucy, can I talk to you for a moment?"

With a heavy sigh, Lucy stood up. "Sure, Mom." She shot me an apologetic look. The two went out into the hallway. I leaned back to eavesdrop. Lucy tried to keep her voice down, but Mrs. Fernández didn't seem to care if I heard every word she spoke.

"What's going on, Lucy?" All the pretense of the cheerful mom was gone.

"What do you mean?" Luce whispered. "I told you, we're working on a project. What's the problem?"

I had the same question. What *was* her problem? She was acting like she had caught Lucy cheating or skipping school. We hadn't done anything wrong. Why was her mom getting so worked up?

"Are you actually teaming up with Ian?" her mom said.

Oh, duh. *I* was the problem. My pulse began throbbing in my hands as I squeezed the cupcake a little too tightly, turning the devil's food cake into a crumbled mess. I couldn't decide if I should stay or go.

"Yeah, so?" Lucy said.

"Were you going to tell me?"

"Of course, Mom. I just didn't want to have this conversation while Ian was around." Lucy tried to remain quiet.

"Why's that?" Her mom said, clearly unfazed by the volume of her voice.

"Because of *this*!" I pictured Lucy gesturing to her mom. "I knew you'd freak out."

"Lucy, dear, I know you have a soft spot for Ian, but he's not reliable. The TechEd Tournament is too important to partner with someone with his track record."

The conversation became increasingly more uncomfortable. I quietly began gathering my things.

"Ian is a genius," Lucy spoke louder as if she wanted me to hear this part. "He has built something incredible. And with my help, I think we can win State—perhaps even Nationals."

"And what if he bails? What if he doesn't show up or do the work?" Her mom's voice was accusatory. And spot on. I was about two seconds away from bailing at that very moment. "What if he takes all the credit?"

That was the final straw. A pit had opened inside my stomach, and I was afraid it would swallow me whole if I stayed. Maybe I *was* the villain in this situation. I wondered if Lucy would be better off without me. One thing was clear. I needed to leave. So I snuck through the adjoining dining room and quietly walked out the front door.

When I got home, I dropped my bag on my desk. It was still littered with pages of handwritten notes and empty bags of chips. I picked up a VR headset and sat on my bed.

"Ian."

I jumped at the sound of Lucy's voice. Her dark eyes peeked behind the crack of my door before she gently opened it. "I'm so sorry you heard that."

I'm sure I was the picture-perfect image of a lost cause in need of rescue. Embarrassed and stupid, I wished I was better at hiding my emotions. But the mixture of sadness and shame on Lucy's face consoled me. I stood up, grabbed the other headset from my desk, and handed it to her. Without a word, we put them on, transporting ourselves into *The Garden*.

I had spent a lot of time inside my virtual world long before I shared it with Lucy. But that didn't dilute its intoxicating allure. It was like an instant mood booster. The sound of the waves crashing against the shore lifted my heaviness. A setting sun offered a welcoming glow. Seagulls sang in the distance while the wind rustled the leaves. It wasn't just the scene's serenity that comforted me. It was the knowledge that I had created it all.

Lucy's avatar stood in the breeze, staring off into the horizon. The silhouette of her body stood resolute and firm. Her eyes followed me as I walked toward the water and stood by her side.

"Do you ever consider staying in here forever?" Lucy asked.

"All the time."

We stayed silent for several minutes. The gentle in-and-out of the ocean perfectly matched my breath. With each exhale, my feet sunk a little deeper into the sand. I could tell Lucy was looking for the right words to say. She grabbed my hand. A jolt struck my heart.

"I'm sorry I keep letting you down." Her words were soft, her eyes sincere.

I squeezed her hand, wishing I had the courage to wrap my arms around her. But as quickly as she had grabbed my hand, she let it go. I followed her lead as she sat down at the water's edge.

"Apparently, I'm the one who lets everyone down," I said.

"That's not true. You can't let my mom bother you."

"You mean like she bothers you?" I shook my head. "Come on, Luce. Is anything ever good enough for her?"

Lucy pulled her knees in, hugging them with her arms. "My whole life has been a long string of attempts to prove my worth to her. No matter how hard I try, I'm never enough." She picked up a seashell and tossed it back into the rising tide. "I'm sure my mom loves me, but sometimes it feels like that love is the reward waiting for me at the end of a never-ending marathon. I live in constant fear of losing it. I've chased an always moving goalpost for years—ashamed anytime I miss the mark."

Lucy always had a way with words. Even when we were kids, I always wondered what it was like to be inside her mind and think so deeply about everything.

"But back at my house? The things my mom said about you?" Lucy closed her eyes, shaking her head. "She made me angry. I was mad that everything was always about *the plan*. Upset that after seventeen years, my mom still doesn't trust me or my decisions. And I was insulted that you were left hurting."

I wanted to pause the moment and comfort her. Hell, I wanted to kiss her. For years, I watched Lucy conform to the boxes placed before her. Now, a glimmer of that nine-year-old who shoved a bully to the ground to save an outcast peeked through.

"Listen to me." She stood up. There was a determination in her voice. "Whatever my mom hoped to achieve from that embarrassing lecture had the opposite effect. I am certain about this project and believe you will help see us through. And I want us to win—not only for me but for *you*, too."

"Do you mean that?" I asked.

"Of course I do! You deserve to have your moment to show off your brilliance!"

But I didn't care about everyone else—only Lucy. For years, I feared the day she'd leave me for her big fancy school. There was no way to follow her with my academic record. I had planned on running into her that first day of school. When I built *The Garden*, I hoped it would impress her, enticing her back into my world, even for a moment. I needed a few more months together before she left for good.

And then fate handed me the greatest gift: The TechEd Tournament. The moment she brought it up, I realized *The Garden* could win it all. And I was more than willing to give it to her. Not only because it meant working together, but because a win could change my life. It could open doors, allowing me to follow Lucy after graduation. I jumped to my feet. "I meant what I said, too. I won't let you down. I want this."

More than that, I needed it. *The Garden* was my chance at redemption.

Lucy nodded her head and shook my hand as if we had agreed to a legal contract. "Alright, that settles it. We're both in— one hundred percent. And we're not going to let anyone stop us. Agreed?"

I tried to memorize the moment. The ocean's pulse matched my breath as the sun's glow melted my fears. Happy with the world around me, things were finally changing with Lucy by my side. My future, I dared to believe, promised to be a little less lonely.

"Agreed."

MESSAGE FROM JAKE

WED, AUG 17

Hey, Lucy. Been thinking about entering that Techno competition you were talking about yesterday. Coach says it could improve my chances of getting a football scholarship at a top university. Want to work together?

You'd do great at TechEd. You should go for it! Unfortunately, I've already partnered with someone else. Otherwise, you know I'd love to work with you.

Damn. Gotta be fast if you want to work with the great Lucy Fernández. Who's your partner? Hope he's worthy of you.

CHAPTER 6
CREATIVE DIFFERENCES

"LET THEM FLY?" I pounded the table. "No, Ian, we can't make the people fly. They need to be realistic."

"Why you gotta be like that, Luce?" Ian said with a mischievous grin. "Don't be a killjoy."

We already had some conflicting visions for the project three days into this partnership. The task at hand sounded simple enough: Define the specifics of our fictional culture. But when anything's possible, it's hard to know where to start—or in Ian's case, when to stop.

Ian took a sip of Coke while I crossed "flying" off our growing list. My lunch was left untouched as we brainstormed features for the simulated civilization. We piggy-backed off each other's ideas—from the silly and absurd to the philosophical and intriguing. There were arguments over crucial details like the time period, clothing, and social structures. We discussed the ripples of a single decision and debated whether those choices were justified. I couldn't help but chuckle at the crazy scenarios Ian imagined.

"Did I miss the party?"

Ian and I stopped mid-laughter. Jake towered over our table

in the isolated corner of the lunchroom. I was very aware of where I was and who I was with. I hated to admit it, but I was embarrassed.

"Hey, Jake," I said, trying to act cool. "What's up?"

"Oh, just curious what all the fuss is about. It looks like you two are having too much fun. You're making the rest of us jealous." Jake tried to sneak a peek at my notebook. "What are you guys doing anyway? Planning a kegger? World domination?"

"Ha!" My laugh sounded forced. "No, we're working on a school project."

"No kidding," Jake said. He glanced sideways at Ian, who had gone mute through the entire exchange. I had never responded to Jake's last text about TechEd. Seeing me getting chummy with Ian must have been the answer I was too afraid to send when Jake asked who my partner was.

Jake sighed. "Well, don't let me stop you from your hard work." With a quick tap on the table, he went to leave but then turned around. "Oh, Lucy, I almost forgot. Are you still on for the post-game party this Friday?"

Painfully aware that Jake purposely left Ian out of the invitation, I was unsure how to answer. "Oh, uh, probably?" Ian buried his gaze in his sandwich, which I pretended not to notice. "I need to double-check my schedule."

Jake nodded with a suspicious smile and walked away.

Ian was quiet for a moment. "Jake Wittingham, huh? What's it like having the hunkiest guy in school single you out?" The sarcasm was thick as he stuffed a few Doritos in his mouth, clearly annoyed. "So, are you going?"

"To the party? I don't know." I finally grabbed my sandwich and took a bite. "Honestly, I don't want to. I have so much going on, and big parties like that drain me. But Jake's nice, and I'd hate for him to think I don't like him."

"Wait, like him? Like—*like* him, like him?"

"No, not *like* him, like him," I said mockingly. "He's my friend."

Ian slowly nodded his head, deciphering my desire to move on. "Sheesh, we've only got another three minutes. Where does the time go?"

"This is harder than I thought it would be." My notes were a flurry of ideas, making it hard to focus. "I never realized how many layers go into making a believable culture. Life is the result of hundreds of thousands of years of evolution. What do you define, and what do you leave to chance?"

"I think it's exciting. I mean, we could have the first race of lizard people!" Ian tried to suppress his smile.

He was baiting me, so I moved on. "I think the more we leave to chance, the better. It feels more authentic—more evolutionary." I leaned back, pondering the idea further. "Besides, aren't you curious what happens when you let the program do its thing?"

"A little," Ian said. "But I'm also drawn to the idea that we can design something *better*."

"What do you mean? You're not serious about bird wings or lizard tails, are you? Because I'm a firm *no* on all of that."

"They can still be normal people, but that doesn't mean we can't give them the world of our dreams. They can be anything we want." Ian seemed slightly irritated that I didn't understand our potential as creators. "Aren't there things you would change if you could? Or is your life already perfect?"

His question hung in the air. Of course, there were things I would change. I would erase my mom's expectations. I'd give myself a full-ride scholarship to MIT and rid the world of the dumb social rules and popularity contests. Life would be easier, more equitable, and more beautiful. Maybe Ian was right. Perhaps *The Garden* was our chance to make the world better. In theory, we had the power to do it all. And that kind of power was tempting—possibly benevolent. But before I could answer his question, the bell rang. Lunch was over.

I was still thinking about our conversation as I walked to seventh period that afternoon. After the enticements of creating a blissful utopia, I reminded myself that, more than anything, *The Garden* needed to maintain its integrity as an educational resource. That was the key to getting to Nationals and acceptance to MIT. After all, what good was a perfect artificial world if it didn't benefit my real one?

Still, I couldn't help but wonder about the program's potential beyond that singular focus of TechEd. What kind of world would I build if nobody was grading me? How would I act if this virtual space was mine alone to design and control? How would I make life *better*? Consumed by my thoughts, I walked into Ms. Howell's classroom, oblivious to everything else around me.

"Earth to Lucy. Hello?" Ian's voice popped my mental bubble.

"Oh! Hey!" I was surprised he was already at his desk. "Did you beat me to class today? And are you in your chair *before* the bell? I must be in an alternate reality or something."

"Very funny," Ian said. "I told you. I'm committed. I don't want you worrying about me. Besides, I've been admiring the sterile white walls and prison-like slats they call windows here. This school is so..." He cleared his throat. "Inspiring."

I rolled my eyes, amazed at how easily sarcasm dripped from Ian's lips. I took my seat as the bell rang.

"Alright, class, I want to start today with a little discussion." Ms. Howell stood tall in front of the room. She was the definition of no-nonsense in her dark gray pants, a light blue cardigan, and a white button-up blouse. Turning to the whiteboard, Ms. Howell drew a house with a giant question mark inside it. With a click of the marker lid, she turned to face us. "Imagine a stranger came into your home to study your family," she said. "How would that make you feel?"

Zarine raised her hand. "What exactly are they doing in my house? Are they interviewing me or what?" Several students nodded their heads as if they had the same question. They all turned back at Ms. Howell expectantly.

"Great question, Ms. Rashid. Let's say this stranger is coming to live in your house for a few months. He'll watch you, help cook dinner or try on your clothes. He might interview you or ask to look at your family albums. How would you feel about that?"

Zarine's eyes grew large. "Weird. Very weird."

The class laughed.

"Why?" Ms. Howell asked.

"Uh, because it is creepy and a major violation of my privacy."

"Okay, good." Ms. Howell moved her attention to another part of the classroom. "Who else?"

I raised my hand, not willing to be outdone by Zarine. "More than *what* the stranger is doing in my home, I want to know *why*. Why is he there? What's his purpose?"

Ms. Howell smiled. "He's there to learn about what makes your family tick. What's normal? Taboo? What are the family dynamics—the spoken and unspoken rules?"

I leaned forward in my chair. "But *why* does he want to learn those things? I still haven't gotten an answer to that."

Ms. Howell turned back to the class. "What do you guys think? Why would someone want to know those things about your family?"

"Because he wants to see a different way of doing things," Ian said abruptly. "Maybe his life sucks, and he's interested in learning how to improve it. Observing different people gives us a chance to question our experiences. It forces us to ask what is normal and possible."

I was surprised Ian joined the discussion, especially with a thoughtful response.

Ms. Howell was delighted. "And tell me, Mr. Gibson, why is that important?"

Ian raised his eyebrows. "Because living one way simply because it is normal or expected limits your ability to do things —*better.*" He shot me a smile as he emphasized his last word.

I smiled back, clearly catching his meaning. It was his not-so-subtle push to use our power to design the world of our dreams. He wanted more control over the people inside *The Garden* instead of leaving it all to chance. But I still wasn't convinced. Nor was I willing to back down. I shot my arm back into the air.

"Yes, Ms. Fernández," Ms. Howell said, pointing to me.

"I agree. We must see the world through other people's eyes. That is the key to progress." I tried to hide the smugness floating on top of my voice. "But that doesn't automatically make it okay to insert yourself into their world. History has proven the devastation that can come when anyone tries to exert their influence on others."

"You're both right," Ms. Howell said, inserting herself into our verbal duel. "Cultural Anthropology is a tricky subject. As Mr. Gibson explained, expanding our worldview and learning from others is vitally important. And as Ms. Fernández pointed out, expanding that view requires a standard of ethics to ensure those lessons aren't the result of—or justifications for—abuse, neglect, or colonization. Or, as Ms. Rashid would put it, to make sure we're not being creepy by invading other people's privacy."

The class laughed again. Zarine blushed.

Ms. Howell segued into the day's topic, outlining the rules cultural anthropologists should follow. From *doing no harm* to *being open and honest about your work in the field*—the responsibilities she presented were eye-opening. I was enthralled with the discussion, mostly because I couldn't stop thinking about how it applied to what we were doing inside *The Garden.*

I left class with even more questions, but there was a drastic shift in my excitement about TechEd. Ian's technology was on a level above my capabilities. But after Ms. Howell's lecture, I realized how important my role would be in establishing an exciting educational component to ensure we stood apart from the competition.

I took that confidence and marched over to Ian's house later that afternoon. I plopped down on his bed and proudly declared, "I've got it."

Ian turned around from his computer. "Got what? Snacks?"

"No. I think I've figured out how we can both be happy and find a balance between design and evolution."

"Hit me with it." Ian reached over and grabbed a bag of chips that had been on his desk for a few days. Once he realized it was empty, he shot me a dissatisfied look. "Seriously, where are our snacks!"

Shaking my head, I picked up my backpack. Ian's face lit up as I pulled out a small plastic bag with two lemon bars inside—leftovers from before. "Oh! Gimme, gimme!" Ian grabbed a bar and took a bite so big his pastry was reduced by half. His shoulders relaxed as a sleepy look swept across his face. "Mmmmmmmm."

"Okay, now that the toddler has his food, can you give me your attention?" I put the bag down next to me, my bar still inside.

"Yeshh ma'am," he said with a mouth full of pastry. "I'm lish'ning."

"Here's what I'm thinking." I began pacing in the small space between Ian's bed and desk. "What if we both have a specific role to play? You—" I said, pointing to Ian, "can wear the hat of the creative director. You're the one writing the code, so go wild on the design stuff. Within reason, of course. I'm still against letting the people fly or giving them long lizard tails. But go ahead and create the kind of *realistic* world you'd like to have."

Ian swallowed hard. "Okay, and what would your role be?"

"I'd be more of an anthropologist. I'd do some participant observation stuff Ms. Howell talked about today. I'd interact, interview, and map out our findings—careful not to unnecessarily influence or insert myself."

"That could work," Ian said with a hint of hesitation.

"What? You don't like my idea?"

"No, I think it is great. But... Well, I was thinking a lot about what you said earlier. And I think it makes sense to stay out of the way as much as possible."

I threw my hands up as I plopped back down on the bed. "Oh, *now* you agree with me." I smiled. "So, how much influence do you think is too much or too little?"

"Honestly, I don't know." Ian took another bite of his lemon bar, talking with his mouth full. "That's sort of what this whole thing is about, right? We're experimenting— finding out the right level of interaction and manipulation as we go."

"Can we use the word *design* instead of *manipulation*? It sounds less dirty."

"Fine, interaction and *design*," Ian said. "But no matter what you call it, I think this project will require a lot of trial and error. We're playing around with life—artificial life, but still. It will respond like life, so I figured we should start with as little influence as possible and add things as needed to make the culture more authentic."

I scrunched my face. "Sooooo... is that a *yes* or *no* to my plan?"

Ian laughed. "You love being in control, don't you?"

"No," I said emphatically. That was a lie, and we both knew it. "But I was excited about playing the role of the anthropologist. I want to interact and get a first-person perspective."

"So do it!"

"Really?" There was a spark of excitement in my voice.

"Yeah, of course. Participate. Be ethical," Ian said while

waving his arms like a crazed conductor. He stood up and stared me squarely in the eyes. "Any experiment requires proper data collection, right? You'll be our field operative learning all the little details. I'll be the guy in the chair checking out the big picture." He slumped back down in his seat. "I'm only saying I agree that we're probably better off easing into things even with these separate roles. Instead of figuring out a bunch of super sophisticated details from the start, let's simplify and let things evolve naturally. We can always adapt and add as necessary."

I felt triumphant—like we had passed another hurdle. "So, how long until the civilization is up and running?"

"Someone's excited," Ian said.

"I am." Patience had never been a virtue of mine. Not only was I anxious because Regionals were coming up, but I was also eager to meet our virtual people—a fact that was all too obvious as my eyes locked on the VR goggles on Ian's desk. I repeated my question. "So, how long?"

Ian followed my gaze and laughed. "Tell you what—before I answer that question, how about we celebrate with a little beach break. What do you say?"

I didn't have to say anything. The best perk about partnering with Ian was our daily beach fix inside *The Garden*. I grabbed a headset and strapped in before he had even finished his sentence.

"Seriously, Ian, this place is stunning." I was gushing again as we sat inside the virtual world. This after-school ritual was like a cleansing from real life. We never stayed too long as there was plenty of work to do, but even five minutes nourished me.

Ian breathed deeply. "Soak it in, Luce. It won't be long until this place is crawling with Simples."

I paused. "Simples?"

"Yeah, Simulated People—or *Simples*. Get it?" Ian chuckled.

"Clever." I shook my head and laughed. As the wide-open space enveloped us, I had mixed feelings about adding people to this digital paradise. Obviously, we didn't have a choice. It was the whole educational angle for TechEd, not to mention the core of our anthropology assignment. And I was beyond curious to learn about the soon-to-be inhabitants. Still, I was hesitant to share this garden with anyone else. I sighed deeply. "I wonder what will happen once we add them."

"You mean, once we add the *Simples*." Ian was determined to make the term stick.

"Right, of course. I'm curious how the Simples will change things, but I'm also going to miss the solitude of this place."

"Me, too. I've enjoyed these quiet moments together these past few days." Ian's blue eyes lingered on my face before his cheeks turned red. He quickly faced the ocean. "Hey! What if we keep this beach to ourselves?"

"What do you mean?"

"I mean, make it ours—only ours. The Simples can have their town over in the garden, and we'll keep this part for us."

I wrinkled my nose, still not sure what Ian was suggesting. "Like, would you put up some private property signs and tell the Simples to stay off our land? Or do we need a watch guard? Like a cranky old guy who yells at anyone who dares step on our beach."

"The second one, definitely." Ian laughed. "*Or* I could program an invisible boundary, so they can't cross over the dunes."

I thought for a moment. "Okay. Walk me through this. Say I'm a Simple inside the village. When I look toward the beach, what's there? A wall? A fence? Can I see the ocean but not go there? Or is it a rule we establish for them that they obey? Like an honor system thing?"

"That's up to us," Ian said. "We decide the rules."

"Right." And just like that, we were back where we started at lunch. No matter how much we wanted to leave the Simple's progression up to chance, we couldn't perfectly mimic the evolutionary process. We didn't have hundreds of thousands of years to let life grow from some bacterial Petri dish. We were skipping ahead, starting with an established baseline that *we* had to determine.

"So," I said, sitting up taller, "you're saying you could program a way for the Simples to stay inside their borders?"

"Yep, almost like authorizing the natural laws they have to follow. It could be a little fun if you ask me." Ian shook his head, reading my hesitation. "Relax. The Simples are not real people. They're a bunch of computer code—a simulation designed to help us learn. Think of it as an experiment on humanity where no actual humans are harmed."

"An experiment." I thought it over before looking at Ian with a smile. "This *will* be fun. So how much longer until the code is ready to go?"

"Oh, it's ready now." He said the words so casually as if he was mentioning the weather. The shock on my face must have been hilarious.

I perked up immediately. "Wait—what? Are you serious? You're done? I thought it was going take longer."

"Well, that was when I thought I was adding lizard tails and wings." Ian chuckled. "But if you need a basic, blank slate, I've played around with that code for weeks. I think I have something that will work and uploaded it last night." He smiled before his handsome avatar vanished from the beach.

I tore off my headset to see Ian sit down in his chair and swivel back toward his desk.

He waved his arm at me. "Put that back on! You're our field operative, remember? Time to go meet your people."

The headset felt heavy in my hand. I couldn't believe this lifeless piece of plastic could take me into a virtual world brimming with digital life. Knowing an entire civilization was waiting to awake for the first time was thrilling. I took a deep breath and strapped on the goggles.

"Let's go meet The Simples."

CHAPTER 7
IAN'S VOICE

A BREEZE TOUSLED Lucy's hair as she appeared on the beach inside *The Garden* for the second time that day. Her hands quickly touched the fabric wrapped around her body, surprised to be wearing a plain, cream-colored tunic that came above her knees.

"Ian?" Lucy said as her hand instinctively reached for her sunflower charm—a clear sign she was nervous. Disappointment washed her face as she realized the necklace was missing.

"I'm here," I said.

She turned around, searching. "Where?"

I smiled, watching her from my monitor. "Here at my desk. I'll be observing everything from my computer in stealth mode."

"Right." Lucy nodded. "That's too bad. I was getting used to your smoking hot avatar," she said with a teasing smile.

"Ha! I knew you liked it."

Lucy chuckled as she pointed to her outfit. "What am I wearing?"

"Oh, that? I'm trying out some designs before submitting them to fashion week. What do you think?"

She tugged on the scratchy fabric, trying to smooth it out. "Don't quit your day job."

"Ouch, fine." I chuckled. "It may not be ready for the runway, but it should help you blend in with the Simples."

Lucy perked up at the mention of their name. She started moving away from the shoreline, lowering her voice as she spoke. As she made her way toward the village, I scanned my desk for something to eat. Behind my monitor, I found some day-old popcorn—the perfect snack as I eagerly awaited the debut of the Simples.

"So, how will this work?" Lucy asked as she walked through the dunes. "Can they—the Simples—hear you? Or only me?"

"Right now, I'm speaking directly to your Amplifier Chip, so only you can hear me. But I can broadcast to anyone, even the whole world if needed."

Lucy's posture shrunk a bit. "This is weird. I'm standing in your room like a half-asleep zombie while you watch some video game version of me. And why do you need to talk to my amplifier chip? We're two feet away from one another."

I admit it was strange. Lucy stood motionless next to my bed with a headset strapped around her eyes.

"Remember," I said, "the amplifier chip hijacks your motor skills. That includes talking. We have to communicate through the chip."

Lucy sighed. "That's why it sounds like you're inside my head. So weird."

"Nah, pretend you're going undercover," I said as I tossed a piece of popcorn in my mouth. "I'm the surveillance guy in your ear. I'll lie low unless you need me."

She gave a thumbs-up and walked through a grove in front of the village. I was excited for her to go beyond the shore for the first time. As she made her way through the wooded path, the roofs of small huts peeked behind the treetops. The sound of muffled footsteps became more distinct the closer she got. Lucy crouched behind some bushes and watched for a few minutes.

I tapped my keyboard, opening up a multi-view snapshot of the village. I had been working on the Simple's code for months, but this was the first time a group of them interacted. I was excited—and nervous. There were dozens of people roaming the village, each dressed similarly to Lucy in neutral-colored tunics. They walked along the pathways, smiling and performing simple tasks like collecting fruit and weaving baskets.

But like my other attempts at simulated life, something still off. There was zero interaction between the people. They were like robots moving through pre-programmed motions—very functional with plastered smiles that made the whole scene a little eerie. I hoped Lucy wouldn't notice. Would she regret working with me?

Lucy stayed hidden as she walked along the edge of the village through the small forest. The trees cleared, and she found a patch of grass nestled next to a pond. Birds and flowers completed the enchanted look. Nobody was around except for a single man resting near the water. With sun-bleached hair and tanned skin, he reminded me of a Ken doll.

"I'm going to start with him," Lucy whispered, still out of the man's view.

"Go in peace." I chuckled, knowing I amused myself more than Lucy.

Lucy smoothed her tunic and carefully approached the man.

"Hello," she said.

The man cocked his head like a curious puppy. "Hello." He smiled before running his hand through the water again. He was much more relaxed than the other Simples. While everyone else completed tasks as if on autopilot, this guy acted like he was vacationing in the Bahamas.

"How are you doing?" Lucy asked, taking another careful step toward him.

"Oh, I'm great." He smiled warmly before turning his attention back toward the pond. Everything about the interaction was odd. The man was so unaffected by Lucy's attempts to connect. He didn't understand this was a momentous first encounter.

"Can I ask you a question?" Lucy sat down next to him.

"I suppose," the man said, mesmerized by his reflection in the pond.

"What are you doing?"

"What do you mean?" He sat up.

Lucy pointed to the pond. "Why are you playing with the water?"

"What else would I do?"

I thought back to the other Simples dutifully collecting food and weaving baskets. Lucy seemed to be thinking the same thing as she spoke.

"Don't you have some task to complete like the others?" she asked. "Are you taking a break? Are you Bored?"

"No." He shrugged. "I like doing this." He took a deep breath, admiring the surrounding scene. "Isn't it beautiful?"

Lucy tried to follow his gaze. "Isn't *what* beautiful?"

"Everything! The trees, sky, and water are all beautiful. I like it here. It makes me happy." He smiled at Lucy.

I couldn't help but smile, too. The man was so relaxed— unrushed and innocent. I had no idea what made him different from the others, but I was fascinated to find out.

"What's your name?" Lucy asked.

"What's that?" he replied.

"Your name?" She raised her eyebrows, confused by his uncertainty. "Like, what do you call yourself?"

"I don't call myself anything," he said. "Why? Do you call yourself something?"

"I call myself Lucy. That is my name." Lucy placed her hand on her chest to make her meaning clear.

"Lucy," he said, gesturing back at her. "I like that. Lucy." He paused for a moment. "Lucy, Lucy, Lucy."

I couldn't tell if he was trying to remember her name or still processing the concept of one. He mulled on the word for a few moments, saying it with different tones and inflections. Like piecing together a puzzle, he let his mouth play with the sounds until they finally settled into place.

"Where can I get a name?" the man asked.

It was a simple enough inquiry—why shouldn't the man want a name? A pop of inspiration struck me, and without thinking, I grabbed the microphone next to my monitor. In my deepest voice, I broadcast my words.

"Your name is Steve," I boldly declared.

The man and Lucy jumped to their feet at the sound. An anxious look settled on Lucy's face as she recognized my voice.

What was I doing? Had I lost my mind? How did I think screaming from the skies was a good idea? I'm sure Lucy was already calculating all the ways I was breaking the rules of anthropology. Forcing a name on someone was probably a big no-no, especially speaking it like some omniscient being. But I wasn't an anthropologist. I had a bigger role. Maybe it was natural for me to interject and help the Simples out. I mean, I did create them.

Right or wrong, I had proclaimed a name for this man, and there wasn't anything Lucy could do about it.

"Steve," the man said as he gazed toward the sky. "Ssssteve. Steeeeevah. Steve." His tongue played around with every sound. He turned to Lucy with a confident smile. "My name is Steve!"

"Nice to meet you, Steve," Lucy said as she nervously tugged on her tunic. She resisted the urge to yell at me as beads of sweat formed on her forehead. "Uh, can you excuse me for a moment?" She quickly turned around and walked into the nearby forest— moving far enough away to ensure Steve couldn't hear. "What the hell was that?" she said, looking into the sky.

I laughed—not the best response. I didn't mean to make light of the situation, but I was having fun. Besides, Lucy was so tiny on my computer. Her size dwarfed her anger.

"Relax, Luce. I told you this was an experiment. We're learning about the things they need as we go. He needed a name, so I gave him one."

"Okay, but can we find a better way to do it? One where these people don't hear a voice from the sky?" She put her hands on her hips, making me laugh harder. She was so cute in her riled-up, miniature form.

"You're forgetting something," I said, trying to regain composure. "Everything is new to these people. So hearing voices from the sky isn't weird. They don't know any better."

I was making stuff up on the fly, but I had landed on a solid point. The Simples didn't have years of conditioning. There was no older generation passing down layers of traditions—no taboos about what was weird or normal. Everything was new, which meant everything was normal. Still, I could tell Lucy wasn't convinced my actions were reasonable.

"Even if it's not weird now doesn't mean it can't ripple out in unexpected ways," she said. She rubbed the sides of her head as if unraveling a million tangled thoughts. "How about we hold off on more sky speeches until we talk things through? Okay?"

"Sure thing, boss. Sorry." I tried to sound sincere, but it was clear I didn't mean it. Lucy began making her way back when I interrupted her again. "I have to say—this whole thing is better than the movies. Good thing I have popcorn."

"Please, focus." Lucy's patience was waning. She started walking toward Steve. I was excited for her to learn more about him—excited and anxious. But to my surprise, Steve was already speaking with another woman.

Full-figured and brimming with desperate energy, the stranger's hair flowed outward with tight, corkscrew curls while her rich, brown skin contrasted the beige tunic she was wearing.

Like Steve, this woman was different from the other Simples. But unlike Steve, she wasn't carefree or relaxed. She had a fierce spark behind her eyes as if thirsty for answers.

"Hello, how are you doing?" Steve said to the woman with forced politeness. I laughed as I realized he was asking the same question Lucy had asked him mere minutes ago.

"What was that voice?" The woman asked him.

"What's your name?" Steve said.

"What was that voice?" The woman said again emphatically.

"You mean the Voice in the Sky? It gave me a name. Do you have a name?"

"What's a name?" It was the same thing Steve had asked Lucy, but there was a hunger to the woman's words. She didn't look afraid. Just determined to learn.

Lucy slowly walked up and interjected. "A name is what you call yourself," she said with a warm smile, her eyes locked on the woman.

"You!" the woman exclaimed, pointing to Lucy. "I saw you behind the bushes beyond the trees. What were you doing?"

"Hi, I'm Lucy," she said, sidestepping the whole bushed thing.

"What's a Lucy?" the woman asked.

"Lucy is my name." She gestured to herself as she had done with Steve. "A name is what you call yourself. I'm called Lucy, and he is called Steve."

Steve beamed with pride at the sound of his name.

"I don't have a name," the woman said, her voice tinged with sadness at this new realization. "Will the Voice in the Sky give me one?"

Shit. Lucy was right. My impulsive thoughtlessness had already come back to bite us in the ass. Should I respond or pull back? Lucy froze—probably hoping I'd be quiet. That was the safest bet. Still, I found myself reaching for the microphone again. But before I had a chance to speak, Steve chimed in.

"Evie," Steve said.

"What?" said the woman.

"How about I call you Evie? Do you like that name?" Steve asked.

The woman slowly nodded her head. "Okay, I'm Evie."

Lucy let out a relieved exhale as she smiled at Steve. He saved us both from having to respond. Lucy reached out her hand. "Nice to meet you, Evie."

Both Steve and Evie shot their hands out, imitating Lucy's gesture instead of grasping her hand. I laughed at the natural evolution of the greeting. So did Lucy, although she tried to stifle it. She lifted her arm up and down in an imaginary handshake motion. Evie and Steve did the same, pleased with the interaction.

Meanwhile, I was hopeful. I'm sure Lucy thought I was being careless with my disruptive Voice from the Sky stuff. I admit I enjoyed the role more than I should, but it wasn't part of some plot to control the Simples. I just reacted because I was worried Lucy would see the weakness in my AI.

Thankfully, my impulsive response worked.

Giving Steve a name sparked some sort of social programming. It was as if the very act of getting a name somehow changed them. While it was still too early to tell if the results would last, it was promising.

Lucy, Steve, and Evie stood silent until some birds flew by, distracting Steve as he chased them. But Evie kept looking at Lucy as if she was trying to understand her.

"You're different, Lucy. Why is that?" Evie asked.

I wanted to ask Evie the same question. Where did her curiosity come from? Why did she possess such an intense passion when the other Simples had none? Was she a glitch or a miracle?

"Why are you different?" Evie asked again. "Why were you watching us earlier?"

"Well, I'm a visitor," Lucy finally said. "I came to learn about your people."

Steve jumped right back into the conversation after the birds had flown away. "People? What are people?" He was like a puppy —big, joyful energy with a teeny, tiny attention span.

"You guys are people—all of you." Lucy gestured toward the town. "I'm a person, too. But I'm not from around here. I was watching you because I wanted to learn about you."

"If you're not from here, where are you from?" Evie asked, stepping closer to Lucy. "Are there other places besides this? Other people?"

Lucy went to grab her sunflower necklace. With it missing, her hand settled on her collarbone. A mixture of overwhelm and enchantment filled her eyes while Evie questioned her.

"I need to go," Lucy finally said. "But I'll be back. We can talk later."

"You promise," Evie said.

"I promise."

A sense of relief spread across Evie's face. She shot her hand back out toward Lucy, like before. Steve didn't quite understand what was happening but was happy to rejoin the gesture. With a small laugh, Lucy put her arm out. The three lifted their hands up and down before Lucy said goodbye and left. As soon as she was past the dunes, she raised her hands to her head and disappeared.

I spun my chair around. Lucy's body reanimated as she took off the headset. She glanced at me, annoyed that I was still casually munching on popcorn while big things were happening.

"Exciting stuff," I said while tossing a kernel into my mouth.

She dropped the headset on my bed. "We need to talk."

LUCY'S NOTES
WEDNESDAY, AUG. 17

Today I made my first contact with the Simples. It was fascinating but also a little troubling. They seem to lack a lot of basic knowledge. I'm not sure they represent the sophisticated culture we need for TechEd.

But Evie's intense curiosity gives me hope. She's different—passionate. Her desire to understand might be the key to sparking the others into something more realistic. There's something special about her, and I'm crossing my fingers that whatever makes Evie unique is the secret to bringing the whole culture to life. That is, of course, if Ian doesn't ruin everything with his ridiculous Voice in the Sky act.

CHAPTER 8
STIFF COMPETITION

"WELL, well, well! Look who decided to grace us with her presence again." Jake winked as he approached me. I had spent the last week or so working with Ian during lunch, but he was gone for a dentist appointment, so I was back at my familiar seat in the middle of the crowd. I scooted my chair over and made room for Jake. He smiled as he sat down. "Good to see you, Lucy."

"You, too, Jake."

It had been several days since my first contact with Steve and Evie. After a stern discussion, I was hopeful Ian would make his Voice in the Sky a one-time thing. We decided to keep our distance from the Simples until we formulated a plan. But that wasn't easy. My focused drive and Ian's tongue-in-cheek indifference made moving forward difficult. How could we make the Simples more lifelike? How could we teach basic concepts like names and greetings without totally influencing their way of life? And how could those lessons evolve into a rich culture worthy of a win at the TechEd Tournament?

With Regionals less than six weeks away, the pressure to find the answers to all of these questions increased. I wanted a clear path that didn't include booming answers from above.

But for the moment, I tried my best to enjoy a normal lunch with my friends.

"I have to admit it, Lucy. Teaming up with Ian was pure genius on your part." Jake bit down on a carrot stick with a loud crunch.

I put my sandwich down. "What?"

"I mean, bagging the whiz kid for TechEd! Brilliant move. Don't get me wrong, I was bummed not to work with you, but after learning what this competition can mean in terms of scholarships, it all makes sense. A win is like a one-way ticket to almost any major university. I would have chosen Ian over me, too. Clever girl."

My heart sank. I wanted to protest and remind everyone that I had won Regionals all by myself the year before. As a junior! Or explain that Ian and I were friends long before I met half the people sitting at our table. I wasn't trying to use him for my own academic agenda. But nobody would believe it. I didn't always believe it.

"It was actually Ian's idea to work together," I said, trying to deflect the accusation.

"Of course it was!" Jake laughed. "The kid is probably pinching himself that anyone is giving him attention, let alone one of the coolest girls at school. Like I said, brilliant move. He's happy, and you're guaranteed a win."

"It's not like that," was all I could muster. I kept my eyes focused on my water bottle so Jake couldn't see how bothered I was—bothered *and* exposed.

"Don't worry about it, Lucy. As I said, I think it is a smart move. In fact, I'm following your lead."

I snapped to attention, looking Jake square in the eyes. "What do you mean?"

"I found my own wonder boy. He's a junior. Freaky genius,

although admittedly not at Ian's level." Jake leaned back in his seat. His arrogance had a playful banter to it that made him annoyingly likable. He wasn't taunting me—more like trying to impress. "I'm going to give you a run for your money, Lucy."

Jake was putting on a show for everyone. For him, teaming up with a nerdy junior helped save his street cred. Jake understood the way things worked and played the game to win. But the truth was, he was smart enough to win on his own.

"Of course, I'd be willing to ditch my guy if you want to reconsider my offer to team up." He said it like a half-joke. Jake knew I wouldn't abandon Ian, but he wanted to make it clear that I was still his first choice.

I laughed nervously, not wanting to speak. I noticed everyone at the table was looking at me—waiting for my final reaction so they could manage their own. Was Jake threatened? Was he flirting? Without my response, they didn't know for sure. It was all part of the calculated rule book of teenage life.

I smiled as warmly as I could. "I'm sure you'll do great at the competition, Jake. With or without your partner. You're a smart dude."

Jake smiled at the compliment. For a second, his bravado faded, and a genuine concern swept across his face. "Promise me you won't hate me if I win."

"Culture is not something you learn simply by being born," Ms. Howell said as she began class later that day. "Even your most basic habits were influenced by the people in your life."

I wanted to focus on what Ms. Howell was saying, but I couldn't stop thinking about what Jake said at lunch. Ian and I had barely started working together, and already people were talking about our partnership as if it was some kind of unsavory deal. But truthfully, working with Ian wasn't a quid pro quo. If anything, it was a rekindling. It was like uncovering a forgotten treasure—a friendship so deep it needed to be unearthed. So while Jake and the rest of the school may think I was using Ian, there was more to it.

I hoped Ian knew it, too.

While I tried to untangle all my thoughts, Ms. Howell called on me. "Ms. Fernández? What about you?"

My face went flush. I had no idea what she had asked. Every eyeball was on me as I stammered. "Uh, I'm sorry. Can you repeat the question?"

Ms. Howell looked more surprised than angry. "I wondered if you could tell us a time when you stayed at a friend's house only to find they do things differently than you."

I tried to think of something, but my brain was spinning its wheels. Frozen with embarrassment, I worried about what Ms. Howell was thinking. I had never been distracted in class like this. But as much as I tried to respond, the words weren't coming.

"For example," Ms. Howell said, coming to my rescue. "I remember sleeping over at my best friend Becky's house when I was a little girl. I was having such a great time until breakfast the next morning. After finishing my bowl of Froot Loops, I put the dish in the sink, and Becky shot me a horrified look. I had not sipped the leftover milk in my bowl, and she insisted I drink it all. The idea was revolting to me."

The class laughed.

"But in her house," Ms. Howell continued, "you didn't waste anything. So I was forced to drink that slightly pink sugar milk."

I smiled nervously at Ms. Howell, silently thanking her for moving on without me. I sat up tall in my chair, determined to be better. *Focus, Lucy.*

Ms. Howell nodded back before continuing her lecture. "As I said earlier, culture is not something you learn by being born. You learn it by living—specifically by living with other people.

The things you did in your house seem normal to you, just like drinking disgusting cereal milk was normal to Becky." The class laughed again. Ms. Howell walked up and down the rows of desks. "We all grow up around different people with different ideas, and that is how cultures form. Our families are their own kind of culture. As is our high school—"

"Go Warriors!" Jeremy White yelled. He was one of Jake's friends on the football team.

"Yes, thank you, Mr. White," Ms. Howell said with a smile before continuing. "Our high school is a culture and is made up of smaller cultures, like the football team." She smiled back at Jeremy. "The cheerleaders, math teams, and drama students all have habits, language, and rituals. Our town, state, and country are built on culture. Culture is all around us. Wherever you find a group that has been influenced by a certain set of rules and beliefs, you are ultimately talking about culture."

I jotted down some notes. Again, I found my thoughts drifting back to *The Garden*. I realized the Simples didn't have any set rules or beliefs. They had no family or social expectations handed down to them. They all came from the same code. Maybe they'd eventually evolve into something more sophisticated, but it was more likely they needed a push. And I realized my fear of influencing the Simples was the very thing keeping them from developing. The Simples were craving influence. They needed to learn from others, and it was up to Ian and me to get the ball rolling.

The bell rang, and I slowly packed up my things, waiting for the classroom to empty. Ian was still at his dentist appointment, giving me the afternoon to cross some things off my to-do list, like securing a faculty advisor for the tournament. After today's lecture, Ms. Howell was the obvious choice.

"Ms. Fernández? Everything okay?" Ms. Howell said, noticing I had lingered longer at my desk than usual.

"Oh, yeah, fine." I walked to the front of the classroom. "I wanted to apologize. I'm sorry about zoning out earlier. I don't usually do that."

"I'm aware," Ms. Howell said. "Is there something on your mind. Anything you want to talk about?"

"Actually, yeah. I was wondering if I could ask you a favor?"

Ms. Howell sat down at her desk and gestured toward the empty seat on the other side. "How can I help?"

I sat down and pulled a folder out of my backpack. "Have you heard of the TechEd Tournament—the national STEM competition for high school juniors and seniors?"

"I'm familiar with it, yes."

"Well, I'm entering again this year. I'm partnering with Ian Gibson. And we need a faculty member to sign off as our advisor." I was talking fast, and I wasn't sure why. Part of me was still embarrassed by what happened in class, while another part struggled to claim Ian as a partner, considering his reputation among the teachers. I was making up stories about what Ms. Howell must be thinking. "You wouldn't have to do much. Maybe check our research or watch our presentation and offer feedback. I know you're busy—"

Ms. Howell interrupted. "—I'd be happy to help. What's the project you're working on?"

I took a deep breath, relieved that Ms. Howell had agreed. "We're creating a simulated civilization inside a virtual world to help students better understand principles of cultural anthropology."

"Wow, ambitious." Ms. Howell leaned back in her chair. "Sounds like you've taken my semester assignment and pumped it full of steroids."

I let out a nervous laugh. "Yeah, your assignment was sort of the last piece of the puzzle. So there will be some crossover between the competition and what we do for your class. I hope that's okay?"

"Of course. The TechEd Tournament is its own thing. I think it's smart to combine the projects."

With a sigh, I handed Ms. Howell a form. "The only thing I need at the moment is your signature for the registration form. Here and here," I said, pointing to the document.

Ms. Howell took a pen, quickly signed her name, and handed it back.

"Thanks." I slowly slid it into my backpack, looking for an excuse to linger longer.

"Are you sure that is all you need?" Ms. Howell said as she tipped her head a little to the side. "You seem distracted by something else. Want to talk about it?"

Ms. Howell was insightful, but now I wondered if she was reading my mind. Unlike everyone else who hoisted me up as the perfect student, Ms. Howell didn't buy the shiny facade. She made me feel vulnerable—vulnerable but seen. I sighed again and met her eyes across the desk. Ms. Howell's rigid professionalism melted into a genuine warmth that put me at ease.

"Yeah, I guess there is something," I said. "This project—*The Garden*, as Ian calls it—is messing with my mind a little. I've always been good at following the rules and doing what's expected of me, you know?"

Ms. Howell laughed, "Yes. You've made quite a name for yourself at this school, Ms. Fernández. You're a favorite among the teachers."

I blushed. "Oh, thank you, I think." I cleared my throat. "The thing is, the rules aren't clear inside this virtual world. I'm not sure they even exist. For the first time, I have to set the rules. And I'm worried I'm doing it wrong."

Ms. Howell smiled as she leaned forward, resting her elbows on her desk. "Sounds like this is exactly the kind of project you need."

"Yeah, I guess."

"Rules don't automatically happen, Lucy." It was the first

time Ms. Howell had referred to me by my first name, which made me feel safer somehow. She smiled. "Somebody has to create the rules. And for someone like you—someone who's always been a follower—it can be easy to view rules as unbreakable laws. But rules of culture aren't like gravity. They're not some invisible force outside of your control. Rules are reflections of the values of the people who made them. So the real question is, what do you value?"

I wasn't sure how to answer that question. My motivation for doing things was intricately connected to the wants and wishes of others—my mom, most of all. I aimed for success because Mom demanded it. Dad didn't want me to ruffle feathers, so I avoided drama. Teachers, friends, and coaches all wanted something from me. Extracting myself from other people's expectations felt impossible.

So, what did I value? I wasn't sure.

Luckily Ms. Howell wasn't expecting an answer. "Think about it," she said as she gathered some papers from her desk and stood up.

"Thanks, Ms. Howell. I will. And I appreciate your help."

"Any time." She glanced at the clock. "Now, one last thing I must know before I head off to a meeting."

"What's that?"

"When will I see this project you're working on?"

I smiled. "Hopefully soon."

IAN'S NOTES
MONDAY, AUG. 22

How much does a name matter, I wonder? After watching the Simples the past few days, I think it matters a lot, which is kind of weird when you think about it. We don't pick our names. They're slapped on us as soon as we're born. And yet, they become a part of us.

I wonder if I had waited to learn more about Steve. Would I have chosen a different name for him? And what about my parents? Ian means "God is gracious." Do you think they would have picked something else for me now? I know I would.

CHAPTER 9
THE GLITCH

"Knock, knock." I softly tapped Ian's bedroom door, eager to talk to him after chewing on Ms. Howell's question for the past few hours.

"Hey, Luce! Come on in." Ian was sitting at his desk, sipping on a milkshake.

"How was the dentist?"

"Painful." Ian moaned as he rubbed his cheek. "But after four fillings and a slightly numb mouth, Mom got me a milkshake for dinner. So, all things considered, not bad."

"Maybe if you ate fewer milkshakes for dinner, you'd have fewer cavities," I joked.

"Touché." Ian took another long sip.

I sat down on Ian's bed and pulled out my notebook. "Good news, Ms. Howell agreed to be our faculty advisor for the tournament."

"Cool," Ian said, clearly uninterested. He turned to face me, perking up a bit. "I want to show you something." He stood up and tapped the seat of his chair. "Come. Sit."

I cautiously walked to his desk and sat down. Ian leaned over my shoulder, clicking the mouse and opening *The Garden* from his desktop. The screen was divided into four sections, each switching to another area of the island every few seconds. The sights were familiar, but everything was stripped of its vitality. Instead of the tangible experience I had come to love, I was suddenly a security guard monitoring the comings and goings of strangers living in a make-believe world.

"I've never seen it like this," I said, mesmerized by its mechanics. I looked at every corner of the screen. "I had no idea *The Garden* was so big!"

"Oh yeah, you've only walked through a small fraction of what's there," Ian said as he hovered over my shoulder. He moved in closer. "Your hair smells like coconut."

Uncomfortable, I leaned away, trying to make more space between us. "Uh, so... What did you want to show me?"

"This," Ian said as he clicked his mouse again. The lower-left corner of the screen expanded, giving us a perfect view of a cluster of huts near the middle of the town. Ian unplugged his headphones and turned up the volume. We could hear a handful of Simples talking to one another.

"You can ask Steve for a name," one woman said to another.

"Did Steve give you a name?" the second woman asked.

"Yes, my name is Sariah," she said proudly.

The others nodded their heads while silently talking to themselves, "Sariah. Yes, Sariah is a good name."

"Steve also gave me a name," said a man. "I'm called Joe."

The others excitedly practiced saying the name. "Joe, Joe. Good name."

The second woman spoke again, "But where do I find Steve? Will he give me a name?"

"What's going on here?" I asked, my eyes glued to the screen.

Ian laughed. "Well, it looks like Steve has become the official name giver. I've witnessed the same conversation dozens of times over the past two days. The only difference is the people involved and the names they've been given. From what I can gather, Steve has named over 100 people since last Wednesday when you went inside—just under half of the 231 Simples I've programmed."

"Are you for real?" My eyes widened as I leaned toward the screen.

"What's interesting is he's become a sort of celebrity among the others. The word spread quickly."

I shook my head in amazement, smiling at Ian. "You did this."

"Did what? Am I in trouble?"

"No, you did what needed to be done. You taught him something simple. His name. But had you not shown him how it works, they'd all still be nameless automatons without any sense of identity."

Ian shook his head. "You know, Luce. Sometimes you overthink this stuff way too much."

"Oh, you have no idea," I said with a faint smile. "But I learned something today. Culture doesn't happen in a void. It is learned. So if we want these people to develop into anything worthwhile, we'll need to teach them."

"Teach them what?"

"First, how to be individuals—to be different and distinct. I think we've been coming at this all wrong, worrying about the rules of the society before we give them a chance first to define who they are as people. Once they've established a sense of *me*, they can work on a sense of *we*. They'll begin to teach and learn from each other."

"As evident here," Ian interjected. "When they have something worthwhile to share, they'll share it. Last week, nobody was interacting. Now, look at them! Who knew a name could be so powerful?"

"Right?" I grabbed the mouse from Ian.

"What are you doing?"

"Checking for any other signs of progress." I clicked, cycling through a few different camera angles. "Look." I pointed to the screen. "Someone's approaching the beach. I thought you were going to make that off-limits?"

"That's weird," Ian said, taking over the mouse. "I programmed an invisible barrier around the town to keep them inside their borders. They shouldn't be able to leave the village boundaries. There must be a glitch—a bug of some kind." He zoomed in. "Who is that?"

I leaned closer to confirm my suspicions. "Evie," I said, slightly amused.

More than simply walking the pathway toward the beach, Evie explored every nook and cranny. She was picking up rocks, lifting leaves, and scanning the sky. Like a pirate looking for buried treasure—this was a woman on a mission to discover anything of worth.

"We need to do something," Ian said. He pushed my chair out of the way and grabbed the microphone next to the computer. Watching Evie move closer to the shore, he finally cleared his throat before speaking in his fake, deep voice.

"Evie," he said. "Stay away from that beach. Go back home."

My cheeks went hot. No matter what progress came from Ian's interjections, they were still off-putting. I held my breath, waiting for Evie's response. Her eyes traced the clouds before lifting her arms above her head. The expression on her face was a mixture of scared determination.

"Who are you?" Evie yelled.

I dug my elbow into Ian's side and shook my head. "Don't say anything."

"Fine, I'll reboot her. She's obviously the source of the glitch."

"No, don't!" I pulled his hand off the mouse. Grabbing the

VR headset next to me, I stepped away from the desk. "I'm going in."

"Why? What are you going to do?" Ian asked.

"I'm not sure. But I know Evie is different. She's what we need for this project to work. Don't you dare reset her."

As soon as my feet hit the sand, I bolted toward the dunes.

"Whoa, slow down!" Ian's voice echoed in my ear. "Evie is heading toward the village. There is no fire, so relax. You don't want to scare her."

"Right." I took a deep breath and slowed my pace. It was weird having Ian always watching. I made it into the village and began scanning for Evie. "Where is she now?" I said under my breath.

"To your right, sitting under that oak tree," Ian said.

I turned to find her looking at the sky. "Hi, Evie."

Evie jumped to her feet. "Lucy! I'm glad you're back."

I was still a little out of breath but tried to act casual as I sat down next to her. "What are you doing?"

"I heard the Voice again."

"What voice?"

"The Voice in the Sky." Evie stared at the sky. "The one that gave Steve his name. Remember? It was that day I saw you hiding in the bushes. I followed you and heard everything." She talked like a precocious child, full of emotion, confidence, and curiosity.

"Right," I said carefully. "*That* voice."

"I heard it again today. It told me to go home."

I reached for my sunflower charm like I always do when nervous. But my neck was bare. I moved my fingers to my lips and started nervously biting my nails. "What do you think the Voice is?" I hoped Evie's response would help guide my answer.

Evie pressed her lips and shook her head. "I'm not sure.

Whatever it is, it knows things. Sees things. It knew Steve's name. It knew I was heading toward the beach."

"And why were you going to the beach?" I asked.

"To find you."

"Me? Why?"

"Well, you said you were from another place. I wanted to go there. But as I got to the edge of the village, a strange resistance stopped me from going further. It was like an invisible wall I couldn't move past no matter how hard I tried."

"So, how did you finally make it to the dunes?"

"I found a small spot, like a hidden crack." Evie grabbed me by the shoulders and pointed to the path between two small huts. The road had a small area where the edges didn't line up— almost like a shifted fault line. "There is no resistance right where that pathway fractures. It is like a secret doorway to the rest of the world."

A glitch. Ian was right about a bug, except it wasn't in Evie's programming. It was a problem with the barrier's coding. I smiled at Evie, inspired by her determination. "How long did it take you to find it?"

Evie sighed. "A long time. I walked the whole perimeter of the village until I found the spot that let me out. When I finally escaped, I was so excited." Her eyes widened, along with her smile, as she grabbed my hand. "How long did it take you to find it?"

"To find what? What do you mean?"

"To find the secret doorway? You said you came from another place. You must have discovered the door before I did. How else could you have made it past the invisible wall to find us?"

I was impressed with Evie's deduction skills. She was so anxious for answers that a part of me wanted to tell her the truth, but that could ruin the project and our chances of winning TechEd. I needed some other kind of explanation.

Evie leaned in closer to me. "So? How long did it take you to find the doorway?"

"Uh, it took a while." I lied. "But I was looking a long time before you."

"And how far away is your home? Is it near the beach or somewhere else? I tried to find you, but the Voice stopped me." Evie shook her head. "He told me to stay away from the beach and turn back. Why?"

"The place I come from can be dangerous," I said. This time I was only sort of lying. After all, Evie was nothing more than code. She couldn't survive in the real world. Leaving her digital world *was* dangerous. But my answer didn't generate the reaction I had hoped. Fear crept into Evie's eyes.

"If it is dangerous, you should stay here," Evie said frantically.

"No, I'm fine. Don't worry about me." I quickly tried to shift the focus. Standing up, I gestured to the beautiful scenery that surrounded us. "Besides, why would you want to leave? This place is perfect. And you have everything you need—food, shelter, community."

"What's a community?" Evie asked.

"A community is a group of people living in the same place." I sat down again and turned toward her. "Everyone in the village is part of your community. And they need you. They need you to stay with them and help them."

"Help them? How? I don't even know them."

"Not yet, but you will. You're all new—uh, I mean..." I shook my head, trying to find the right words. "You're all *young* and have a lot to learn. But you're special, Evie."

"Special? What does that mean?"

"It means you're different. You have questions. You want answers. And your curiosity can help you find them. I mean, look at you! The way you searched and worked to find a way past the invisible barrier—you're amazing!"

Evie stood tall. Her smile grew. "I can help my community find their way out, too!"

"No!" I jumped to my feet.

With a deflated look, Evie sank back down on the rock.

I immediately regretted blurting it out. I cleared my throat, took a deep breath, and tried again. "No," I said calmly. "As I said, there is danger outside the village. You need to stay here. Everyone needs to stay here. You can help your community by keeping them inside the village and teaching them."

"Teach them what?"

I paused. It was up to me to plant the right seed to help the Simples progress. But what could I tell Evie that would help her lead without ruining the experiment? I still didn't understand why she was so different from the others, but it was clear Evie was the key to the project's success.

"Well, Evie. You can teach them a lot, like how to ask questions. You've got a knack for it."

"But I only ask questions because I don't know anything!" Evie said, slightly exasperated.

I grabbed Evie's hands. We locked eyes. "That's how you find answers. They don't drop from the sky. It comes from asking questions and looking for solutions."

"You're right," Evie said as if churning the words in her mind. "Steve had a question. He asked what a name was, and *then* the answer came from the sky!"

My head dropped. With a heavy sigh, I tried again. "That's not exactly what I meant. Yes, in Steve's case, the answer came from the sky. But your question about getting past the invisible wall—that answer came from you."

"But I never asked a question."

"Not out loud. But you asked it here." I gently tapped Evie's head. "Your mind has been asking questions this whole time. It asked what was beyond the village. It asked how to move past the invisible wall. And those questions inspired you to search for answers."

"I understand. I was thinking those things, and those thoughts led me to answers. Like, I now know there is a beach over there," Evie said, pointing toward the dunes. "And there is an invisible doorway between those huts."

"Exactly."

"But do you think the Voice in the Sky could also give me answers?" Evie asked. "It would be faster. The Voice knows everything."

I smiled, shaking my head. "Nobody knows everything."

"The Voice in the Sky does."

I tried to stifle my laughter. On the one hand, Ian knew more than most, but not everything. Then again, Ian knew all the inner workings of *The Garden*, from the coding to the hardware and how it all connects—a fact that made me jealous.

"The Voice in the Sky understands a lot," I finally admitted. "But I'm not sure he will always be around to tell you what to do. Maybe he has some answers for you. Maybe he doesn't. But part of growing up is figuring things out for yourself."

"I guess," Evie said with a slight smile. "I'm excited by how much I can learn. And every time I learn something new, it makes me feel safer—less confused." She closed her eyes. "But it is also a little scary."

I sat mesmerized for a moment. I loved seeing the world through Evie's eyes. Everyone at school was so concerned with fitting in. Evie's determination to find her own way was refreshing. I wanted her passion to rub off on me.

"I understand," I said. "But that's what makes it all worth it. The best things in life are often a little scary." I leaned over and hugged Evie.

"What are you doing?"

"Hugging you. It's a way to show affection. You're my friend,

Evie. You're someone I like and trust. A friend is someone you can count on, even when they're gone."

"Wait. Does that mean you're leaving again?"

"For now," I said, standing up. "I've got to go. But I'll be back. In the meantime, why don't you try interacting with the other people here? Learn their names. Teach them how to ask questions. And together, you might find the answers you're looking for."

"I'll do my best," Evie said. "Thank you, friend."

CULTURAL ANTHROPOLOGY

Culture cannot form in a day. Time is a necessary ingredient. Time changes people and landscapes. Time makes room for new ideas, as harmful or outdated ideas die out. With enough time, all cultures will adapt and evolve.

<u>Cultural Anthropology: Diversity in a Global Age</u>, 21st edition
Chapter 2, page 17

CHAPTER 10
TIME TO EVOLVE

THUD. My anthropology book hit the lunchroom table.

"Time," I said.

Ian grabbed his chest. "Sheesh, Luce! Don't do that. You scared me."

I pulled my chair out and sat down, directly facing him. "I couldn't sleep last night after I met with Evie. I've been so worried that I am influencing them too much or too little. I always have a million questions running through my head."

"Okay... and?" Ian said.

"Well, I started reading our anthropology textbook, trying to find answers. And look what I found." I opened my book to page seventeen and pointed to a sentence. "Read," I said, pushing the book in front of him.

Ian rolled his eyes but smiled and obeyed. "Culture cannot form in a day," he said, reading from the page. "Duh, so?"

"You're missing the point." I tapped the book. "The Simples need more time. That is the answer. I've been racking my brain, figuring out how we program an authentic culture into the system, but real cultures form over time."

"Yeah, and?" It was like Ian was too lazy to connect the dots.

"So," I said firmly, "the regional competition is one month from today, which is not enough time for the Simples to evolve in any meaningful way."

"What do you want to do about that? You're not suggesting we change projects, are you? Because that would be crazy."

"No, I don't want to change anything. All I want to do is speed things up and give the Simples more time. Is that possible?"

"Speed things up. How?"

"Well, there have already been hints of progress in the short time we've been working. Right? We met Steve and Evie, and then things started to change. The community started coming together. People were getting names. Questions were asked. It is all promising."

"It is. I agree."

"The problem is that at this rate, we're not going to have enough research about these people for TechEd. And I've been trying to figure out the best way to program culture from the start. But that is not how it works."

"You're saying culture takes time."

"Exactly. So, we need to stop worrying about coding some artificial rules and instead give them the time to evolve independently."

Ian nodded—as if calculating a complex problem in his mind. "You want to know if we can speed things up inside *The Garden* to track changes over a longer period. For example, while an hour of *our* time passes, the Simples would experience several hours. Is that it?"

"Or days—maybe even years. Yes," I said.

"Yeah, I can do that. Pretty easily, I might add." A cocky smile spread across Ian's face as he shoved a few Cheetos in his mouth.

"Really?"

"Really. Changing the world's internal clock requires a few edits."

"Okay, so let's do it!"

"Hold on," Ian said. "Changing time isn't hard. The tricky part is that there is no birth or death programmed into the system. So even if you speed things up, their reality isn't quite like ours. The Simples don't age. No younger generation will come in and replace the older one. Is that a problem?"

"That's a good question." My spirits deflated. "How hard would it be to add those things—birth, death, and aging?"

Ian shook his head. "I'm not sure, but I can start working on it. It might not be ready for the regional competition, but hopefully, before we head to State." He tossed a few more Cheetos in his mouth, crunching as he thought. "But in the meantime, I think you're onto something with this time thing. It is a start toward giving them a more realistic experience, so let's do it."

"Agreed." I peeked up at the clock. "Shoot. Speaking of time —lunch is almost over. So what's our next step?"

"Give me an hour or two after school to work on this time thing. Why don't you come over after dinner, and we'll give it a whirl."

"Sounds good. So how much time are you going to add? Are you going to move them a few months into the future? A few years? What are you thinking?"

Ian paused while his mind went to work. There was an ease in his thinking process. He probably didn't experience the same tormenting internal dialogue I did when wrestling with a problem. Ian was calm and calculated—taking pleasure in imagining all possibilities.

"How about this," he said confidently.

"Yeah?"

"What if it was like a dial? Say you want to fast-forward a year, or ten, or—whatever. I could add a feature that allows us to speed the Simples up, slow 'em down, or even pause. That way, you can pop in as often as you like. After ten years, you could check in and then push them forward another hundred. We'd have total control over all of it."

"You can do that?"

"I think so."

I smiled and shook my head. "Promise me you'll never use your freaky genius powers for evil, okay?"

He laughed. "I promise. So, are we doing this?"

"Oh, we're doing this. Your house at seven?"

"Seven, it is."

"Put your hand out like this," Ian said, reaching his arm out. After spending the last few days monitoring *The Garden* from his desk, he seemed happy to be back on the beach next to me. I copied what he was doing, extending my hand out in front of me. The sun was getting low, casting a beautiful reflection against the gentle waves.

Ian leaned in closer. "Now, point your index finger and tap the air in front of you—just like you would an app on your iPad."

I tapped, and a small dial appeared out of thin air. I took a step back, surprised by its sudden appearance. Similar in shape and size to the thermostat in my house, the black cylinder was shiny and sleek. A silver ring ran along the edge, and in the middle was a simple backlit triangle—like a play button.

"Whoa, is this the time dial?" I glanced at Ian, who signaled for me to try it. I reached out and gently touched the button in the middle. As soon as I did, it instantly switched to a pause icon. Suddenly, the sound of the waves stopped. Everything froze. There was a bird stuck, mid-flight off to the right. The wind no longer tousled my hair. The ocean stood motionless like a photograph. "Uh, what just happened?"

Ian was thoroughly amused. "You paused everything. Go ahead, touch the button again."

I tapped the button, and it switched back into play mode. The bird flew past our heads while the ocean's gentle hum continued.

"Okay, this is trippy." I laughed nervously. "I mean, I've paused my fair share of things—music, videos, games. But with the Reality Amplifier, I'm pausing... *life*. It was so strange when the breeze disappeared, and the smell of the salty air vanished."

Ian laughed. "If you think that is crazy, reach out and turn the dial *slowly* to the right a tiny bit."

I placed my fingers around the edge of the outer ring and slowly twisted my hand. A set of numbers appeared above the dial. As I turned my hand, the numbers quickly sequenced from 1-H to 312-Y. I let go. The sky went dark and then bright again as the sun sank and rose in a heartbeat.

"I said slowly!" Ian quickly hit the play button, bringing the world back to the normal flow of time. He laughed. "You're always so eager to go for things, aren't you?"

"What did I do?"

"You *almost* fast-forwarded time more than three hundred years. But I stopped it, so you probably only moved things forward about twelve hours or so."

"12 hours? Wow. So, the dial is pretty sensitive. A little nudge goes a long way."

"Yeah, it needs to be sensitive to speed things up a little or a lot."

"How does it work?" I was eager to learn.

"When you move the dial, you're setting a time in the future. The numbers above the dial show you how far ahead you're going. The 'H' stands for hours, 'D' for days, and 'Y' for years. As soon as you let go, everything inside the garden will move forward, like a time-lapse, until it reaches whatever time you set. The further in the future you go, the faster things move. But for the Simples, they won't notice a thing."

"Can you stop it once you've set it?" I asked.

"You can hit the play/pause button, like I did. That will stop the timer. But if you set it to go way off into the future—like you did, you'll need to hit that button fast as things will immediately start moving forward."

"Can time go backward?"

"No, since we're trying to mimic real life, that didn't seem right. Time is a one-way street, even here. The only way back is a total reset of the entire civilization."

I nodded my head, taking everything in. "Okay, one last question. Let's say I set the dial to move forward 100 years. What happens after cycling through that setting?"

"It automatically moves into play mode, back to our normal flow of time."

I was beaming at Ian. "This is incredible. You built this in like—what? Three hours? I can't believe it."

He blushed. "Well, like I said, changing the program's internal clock wasn't that hard. Coding the dial was a bit trickier. But I'm glad you like it."

Ian stared at me, something he often did. But lately, there was an intensity to his gaze that was unsettling. A sudden panic pricked my nerves as I wondered if he liked me—an idea I quickly pushed away.

"Well," I said, eager to move on, "should we put this thing to the test?"

I made my way toward the village as Ian unstrapped from the headset, ready to watch from his desk. As I walked through the dunes, I couldn't get the image of him staring at me out of my mind. My brain, always in planning mode, started calculating all the potential ways any romantic inclinations could sour this experience. I shook my head, telling myself to forget it.

"So, how far in the future should we go?" I asked.

"How about a year?" Ian said. "That should be long enough

to develop some changes without things going totally off the rails should there be a problem."

"Sounds good." I made my way to the village. Full of nerves, I fumbled behind some bushes at the edge of town. I reached out and tapped my finger in front of me. The time dial appeared before my eyes. With a careful turn of my wrist, the numbers moved forward until they hit the one-year mark. "Alright," I muttered. "Let's see what happens."

With a deep exhale, I let go of the dial. Day turned to night and back into day. Over and over, the sun rose and fell. I peered through the bushes. My mouth dropped. A blur of motion raced throughout the town. Everyone moved so fast, making it impossible to track what they were doing. Like smoke around a fire, ghostly trails of life rushed in every direction. Finally, everything locked into place, jolting my senses as the cloud of movement crystallized into a buzzing town.

"Lucy!" Evie exclaimed. "You're back! I was so worried about you."

I turned around, my heart racing from the dramatic shift in time. Evie ran up and threw her arms around my neck. Surprised by the sudden burst of kindness, I settled into the embrace, squeezing tightly around her body. "Hello, Evie. I'm happy you're here." And I meant it.

Evie pulled back, her hands still on my shoulders. "What happened, my friend? Why were you gone so long?" There was a genuine look of concern in her eyes.

"I'm sorry. Sometimes I have a hard time getting away from my home. But please don't worry about me. I promise I was safe."

Evie smiled and linked her arm through mine. "Come, everyone will be so excited to see you."

"Me? Why? They've never met me."

"Oh, I have talked about you a lot."

Evie guided me toward the center of the town, pointing out

different people and places. I couldn't get over how articulate she was.

"Everyone! Lucy has returned!" Evie announced as she neared a group of Simples.

Steve burst through the crowd and ran toward me, giving me a big hug. "Lucy! Welcome back! Do you remember me? I'm Steve!"

I smiled. "Of course, I remember you, Steve."

Steve took me by the hand and pulled me toward the group of Simples. "Let me introduce you to the others," he said confidently.

Over the next few minutes, Steve introduced me to a dozen or more Simples. As I shook their hands, my awe increased. The change in the people's energy was incredible. Their once robotic mannerisms were gone. Individual traits bubbled to the surface, bringing a dynamic interaction to the group. They laughed and hugged as if connected by a particular set of social rules.

"Alright, everyone, we don't want to overwhelm Lucy," Evie said. "I'm going to help reacquaint her with the village." The other Simples responded to Evie with reverence, separating her as a leader.

Evie guided me through the small paths that connected the village. On the outside, things weren't much different. Small huts and fruit baskets still spotted the town. Likewise, the Simples themselves dressed much like they did before. The only notable change I noticed was that everyone was wearing a seashell necklace.

"That's lovely. Where did you get it?" I pointed to the string of puka shells around Evie's neck.

"I made it."

"Oh! Wow. It's beautiful. But where did you find the seashells?"

Evie paused with a slight blush. "I got them on the beach," she said softly.

There was a twang of disappointment. "You went back to the beach?" I chose my words carefully, not wanting to upset Evie. "I thought I told you to stay here. Remember? It is dangerous outside this village."

"I do remember. And I stayed away for a long time. But I was worried something bad had happened to you when you didn't come back."

I smiled sympathetically.

Agitated, Evie sat down. "I wanted to ensure you were okay and help if you weren't. So I went through the invisible doorway again, even though I said I wouldn't. I'm sorry."

"How far did you go?"

"I made it to the edge of the waters. I walked along the shore for many days."

"Days?"

"Days. And I couldn't find you or any signs of another town. I was beginning to wonder if such a place even exists."

"I'm sorry, Evie. That must have been scary."

"It was." Evie pushed some dirt with her foot before looking back at me. Her eyes were dewy with tears. "But when I came back, I found all these seashells in the sand. They were so pretty. So I gathered some and made this necklace."

"It is beautiful," I said.

"Thank you. The others liked it, too. So I went back to the beach and gathered more shells. And each time I made a necklace for someone, it made them happy, which made me happy. So I kept going back." Shame marked Evie's expression. She took a few shallow breaths and then began to cry. "I'm sorry, Lucy. I said I wouldn't go through the invisible doorway, but I did. I kept going back." She gently sobbed into her hands. "I'm a bad friend, aren't I? I didn't listen to you. I'm so, so sorry."

"No, you're not a bad friend—not at all." I wrapped my arm around Evie. "You were doing what you thought was right. You were trying to help me."

"I missed you," Evie said.

"Me, too." It was strange saying it since I saw her just the other day. But I did miss her, and I felt terrible that I had caused her so much grief. "Please promise me you won't go back to the beach. It can be very dangerous."

"But it isn't! I went there dozens of times and never had a problem. The beach is so peaceful."

Evie was right. The beach wasn't any real danger to her. But Ian and I had agreed to keep that space just for us. It had become a haven for me—offering me solace amidst my stressful life. I didn't want to share it, but I also didn't want to hurt Evie. I searched my mind for the right words and was about to speak when a loud voice ripped from the clouds above.

"Evie, you shall not go to the beach again! This is your last warning." Ian's theatrics were at an all-time high as he made his proclamation in his most resounding voice.

Evie fell to her knees, terrified by the booming sound. "The Voice in the Sky! I'm sorry! Please forgive me."

Not again. I was getting more annoyed with Ian's dramatic interruptions. But I had to admit, I was also a bit relieved. As unrealistic as his all-knowing Voice in the Sky was, it produced some impressive results. The only question was, at what cost?

"It's okay." I pulled Evie back to her feet.

"No, you warned me, but I didn't listen. And now the Voice in the Sky is angry with me." Tears welled up inside Evie's eyes again. "I've cried out to the Voice many times, asking him for answers, but nobody has heard from him in a long time. And now I've angered him. I'm a bad person."

"You're not!" I grabbed Evie by the shoulders. "You're a good person who made a mistake—a mistake made trying to help a friend. But now you must trust that I'm okay, listen to the Voice, and stay in the village. Help your people. Create more beautiful things," I said, pointing to Evie's necklace.

She sighed and gave me a weak but sincere smile.

"I wish I could stay longer, but I have to go." I stood up. "I may be gone for a long time, so please don't worry about me. Can you promise me something?"

"Yes, I'll stay off the beach," Evie said quietly.

"That would be great, but there is something else."

"What?"

"Promise me you'll keep asking questions."

Evie scoffed, shaking her head. "I think all my questions are getting me in trouble."

"No, your questions will save you. Trust me." I let my eyes meet hers, hoping Evie would understand my sincerity. "Keep asking questions, okay? Promise?"

Evie pressed her lips, slowly exhaling. "I promise."

I hugged her and pulled back. My eyes searched her face, trying to understand her better. With a quiet *goodbye*, I began my journey back to the beach. As soon as I was far enough away from the village, I ripped off my headset.

"Seriously?" I threw my VR goggles on Ian's bed and shot him an annoyed look.

"What?" Ian said, trying to act innocently.

"This whole Voice in the Sky thing is getting a little out of hand, don't you think?"

"It worked, didn't it?" Ian turned back around, looking at the screen. "We can't monitor them while they're fast-forwarding. I want to make sure they stay put."

"Why not fix the glitch?" I asked.

"Eh, nobody else cares about the barrier," Ian said. "And trying to find the bug among tens of thousands of lines of code could take hours. My solution worked. Let it go."

"But did you see how afraid Evie was?"

"A little healthy fear can be good. It keeps 'em in line. Besides, they aren't real people, Luce. You know that, right? I think you're getting a little too emotionally attached to this Evie character. Don't let your feelings interfere with the research."

Ian was right. Scoring a win at the TechEd Tournament was the goal. "Fine, I'm sorry. I'll try to let it go, but I'll never be comfortable with your dramatic proclamations from above."

"It won't be an issue. We're going to fast-forward again, and it will become a distant memory. Besides, only two of them have heard the Voice. They don't have enough evidence for it to stick around as anything other than some mythic legend."

"I hope so." I sat down on Ian's bed. "I think another big push into the future might be good. It takes us out of the equation and focuses on the experiment. What do you say? Should we fast-forward them another hundred years?"

"A hundred? Wow." Ian nodded his head, mulling it over. He shrugged. "Sure, why not? If you want, I can do it now, and we can check in tomorrow after they're done simmering for a bit."

"Sounds good."

Ian swiveled back to his computer and pulled up the dial from his desktop. He typed out *100-Y* before giving it a final tap of the mouse. "And they're off."

A blur of motion danced across the screen. It was much less intense viewing it from Ian's computer. Watching a million little moments unfold was nerve-wracking. A lot can happen in a hundred years.

"Who knows what tomorrow will bring," I said as I grabbed my things to go.

Ian turned off his monitor and sighed. "Could be a whole new world."

MESSAGE FROM DAD

WED, AUG 31

I wanted to say bye before I left, but you were still at Ian's. You two seem to be spending a lot of time together.

Sorry I missed you! Yeah, we're preparing for TechEd Regionals. Lots to do. When do you get back? Be safe!

I'll be home in four days. Don't worry. I've still got the plastic shamrock you gave me for good luck. I never fly without it.

I found that in the gutter when I was four. You don't need to keep it. I'm old enough to know it is meaningless.

The cool thing about being human is we each get to decide what's meaningful. That little clover makes me think of you when I'm gone. I'm keeping it forever. Love you, mijita.

CHAPTER 11
IAN'S GIFT

LUCY TREKKED through the dunes in her cream-colored tunic. "This is nerve-wracking."

"Why?" I carefully watched from my monitor. It had been twenty-four hours since we pushed The Simples forward. Now it was time to examine the results of our experiment.

"A lot can happen in a hundred years," she said. "Wars, poverty, uprisings—what if their entire village is in chaos?"

"Dramatic, much?" I laughed. Sheesh, this girl worried about everything. "Don't forget, Luce. The Simples live very different lives. They have easy access to food, clothing, and shelter. There is no death or aging. All of that gives them a leg up."

"True. But you're working on updating the code for all that, right?"

"Yes, ma'am."

As Lucy neared the edge of town, she lowered her voice to a whisper. "Are we sure we need to add those things? It is kinda cruel."

"Life is kinda cruel." I couldn't hide the bitterness in my voice.

Lucy put her fingers to her lips, signaling me to keep quiet. She maneuvered through some tall bushes, trying to stay hidden.

I rotated through different camera angles, checking for any changes. Sturdier buildings made from wood, stone, and even brick stood in place of the old grass huts. Vibrant hand-dyed sarongs, tailored shirts, trousers, and dresses embellished with shells, beads, and stitching hung from clothing lines.

"Luce, don't move."

She froze. "What? Is something wrong?"

"You're fine. But you need a wardrobe update. Hold on." I pulled up a menu and scrolled through various outfit codes I had swiped from an old video game. I quickly copied and pasted what we needed in Lucy's avatar profile. A second later, she was dressed in a tasteful violet wrap dress.

Almost perfect—just one tiny tweak.

I quickly tapped out a few more commands, and a small sunflower charm carved out of wood formed around Lucy's neck. Her hand instinctively moved to touch it. She smiled, admiring the old-fashioned version of the gold necklace she wore every day.

"Thank you," she whispered.

"Go get 'em, boss. You've got this."

Lucy stepped out from her hiding spot. She walked along what used to be a dirt path, now paved with cobblestones. About fifty feet in front of her were a man and woman. They appeared to be bartering over some loaves of bread.

"Excuse me," Lucy said, interrupting them. "I'm looking for Evie. Is she around?"

"Who are you?" the woman said, stepping back. "You aren't from around here."

"No, I'm not," Lucy said carefully.

"How did you get here?" The man stepped in front of the woman. His manners were rigid, as if he were ready to attack. "There's no way in or out of the village."

Lucy stepped back, raising her hands slightly to show them she meant no harm. "You don't need to be afraid. I have been here before, even though it has been a while. I'm looking for Evie."

"Wait..." The man leaned forward. "Are you Lucy?"

"Yes, I am Lucy!"

He stepped back and whispered to the woman. "That means Evie was right. There are other people and places beyond Fredena."

The woman let out a small gasp. Lucy inched closer to the trio of Simples who each took a step back.

"What's Fredena?" Lucy asked.

"Fredena is this place. Our home," said the woman. She quickly packed up her things. "I'm sorry. You must excuse us. We need to speak with the others." She and the man hurried across the street and disappeared inside a small building.

"That was weird," Lucy said under her breath.

I agreed. "Very."

With the two Simples gone, I took advantage of the quiet moment to investigate the village as I clicked through camera angles. There was a wooden windmill and several vendor booths on one side of the town square. Buildings with window displays and signs with strange symbols lined the streets. "Wow, this place has changed a lot."

Lucy shook her head, eyeing the horizon. "I need to find Evie."

The streets were mostly empty. A few Simples wandered through the streets. Some were constructing new homes. Others were selling textiles and pottery. Lucy's eyes darted from left to right until she finally locked on to Evie's familiar corkscrew curls and broad shoulders in the distance. Evie wore a long, flowy skirt—hand-dyed with vivid reds and yellows. A piece of white fabric wrapped around her neck and torso, creating a sort of halter top that hugged her curves.

"Evie!" Lucy shouted.

Evie turned around slowly. Her eyes widened, and a smile spread across her face. She dropped the basket of beads she had been carrying and ran to meet Lucy.

"Lucy? Is it really you?" Evie swung her arms around Lucy's neck. "I told everyone you'd be back. We all waited for it." She walked in a circle, observing Lucy from every angle. "After a while, some people started to doubt you existed, saying you were a creation of my mind. But those of us who had met you—we dreamed of your return. You told us you would. And here you are, finally."

"I'm sorry I was gone so long," Lucy said. "But I'm happy to be here."

I was surprised by the warmth in Lucy's voice. Not that I expected her to be cold, but her regard for Evie was unmistakable, even from where I sat.

"I'm happy, too. Now that you're back, everyone will see that you're real. And then they will believe the Voice in the Sky is real."

My senses perked up. I was anxious to hear what Evie had to say and surprisingly satisfied that she mentioned the Voice in the Sky—even though I'm sure Lucy hated it.

"What do you mean?" Lucy asked, clearly taken back.

"A few people don't believe you or the Voice in the Sky exists. But now that you're here, it will prove we were telling the truth."

Evie grabbed Lucy's hand, leading her toward another part of the town.

"Where are we going?" Lucy asked.

"I want to show you something."

The path they traveled on was long. So, I skipped ahead, bouncing through camera angles to determine where Evie was taking them. They went past the center of the village and headed toward the grove of trees near the pond. It was the same place Lucy had first met Steve. I switched my view and gasped. Next to the pond, in the patch of grass, the Simples had built some kind of massive altar. There were layers of stone on top of a broad foundation reaching toward the sky nearly twelve feet high.

"What the hell is that?" I said quietly as Lucy and Evie stepped into view.

Lucy's eyes grew as she walked around the immense structure. "Evie, what is this?"

Evie proudly placed her hand on one of the stones. "This is where we communicate with the Voice in the Sky. We give our thanks, offer gifts, ask questions, and pray for his answers." She stood stoic before dropping her head and sighing. "Although we haven't heard from him in many cycles."

I zoomed in on the impressive structure. There were dozens of polished rocks, handmade ornaments, and other trinkets tucked in between the layers of stone.

"I don't understand," Lucy said. "Why did you build this? Why here?"

Evie gestured to the sky. "Remember? This was the spot where the Voice first spoke to Steve. We've been waiting for his return ever since. We've offered him our beautiful things, hoping for answers. Now that you're back, the Voice will also likely return."

"Why do you think that?" Lucy asked.

"You're connected to the Voice! Think about it. You were there when Steve first heard him. You found me right after the Voice warned me to stay off the beach. And you were by my side when he chastised me for not obeying his commands. You and the Voice are connected. I know it."

Evie certainly was perceptive. Lucy and I *were* connected, even if Lucy didn't want to accept it. And as much as Lucy protested my dramatic interventions, I was astonished by the results they had produced. I thought about the great pyramids of Egypt, Stonehenge, and the Mayan ruins. The most distinctive cultures built stunning structures to display their rituals, beliefs, and culture. Maybe *I* was the key to ensuring our people were also memorable. My voice inspired them.

Lucy's eyes remained glued to the giant structure. "Wow. This is... something."

Evie carefully walked up a set of stone stairs next to the altar. She took off her puka necklace and placed it at the top of the structure. "Voice in the Sky, we are pleased Lucy has returned. I offer this gift—a token of my gratitude. We hope you will grant us your guidance."

I'm no mind reader, but Lucy's expression was easily decipherable. Stunned, panicked, and disgusted, Lucy nearly toppled over as Evie bowed her head in solemn prayer to me.

But I felt differently. After so many attempts at creating artificial life, this one had taken root. These people weren't just predetermined algorithms. They were creating meaning. Right in front of my eyes was a civilization, made from my own hands, that possessed the same storytelling abilities that have made humans so unique.

And at the center of their story was *me*.

Evie took Lucy's hand. "Now we wait."

"I am pleased with your gift!" My voice boomed from above. The loud rumble of my words echoed throughout the village, nearly knocking Lucy and Evie over.

Evie dropped to her knees. "Oh! Thank you! Thank you, most wise Voice!"

Lucy's mouth dropped. If looks could kill, I'd be a dead man.

Evie pulled Lucy down to the ground, smiling. "Yes, I told you! You *are* connected. And now, perhaps the Voice will tell us more about who we are and why we are here."

"Wow, this is all—" Lucy stood back up. "Something." She shook her head as if trying to formulate a new plan. "Uh, Evie, I'm sorry, but I have to go."

Evie's mouth dropped. "No! Don't go. You can't leave us

again. Not now! We will honor the Voice with celebration. You must join us. Please."

Celebration? For me? I admit I was enjoying it all a little too much. Lucy clearly didn't share my joy. "I'm sorry," she said. "I need to leave. But I promise I'll be back—*soon*."

"In time for the grand party?" Evie asked.

Lucy sighed. "Sure, when is it?"

"It will take time to prepare. Can you come back in two days?"

"I can," Lucy said with a faint smile.

"Then I must also go! I will tell the others. There is much to do!"

Lucy waited for Evie to leave before she disappeared from my screen. I turned around as she ripped off the headset. Her penetrating scowl pierced me. "What the hell, man?"

I laughed, which was always the wrong move with this kind of stuff, but I couldn't help it. Lucy was taking things so seriously. "Come on, Luce. I'm having a little fun. Besides, look how happy I made Evie."

"Ian, this is bad. The Simples have built an entire belief system around *you*! They think you're some sort of god or something."

"And they couldn't have chosen a more benevolent one to worship," I joked.

Lucy put her hands on her hips. "I'm serious."

"Luce, this isn't a bad thing. Like thousands of civilizations throughout history, the Simples have created their own stories to help them understand their world."

Lucy hated to admit it when I was right—especially when I was acting like a total ass. But I *was* right, and she knew it.

"I mean, look at this!" I pointed to the screen, zooming in on the altar next to the pond. "If anything, this proves the validity of this project. This is more than a video game with a loose storyline. This is artificial intelligence creating new ideas based on their experiences. You should be thrilled!"

"But their beliefs revolve around some Voice in the Sky. That's not realistic." Lucy slumped down on my bed.

"Says who?" I wasn't going to lose this argument. "How many cultures have believed in spirits or visions from heaven? Humans have believed in countless crazy things to make sense of life. We're helping speed things along by inserting ourselves from the get-go."

Lucy dropped her head into her hands, rubbing her temples before looking up. "I guess it doesn't matter if I agree or not— what's done is done. So now what?"

"Now we gear up for the competition. I think the changes over these hundred years have given us a lot of great research. I'm still working on updating the code—adding things like death, disease, and all that other *fun* stuff."

"You're sadistic," Lucy said as she rolled her eyes.

I chuckled. "And I'm guessing *you* have some work you need to do, too? Like making sense of the research and polishing a presentation?"

"You're right. There's plenty to do." Lucy sighed.

I lifted my eyebrows and shot her my signature smile. "And then, in two days, we've got a celebration to attend."

"What celebration?"

"Uh, the Simples' celebration, remember? Evie *just* invited us."

Lucy stood up, pursing her lips. "What do you mean, *us*? You weren't invited."

"Uh, hello. They're having a celebration in *my* honor. It would be rude not to make some kind of appearance or give a little speech."

"We're screwed," Lucy said, only half-joking.

"Nah, it'll be fine. I promise I won't do anything to derail the project. You've got to trust me on this one."

Over the next two days, Lucy kept her distance. She said she was preparing for Regionals, but I think she was still mad about my dramatic outburst at the altar. Still, there was a lot of work, and Lucy never backed away from a deadline.

Lucy asked me to upload *The Garden* onto her laptop so she could monitor the Simples on her own time. She wanted to track their habits, dress, language, food, and rituals. I was hesitant to comply, honestly. Sharing my code was like giving away the only power I had. But I trusted Lucy, even if I didn't trust anyone in her world. Besides, I didn't need to give her everything, just enough to gather data. And while she was adamant about learning how the program worked in the backend, the viewer-only access I provided would be enough to keep her busy until Regionals.

"So, what do you have planned for tonight's big celebration?" Lucy asked as she picked up a headset.

"Oh, nothing much." I leaned back in my chair, cracking my knuckles. "I thought I'd turn the moon into blood or drop all the stars from the sky."

Lucy's eyes filled with a threatening rage. "You wouldn't."

"Sheesh, Luce, I'm kidding."

"Seriously, though, don't do anything crazy. The Simples are in a good spot. I don't want to mess things up."

I put my hand on my heart. "Nothing crazy, I promise. I was thinking of some kind of subtle sign. You know, something that shows I'm paying attention, but nothing too weird."

"Okay. Just, *please*—behave." Lucy put on her headset and plugged in. I spun my chair around, eyes glued to the monitor.

The sun had already vanished behind the ocean horizon. Stars scattered against the growing night sky as Lucy headed toward the village.

"Man, I will never get over this view," she whispered.

"Me either," I said, staring directly at her.

As Lucy made her way to the edge of the village, the faint sound of music buzzed in the distance. I tapped through a few camera angles, trying to locate its origin. The sound became crystal clear as soon as the grassy patch next to the altar popped onto my screen. A dozen or so musicians created a lively atmosphere for the evening. Voices in harmony drifted along with the clouds. Drums rooted the melodic song with powerful percussion. It was enchanting, and I could only imagine how magical it was in person.

Lucy came into the scene through the grove of trees. Her eyes lit up when she saw rows of bouquets, torches of light, and a table full of different foods set up along the perimeter. She nodded her head to the beat of the music as if hypnotized by it.

The Simples gathered in small groups spread throughout the patch of grass near the pond. Lucy meandered through the crowd. Everyone's mouths were moving, but I had difficulty hearing what they were saying over the music. That was a simple fix. I muted the music track with a few taps of a button, leaving their conversations easy to decipher. Everyone was excited and curious about how the night would unfold—especially Steve.

Lucy noticed him across the grass and ran toward him. "Steve!"

"Lucy! You came!" He hugged her. "Can you believe this? Isn't this all so amazing?"

"It's fantastic."

Steve's eyes danced around, taking in all the sights and sounds. "None of it would have happened without Evie. She was determined to make this the best night ever. She thinks if the Voice in the Sky is pleased, he might help us."

Lucy tilted her head. "Help you. How?"

"Help us break free from the village."

Break free from the village? Shit.

Lucy was shocked. She leaned in closer to Steve. "Wait

—*what*? What do you mean? Why do you want to leave this place?"

"Oh, I don't." Steve scanned the growing crowd, still charmed by the night's splendor. "Everything is perfect here. Most of us think so. But Evie believes there is more beyond Fredena. She's probably right. You're from outside the village, aren't you? Evie said so."

Lucy nervously nodded her head.

"Well, she doesn't understand why the Voice has forbidden us to stay here. But I don't want to leave."

Lucy furrowed her brow as if trying to understand. "So, Evie hopes that by pleasing the Voice in the Sky—he'll allow you all to leave the village?"

"Yep, she's probably right. I mean, she knew you'd come back. She was right about the Voice being connected to you. So maybe she's right about what's beyond Fredena. There could be something better."

Steve peered over Lucy's shoulders. "Oh! Jenny brought her famous boowa! I have to grab one before they're gone!" He ran off toward a woman carrying some delicious-looking custard tarts. For a second, I contemplated strapping on a headset so that I could taste it myself. Thinking about it made me hungry. I reached over and opened a bag of Cheetos from my desk.

"Did you hear that?" Lucy's voice snapped me back to the problem at hand. She had vanished from my screen. With a few clicks, I switched views until I found her hiding inside the grove of trees.

"Yeah," I said. "That Evie is relentless—such an explorer."

"So what do we do? We can't let them leave the village. There is nothing out there for them to visit!" It was clear Lucy was stressed about this new development.

I took a deep breath for both of us. "Okay, first of all, *relax*. This isn't a big deal. Evie is the only one eager to leave, so I'll give her a better reason to stay."

"Better reason to stay, what do you mean—"

"Lucy?" Evie's voice interrupted us. Lucy quickly turned around, throwing her arms up awkwardly. "Evie! There you are!"

Evie walked toward her. "Who are you talking to?"

"Talking? I wasn't talking to anyone." Lucy wipe her hands on her dress and tuck her hair behind her ears. I could always tell when she was searching for a lie. It was adorable. "I was, uh, thinking out loud."

"Oh." Evie leaned a little, trying to look behind Lucy. "Well, the ceremony is about to begin. Won't you join us?"

"I'll be right there."

As soon as Evie was gone, Lucy let out a deep sigh. "Ian? You still there? What did you mean by giving her a better reason to stay?"

"I've got an idea," I said. "Trust me."

CHAPTER 12
THE COUPLING

"My fellow Fredenians, I am so happy you've joined us for this momentous occasion." Evie stood tall and composed as she addressed the Simples.

I made my way back from the grove of trees, slipping in near the front of the crowd. My armpits were a sweaty mess. I had no idea what Ian had in store, and his track record left me worried.

Steve motioned me to join him. He whispered as I stood by his side. "Isn't she great, Lucy?" His gaze was locked on Evie like a puppy patiently waiting for crumbs from his master's table.

"Yeah." I smiled. "Evie is special."

"Thank you to everyone who helped with tonight's festivities." Evie pointed toward the large table in the back. "The food smells fantastic. The decor is breathtaking. I'm sure the Voice in the Sky is pleased with all your efforts."

The Simples cheered loudly.

"And now, as we come together, we humbly ask the Voice for his guidance." Evie lowered her arms. The crowd grew silent as every Simple slowly bowed their head. "Oh, wise Voice, will you finally grant us permission to leave the village and learn more about this world you have created?"

Unsteady, my mind raced, trying to predict Ian's next move.

The ground shook as a loud voice thundered from above. "I am pleased."

Everyone looked up except me. My eyes were stuck on Evie, who dropped to her knees when she heard Ian's words. As everyone followed Evie's example, a murmuring of gasps and exclamations rolled through the audience.

"The Voice! It is real!"

"He is pleased!"

"He has spoken!"

With a slight tremor, Evie spoke. "We are so happy you are pleased. Does that mean we have your permission to leave Fredena?"

It was the moment of truth. I held my breath. What would Ian do? Did he have a real solution, or was he destined to ruin everything?

"Why should you leave?" Ian said firmly. "Are you not pleased with this home I've given you?"

Evie's face dropped. "Of course, we love it. But we also want to explore beyond our village borders. To find other people and learn from them."

The other Simples remained on their knees. Their eyes focused on the ground. I slowly lowered my body, mirroring the actions of those around me as I didn't want to stand out any more than I already did. After listening intently, I waited for Ian's response. All around me was the distant hum of crickets. A breeze rustled the leaves of a nearby tree. Everyone stood still with bated breath. There was an electrifying buzz of anticipation until—*whoosh*. The energy vanished.

Startled by the jarring silence, I stood up. Everything was frozen. The crowd of Simples behind me stood like garden statues. Their marbled expressions ranged from scared to excited. I had no idea what was going on.

Ian's voice broke the silence. "I need a few minutes." The sound of Cheetos crunched in the background.

"Ian? What did you do?"

"I hit pause. I need more time." His snacks muffled his words.

"Time for what?" I sighed, rubbing the side of my head. My patience was all but gone.

"Hold on."

I tossed my arms up in the air and walked through the rows of people. I placed my hand on one woman's shoulder. There was no response. "This is creepy."

"Don't worry. They're fine. I'm finishing up a little code before updating the system. Hopefully, the changes I'm uploading should keep Evie happy, encouraging her to stay inside the village. Plus, it will prepare everyone for the bigger updates we have planned later on."

"Wait. What?" My heart rate spiked. "Like the death update? I didn't think you were ready for that yet?"

"I'm not. Relax. I'm not killing anyone. This is a different update—small and painless."

I exhaled sharply, trying to relax, which wasn't easy with Ian always scheming. I walked near the altar. Even frozen, Evie radiated life. Her face told a story of passion—her heart reaching upward. I scanned the crowd of Simples and then back at Evie. While everyone else cast their eyes down, Evie searched the sky. The only other person not staring at the ground was Steve. His gaze was still locked on Evie.

"Do you think Steve has a thing for Evie?" I asked with a smile.

"Funny you should ask," Ian said. "He admires her. But with the current code, the Simples don't understand romantic attachments. Hopefully, that will all change in about seven seconds."

The air rushed out of my lungs. "What? Ian! What are you doing?"

"Not enough time to explain. You'll see soon enough. The update is finalizing in three, two—get back to your place, Luce! They're about to go live."

I ran to my spot as everything sprung back to life. A breeze raced across my cheek. The symphony of crickets played again in the distance. The crowd's murmur devoured the stark silence from before, but nothing was as loud as Ian's roaring voice that echoed from above.

"You cannot leave the village. It is forbidden and dangerous!"

Evie's body sank. Her head dropped.

Ian softened his tone a bit. "The thing you are searching for isn't beyond the borders. You need companionship. It is not good to be alone."

This was Ian's solution? Since when did Ian care about companionship? The guy was a total hermit!

Without hesitation, Evie stood tall. She gestured toward the crowd in front of her. "But I'm not alone. I have my community —my people."

"You deserve more," Ian said. "Steve, stand."

"Me?" Steve slowly rose, shifting his gaze between Evie and the sky.

"Evie, from now on, Steve shall be your companion," Ian said. "Go to him."

Evie scrunched her face, obviously confused by this sudden revelation. I shrugged my shoulders. I had no clue what to do.

"Uh, excuse me—Voice in the Sky?" Steve's voice cracked as he tried to speak loud enough for everyone to hear. "I'm not sure what a companion is, but I have a question about Evie and me. Something has changed. I feel kinda funny."

"Explain yourself," Ian said.

I rolled my eyes. I couldn't help it. Ian's over-the-top theatrics were painful to witness.

Steve made his way toward the altar. "Well, I've always thought Evie was great. But now, my stomach gets twisted when

I think about her. And I have this urge to put my lips on her face. That sounds weird. Like, *so* weird. But it is true." He turned to face Evie, who still seemed deflated. "So, uh, did something happen? What's going on?"

"What you're describing is love," Ian said.

I plopped down on the ground and dropped my head in my hands. Like a runaway train, I had little hope of stopping Ian from roaring forward.

"Love?" Steve said. "So, love is a tingling feeling that makes me want to do weird things? Is that companionship?"

I couldn't take it anymore. Jumping to my feet, I interrupted —determined to take back control. "Not quite." Everyone turned to the sound of my voice as I walked toward Steve and Evie. "Those things you're feeling aren't necessarily love. Sometimes, you experience those sensations when you're attracted to some- one. That attraction can develop into love, but not always."

"So, what is love?" Evie asked.

"Love is a deep affection you feel when you care about some- one. When you love someone, you help them and want the best for them."

"Oh, well then, I've always loved Evie," Steve said with a big smile.

"Exactly." I turned to face Steve. "Friends love each other. But the things you are describing—the changes you're experiencing —could be a sign of a different kind of love. A romantic love." I couldn't believe I was trying to explain romance to the Simples, considering my non-existent love life. But there I was. I turned to face the crowd. "And romantic love is... complicated."

"I don't think so," Steve said. He turned toward Evie. "I can't explain what happened or how, but I love you. I want to be with you and nobody else."

Steve put his hand on Evie's cheek and slowly inched his face closer to hers. Evie pulled back a bit. Her eyes were wide with curiosity, but her face was tense. Gradually her shoulders relaxed, and she leaned in for a kiss. The crowd responded with a gentle "aww."

"This is good," Ian's voice declared from above. "I want everyone to be this happy."

And just like that, an almost magnetic force rushed through the audience. Pairs of Simples locked eyes and confessed their love to one another. Like a romance movie on steroids, dozens of cheesy one-liners echoed throughout the group. Two heads turned into one—again and again—as the Simples discovered the pleasures of kissing.

I took advantage of everyone's new distraction and moved away from the crowd. "This is awkward," I said as I hid behind a nearby tree. "I mean, I've had my moments of being the third wheel before, but nothing like this."

"It's nice," Ian said quietly in my ears. "I love love."

I laughed a little too loudly. "Didn't realize you were so romantic?"

"There's a lot you don't know about me, Luce."

The tone of Ian's voice made me pause. He was hinting at something I didn't want to consider.

"Now what?" I said quietly. "I'm afraid this is turning into a bad soap opera. None of this is natural. I'm not sure this was a good idea. Don't you think this could derail the progress they've made?"

"Nah, love is an important step before introducing babies, aging, and death. Besides, this is a honeymoon phase. I say we push time forward again, and we'll be back on track."

"Are you serious?" I gestured toward the sky. "You think we should walk away, add a hundred years, and somehow everything will be okay?"

Ian laughed. "Well, you can say *goodbye* first, if you want. Trust me. This make out fest won't last forever."

"Fine. I'll talk to them—assuming they ever come up for air.

But I need to collect some data before adding another hundred years. Give me a few days before jumping ahead."

"Whatever you say, boss. Don't forget I'm heading out of town for the weekend. Do your research and move them forward when you're ready."

"Will do. And Ian?" I took another deep breath. "You've got to stop interfering like this. Please."

"Pinky promise," Ian said.

With notes sprawled all over my bed, I spent the next several days preparing for TechEd. With only two weeks left until Regionals, the pressure to prepare was on. Ian was gone on a family vacation for the weekend, which gave me some time to collect data from our initial hundred-year jump before moving the Simples forward again. I desperately wanted to go back inside *The Garden* and explore the world as a participant. But getting pulled into the drama was too easy, so I decided it was safer to speed things up from Ian's computer.

"I'm heading over to the Gibsons," I said as I headed down the stairs.

Mom walked out of the kitchen and leaned against the railing. "What for?"

"I'm watering their plants while they're in Oregon, remember? Plus, Ian said I could use his computer to prepare for Regionals."

Mom cocked her head to the side as if trying to read my thoughts. "And? How's the project going?"

I know she meant well, but this kind of non-stop questioning made me an anxious mess. There was so much pressure to perform—as if it were Mom's dream I was working toward instead of my own.

"Everything is good, Mom. *Really*. I showed Ms. Howell my

research outline, and she said it was promising. And we haven't even shown her the tech yet, which is incredible."

"And Ian is pulling his weight?"

I sighed, holding back the urge to roll my eyes. "Yes, it would be nothing without him. Stop worrying."

"A mom never stops worrying, honey." She leaned over and kissed me on the forehead. "I'm glad things are going well. I'm eager for Regionals."

I grabbed my bag. "I'll be home for dinner." I opened the front door and jumped back. Jake was standing there with his hand mid-air, ready to knock.

He dropped his arm, his eyes wide with surprise. "Oh, Lucy. Hi!"

I grabbed my heart. "Jake! You scared me." I chuckled and took a deep breath. "What's up?"

"Sorry, I didn't mean to startle you. Is this a bad time?"

"Kinda. I'm heading to Ian's to work on a school project."

"On a Sunday?"

"Guilty." I laughed awkwardly.

"Well, I won't keep you. But I did want to ask you a quick question." Jake shifted his weight and cleared his throat. "Actually, I was wondering if you'd be my date for Fall Ball."

"Oh, is it that time already?" I couldn't stop myself from stammering.

"Not for two months, but after being too slow with TechEd, I wanted to ask you before *anyone* else did." He glanced toward Ian's house.

I caught his meaning, but I was sure Ian had never been to a school dance. I couldn't imagine him asking anyone out—not even me.

"I'm flattered, Jake. And I would love to go with you."

Jake's eyes lit up. "Sweet! I'll give you more details as the big day gets closer. For now, uh—I'll let you go." He turned to leave, stopping halfway down the stairs. "Say *hi* to Ian for me."

"Oh, he's out of town," I said. "I'm sorta plant-sitting for the Gibsons and taking advantage of Ian's computer while he's gone."

"Well, in that case... Would you like some company?"

"Uh." I stammered. Ian wouldn't want Jake near his stuff, and I was eager to do some work. But I also needed a fresh pair of eyes on the research—someone less entangled with the people. "For a little while, sure."

I gave Jake an overview of *The Garden* while I watered the houseplants. I told him all about the Simples and their beliefs around the Voice in the Sky. Jake was clearly amused by Ian's antics.

"So, wait—Ian uploaded some sort of love potion, and then they all started making out?" Jake shook his head, laughing. "Oh man, I wish I could have been there. It sounds hilarious."

"It was so weird," I said while putting away the watering can. "I'm sure it sounds funny, but I don't want the judges laughing at us. I need your help."

Jake took a deep breath and wiped away a tear. "I'm sorry. I'm not laughing at the project. It honestly sounds amazing. But why do you need my help? Isn't that like fraternizing with the enemy." He winked.

"Well, I need to fast-forward the Simples another hundred years, and I'd love to hear your first impressions after I do. I'm not asking you to review our code or share your secrets. But I need another perspective because I'm a little too close to it all." I led Jake upstairs and opened the door to Ian's room. "Promise me you won't touch any of Ian's stuff. He's very particular about his gadgets."

"Sure thing." Jake dragged his finger along the edge of Ian's desk. "Wow, he's got quite the setup here, doesn't he? So, how smart is Ian? Are the rumors true?"

"He's a freaking genius. Honestly, it is a little intimidating." I shook my head and chuckled. "And sometimes very annoying."

Jake picked up a VR headset. "So, have you ever, like, had feelings for him?"

"For Ian? Ha! *No.*"

Jake laughed. "Of course not. The kid's a freak. But you know he has a major crush on you, right?"

I scoffed, trying to sidestep Jake's insult about Ian. "That sounds like a ridiculous rumor." Jake smiled at me, lifting his eyebrows. I grabbed my sunflower charm and turned away. *Ridiculous.* I cleared my throat, ready to change the subject. "Okay, ready to see inside *The Garden?*"

"From here?" Jake said, pointing to the monitor on Ian's desk. "No VR goggles?"

"Sorry, not today. Ian would kill me if I let someone else go in without his permission. But trust me, the program is still pretty cool watching from the chair."

Jake pulled his seat close to me. I shifted, giving myself a little more room. With a few mouse clicks, I launched the program and rotated through different camera shots. Several Simples walked hand in hand through the village. Another couple was wading their feet in the pond. Everyone was still cozy from the other night.

"This is amazing." Jake leaned closer to the monitor. "Where is this Evie character you were talking about?"

"Uh, let me find her." I tapped through a dozen or so views. "There she is." Evie stood on a rock at the edge of the village border, staring out beyond the dunes.

"Why is she alone? Everyone else is paired off. Where's her man?"

I clicked the mouse again until I found Steve. He was sitting in a grassy field, twirling a flower. "Weird. I wonder why they aren't together." I zoomed in on his face. He was smiling and swaying slowly back and forth.

Jake chuckled. "The dude is in love, alright. I mean, check out the cheesy grin. He's thinking about someone." He leaned back in his chair. "Maybe Evie has higher standards than these other love struck fools."

"Yeah, Evie has always been different. But she has also always valued Steve."

"Valuing someone isn't necessarily love. Maybe she has a bigger vision for her life—unwilling to settle when she knows something better is out there."

I liked that. Evie didn't have the same goofy, over-the-moon expression everyone else did. *What made her different?* I shook my head. I couldn't dwell on that question for too long. "Well, are you ready to add a century to their lives?"

With a big smile, Jake nodded his head. I brought up the time dial and typed in another hundred years before hitting enter.

"Whoa! This is insane!" Jake moved in closer to the screen. "You can barely track what's happening. They're all moving so fast. The rapid-fire sunrises and sunsets are wild."

Thousands of motion blurs raced across the screen. Periodically we'd witness buildings collapse and reform into more modern structures. The trees and landscape grew taller and lusher until pieces were trimmed away. Every inch of scenery morphed into something new while still retaining traces of its past. With a sudden jolt, the world reformed with perfect clarity.

"All done? Already?" Jake's eyes were still glued to the monitor.

"Yep, now we assess." I pulled out my notebook from my backpack. "There are a ton of details I'll need to catalog, but first, I want to hear your thoughts as we take a tour through the town. Ready?"

"I think you're going to murder us at Regionals." Jake laughed as he leaned back in his chair.

I smiled. "That's not the kind of thoughts I was hoping for. Besides, I'm sure you and your teammate have something amazing. What is your project anyway?"

"Dylan has been working on an interactive projector of sorts for months. He was thrilled when I offered to team up with him since he's so shy. He does most of the hard work, and I'm the face of the project—a perfect situation, right?"

I had no idea how to respond. Jake obviously assumed I had a similar arrangement with Ian, but I'd like to think I was more than the spokesperson for our team. Perhaps showing *The Garden* to Jake was a mistake. I was eager to wrap things up and send him on his way. "So, what are your thoughts about *the town*?"

"Right, that." Jake laughed as he scooted his chair a bit closer.

Grabbing the mouse, I opened up the first view of the village, spotting some significant differences in the town's architecture right away.

"Everything is more... creative. Don't you think?" Jake said.

"Yeah, it all looks more meaningful—like every design has some hidden symbolism. Everything was more utilitarian before. Now there are dozens of artistic embellishments scattered throughout." I hopped from one angle to another, looking for Evie. I finally found her, standing alone, staring out toward the ocean. What was she doing out there? I clicked to another view. The Simples had built a gazebo next to an open area where several couples were dancing. I turned up the volume of the monitor.

"Music," Jake said. "Did they have that before?"

"They did. But it was more percussive and simple. It looks like they've created some wind and string instruments." I closed my eyes and gently swayed to the sound. "Beautiful."

"It really is." Jake stood up and offered his hand. "Care to dance?"

"What? Here?" I shook my head. "No, I am *not* a dancer."

"Come on," he said. "Consider it research."

I reluctantly stood up and took his hand. Not because I wanted to, but because I had a hard time saying no to people.

Jake moved the chairs out of the way, and we began swaying to the intricate melody. I tried to relax. Jake was handsome and charming. Part of me wanted to succumb to his flirtations because all our friends expected it. But then I thought about how Steve had described his changing feelings for Evie. I didn't feel that for Jake. Or Ian. Or anyone yet.

"Those hundred years brought out the best of the Simples, don't you think?" Jake said as he carefully twirled me around.

"What do you mean?"

"They look happy. Like they've gone through some sort of renaissance, you know? More art, music, connection—it's nice."

"I guess you're right." I kept cataloging the changes in my mind. The Simples did seem to be enjoying their life. Nearly everyone was smiling. Everyone except Evie. Was she happy?

Jake pulled me in a little closer. He closed his eyes and pressed his lips against mine. I pushed him away. "Whoa, what are you doing?"

"Oh, shit. I'm sorry." Shocked and then embarrassed, his skin turned pale. I'm sure nobody had ever rejected his advances.

"No, I'm fine. But I think you should go now."

"Oh, okay." Jake grabbed his phone from Ian's desk. "I'm sorry. I guess I was reading into things. Hopefully, this won't change your mind about Fall Ball?"

I felt dizzy, angry, and awkward. I wanted Jake gone, but I didn't want to make him mad—or, more accurately, mad at *me*. "Of course not. I look forward to it. But I need to do some work now." I opened the door for him to leave.

MESSAGE FROM JAKE

Sorry about today. I am such a jerk.

> Don't worry about it. You just caught me off guard. I've got a lot on my mind.

You're a lot like Evie. Bigger dreams than most of us. It's why people are drawn to you.

CHAPTER 13
IAN'S PRIDE

I TAPPED LUCY'S SHOULDER. "You nervous?"

She slowly exhaled. "A little."

We stood in the wings of the stage of Orchard High's auditorium. Lucy was excited that our school was hosting this year's regional competition. She said it gave us a home-field advantage. I doubted it. I hated the place and would have preferred a long car drive with Lucy anywhere else. But it made things more convenient, I guess.

As the final pair of the tournament, Lucy and I had spent the last five hours watching dozens of other teams show off their work. There was only one team left before it was our turn. We'd have ten minutes to present and five minutes of Q&A with the judges. Lucy kept rehearsing the presentation in her head—I know because she occasionally muttered lines, perfecting each word. She was a mess—a composed, perfectly poised ball of nerves.

"So tell me," I said, trying to lighten the mood. "What projects do you think we need to worry about? Are there any winners that stand out to you?"

Lucy straightened her blouse. It was weird seeing her in a

skirt and button-up shirt. "Not many," she said. "As usual, there are a lot of throw-away projects. Lots of solar ovens and barely working robots—none of them have a chance."

"Come on! That robot dog was adorable." I laughed. "I mean, sure, it looked like a fifth-grader built it, but it was cute."

Lucy chuckled. "Lucky for us, cute doesn't matter." She kept her eyes on the stage, trying to size up the presenting team as they finished. "There were a couple of impressive projects, though. The Lincoln High team, with their Classroom Smart Board, was good. And Jake and Dylan's Interactive Projector was better than I anticipated."

"Yeah, that one stood out to me. Their software was fantastic. I still can't believe Jake charmed his way into that project. Lucky jerk."

Lucy bit her lip and shook her head. "They nailed the educational angle. And I'm guessing the tech would be cheaper to integrate within a classroom than ours. The judges consider those things." She took a deep breath, trying to hide her nerves, but I could read the signs. Still, she managed to stay put together. "I think we've got the best project. Nothing beats your Reality Amplifier. It is on a whole other level." She pinched her sunflower charm and smiled.

I smiled back while my stomach did somersaults. The look on her face reminded me why I offered her *The Garden* in the first place. Not only did it give me the chance to spend weeks by her side, but I really wanted her to be happy.

"Then let's go do this thing!" I said as I patted her on the back like a total dork.

We had five minutes to set up after the other team finished. I pulled out the VR goggles and Amplifier Chips while Lucy hooked up her laptop to the projector. The audience buzzed as everyone waited for the next presentation. Lucy's parents sat next to Ms. Howell. Her mom nodded while her dad gave two big thumbs up. My eyes bounced row after row, wondering if my parents had made it. Mom said they were swamped with the business but would try to come. I wasn't surprised when I didn't see them. But I did spot Jake making googly eyes at Lucy.

"Looks like Jake can't keep his eyes off you," I whispered as I rolled my eyes. "That guy bugs me. I wish he would have bombed his presentation."

Lucy's cheeks turned red, and she quickly turned her back. "But he didn't," she said. "So let's do even better, okay? Focus." She squeezed her necklace again and nodded. It was time.

"Let's welcome our final team to the stage for the Arizona Central TechEd Tournament. Representing Orchard High, put your hands together for Ian Gibson and Lucy Fernández!" The announcer's voice echoed through the auditorium, followed by a roar of applause.

Lucy smiled at the judges in the front row, and it hit me. I was on stage—in the spotlight. In front of people. I hated people. They hated me. *How the hell did I get here?* Sure, a win would mean moving on to State—giving me more time to work with Lucy. But what if we lost? I had spent so much time teasing Lucy about her obsession with this tournament that I forgot what was a stake. My heart began racing, and sweat pooled in my armpits.

Lucy, suddenly calm and collected, smiled at me. It was like being back in fourth grade. I pinched myself that I got to hang out with her. Her big brown eyes melted into mine as she winked, reminding me everything would be okay.

With a deep breath, Lucy began. "What would our world be like had we never ventured beyond our borders? What foods, beliefs, and traditions would be missing from our lives if we didn't step outside our own homes?"

A series of images of people from all over the world popped on the screen above our heads. "Cultural anthropology is like a window to new worlds. It gives us the chance to study human existence—providing the tools to question our assumptions while discovering new ideas."

The final image on the screen was a picture of Lucy with her parents. "But when we learn about other people and their way of life, we don't just understand *them* better. We understand *ourselves* better, too." Lucy's Dad sat tall with pride as she spoke. "Sometimes, the best mirror is someone else's perspective. Witnessing other people puts a magnifying glass on our own reality that can challenge long-held assumptions and reveal our infinite potential."

I scanned the audience again. Jake's gaze was still locked on Lucy. I cleared my throat.

Lucy was so articulate, contrasting my awkwardness as I stood beside her. She continued. "But the problem with studying anthropology through traditional means is that a culture's humanity vanishes when it is reduced to a paragraph of text or a question on a test. Without the right tools—we may ignore, misinterpret, or even harm the very cultures we want to understand."

The image on the screen switched to a photo of Ms. Howell with a group of people in Tasmania. Lucy smiled. "Most of us will never travel to the islands of Australia like my teacher pictured here. We won't spend a year exploring Japan to learn about the Shinto communities. Fully immersing oneself in a different culture the way a professional anthropologist can is impractical for most high school students."

Lucy gestured to me. "And that's why we created *The Garden.*"

That was my cue. I took a step forward, determined to nail this presentation. My shirt and tie needed an iron, but I tried to make up for my disheveled appearance by summoning all the confidence I could muster. For a moment, I imagined myself as my avatar. My alter ego knew exactly how to behave in front of a high school audience.

"Virtual Reality is the future of education," I said firmly. "It allows students to do more than read about the subjects they are studying. It gives them a front-row seat. But we want to take that visual experience even further. We want students to *live* in these worlds." I held up a small disk. "This Reality Amplifier Chip—combined with our VR and AI programming—creates a one-of-a-kind virtual classroom. Inside *The Garden*, students don't just view what life is like for other civilizations. They experience it. They'll learn about the delicate balance between observation and influence, opening the doors to vital conversations around colonization, diversity, respect, and power."

I signaled to two of the four judges. "If you please, I'd like to invite you to try it out." A plump older man and a young, energetic woman walked onto the stage. I helped them strap into the headsets and insert the Amplifier Chip while Lucy talked.

"We want to give you a quick taste of *The Garden* experience," Lucy said. "We've adjusted the settings so that none of the people inside can see or hear you." She gestured to the screen. "The rest of the audience will be able to watch what's happening on the projector here."

I waved at the two judges. "Are you ready?"

"Ready," they both said.

I tapped a few buttons on the laptop. The screen above our heads lit up with a beautiful ocean view.

"Whoa," the man said.

There was a wave of murmurs from the audience. The energy in the room was palpable.

"This is amazing," the woman said. "I can smell the ocean air!"

I flashed a smile at Lucy before turning to the audience. "The Reality Amplifier triggers the brain's sensory output. Inside *The Garden*, you do more than see and hear things. You can smell, touch, and taste them, too."

Lucy pointed at the screen again. "There is the village—home to 231 simulated people."

"Or Simples, as I like to call them," I said.

The audience laughed.

Lucy shook her head with a smile. "Judges, if you'd please turn around and start walking toward the dunes, you'll find the town nestled behind them."

On the screen, the judges moved along the path. Every twenty seconds or so, one or both would gasp in delight. "The details are incredible," the man said as a butterfly landed on his shoulder.

"If I didn't know better, I'd think I was on a real beach," the woman said.

Lucy beamed at the comment. "One of the tenets of cultural anthropology is that culture takes time, so we programmed the ability to pause and speed up the Simples timeline. What started as a simple computer code has evolved over roughly 200 years."

"We've already noticed significant changes over that period," I said.

The audience gasped as the judges entered the edge of the village. There were dozens of Simples meandering along the cobblestone pathways. Some were playing music. Others were selling handmade jewelry. The rich colors of their clothes and the intricate carvings on their buildings dazzled everyone.

"In a few short weeks, we've tracked more than one hundred significant changes within the culture," Lucy said. She was looking at her mom, whose posture was as rigid as ever, but there was a glimmer of pride in her eyes. "Shifts in language, art, social structures, and beliefs have been among the most dramatic adaptations."

On the screen, the judges wandered through different parts of the village. They got a peek at the large altar, which was worn down from the hundred years since it was erected.

"We were surprised by what we discovered about our influence on the Simples," I said. "Even the smallest interactions rippled out into their world. For example, I taught one man what a name was, and within a couple of days, that man had given everyone in the village a name."

Lucy chimed in. "And that simple act gave the people a sense of individuality. Which taught us one of anthropology's profound truths: The individual is an important part of cultivating a group identity."

The judges inside the village turned a corner and nearly bumped into Evie. "Whoops," the judge said. "They can't see or hear us, right?"

"No, you're fine," I said.

Evie turned around, and the audience shifted to the edge of their seats. Her intense curiosity lit up the screen. She glanced over her shoulder and then turned the other way. "Is someone there? Hello? Hello?"

Lucy shook her head at me. I shrugged, unclear what Evie could have possibly detected. I quickly walked up to the judges and helped them remove their headsets. "That's all the time we have for now."

The two judges joined the others at the table. They had the same glow Lucy had after first entering *The Garden*. I couldn't help but smile. My technology was superior to anything anyone else had showcased. Maybe people would think of me differently now. As the judges began their five minutes of questioning, I could barely feel my legs. Thinking back to the gutwrenching process of getting Lucy to trust me, I was glad I didn't give up. I was ready to prove that this project wasn't just worthy of moving us to the next level. I believed *The Garden* could win it all.

I took a long sip from my milkshake. It had been almost ninety minutes since we finished our presentation. "Sheesh, how much longer until they announce the results?"

Lucy looked up from her phone. "Not sure," she said. "They didn't take this long last year."

The judges had given everyone a sixty-minute dinner break while they tallied scores and determined the winners. Lucy's Dad grabbed some Happy's Hamburgers for us, and we all sat in the courtyard waiting for the results. No longer in the spotlight, my nerves had calmed down significantly, but I could tell Lucy was still rattled. She barely touched her food.

"So, how does this work?" I asked as I stuffed the last bite of burger in my mouth. After a few chews, I swallowed hard. "Do the judges rank everyone who competes? Or do they only determine the winners?"

Lucy peeked over her shoulders again, looking at the auditorium doors. Still closed. She shook her head and nibbled on a cold french fry. "Last year, they announced the top five projects. All five move on to State."

"And the other sixty or so teams are out?" I snuck a french fry from her pile. "Wow, kinda cut-throat, isn't it?"

Lucy slowly nodded. "But not as cut-throat as State. Only the top two teams move on from there." Despite my confidence in our project and presentation, I still couldn't help but imagine the worst-case scenario of not placing at all. I wondered if Lucy would survive it.

"Hey guys, the judges are ready," Ms. Howell said as the auditorium doors opened. "Everyone needs to head back to the theater."

Lucy walked a bit unsteady as we made our way to our seats. The room was buzzing with anticipation as sixty-seven teams and their parents gathered together. I could hear several people talking about their favorite projects.

"I think the Interactive Projector will win," one person said.

"No way, the VR one trampled the others," another replied.

A jolt of pride struck me as I overheard the kid. I nudged Lucy in the ribs, "Did you hear that? They liked our project."

Lucy's eyes were closed, and she slowly exhaled. I put my hand on her shoulder. "You okay? You look kinda pale."

"I'm fine. Ready for the results." She opened her eyes and squeezed the sunflower charm around her neck.

"You guys did a fantastic job," Ms. Howell whispered. "I would love to have your tech inside my classroom. If I were a judge, you'd be the no-brainer winner."

I agreed, but anytime I focused on Lucy, my confidence waned. The heaviness in her face read like a bad omen.

The house lights dimmed, and a spotlight shined brightly toward center stage. One of the judges—a lean, bookish-looking man—made his way to the pool of light. The hum of the audience diminished until only the occasional cough or rustle of paper could be heard. The judge leaned into the microphone. His nasal voice reverberated throughout the auditorium.

"After a thrilling day of innovation and leadership, we are thrilled to announce this year's winners for the Arizona Central TechEd Tournament." The audience erupted with cheers and applause. "Everyone who participated should be proud of the work they did today."

"Eh, not everyone," I said, probably too loudly.

"Shush," Lucy said, giving me the stink eye. But she couldn't hide her muffled laughter.

"In fifth place, from Chandler, Arizona—congratulations to Abigail Frank and Cynthia Brown for their SmartWatch Translator!"

The crowd cheered as the two teenagers made their way to the stage. Lucy's leg was bouncing so hard that my chair vibrated. I reached over and grabbed her hand. She smiled weakly before slowly crossing her arms. *Dumb move, Ian.*

As the fourth and third place winners were announced, Lucy leaned forward while her eyes zeroed in on the floor. She was muttering something. I moved in, trying to understand. As if willing the announcer to speak her name, she quietly chanted it to herself. Lucy Fernández. Lucy Fernández.

"...Lucy Fernández and Ian Gibson from Orchard High with their Virtual Reality Anthropology Classroom!" The sound echoed through the theater.

I perked up, confused. I had been so focused on Lucy that I wasn't paying attention to the place number. Based on Lucy's face, neither had she. *What place did we get?* I quickly glanced over at Ms. Howell, whose scowl told me everything.

"Second place? Are you kidding me?" Ms. Howell huffed.

The audience cheered as we walked up to the stage to accept our trophy, but it sounded like a distant echo. I wanted to know what Lucy was thinking. Second place meant we moved on. I was okay with it. Hell, I was thrilled. But I could tell Lucy was upset. She faked a half-smile as she took the trophy, not fully present. I wrapped my arm around her shoulders, guiding her back to our seats.

"Second place is good, Luce. We still move on to State."

With a vacant expression she tapped the trophy in her lap. "So why do I feel like a failure?"

The audience erupted in another round of cheers as the man announced the first-place winners. Jake and Dylan's Interaction Projector won.

DEAR DIARY
LUCY, AGE 8

Today we went to the circus. It was the most amazing thing I've ever seen! People were swinging from these bars that hung way up high from the ceilings. They looked so free as they flew across the stage. Mom says they are called trapeze artists. I told her I wanted to do that when I grow up. But Mom says the circus is not a real job. I don't understand because it seemed real to me. So what makes something a real job? And if it is not real, do the trapeze artists know it?

CHAPTER 14
NEED FOR STRUGGLE

"Come on, Luce. I hate seeing you like this."

I tried to summon a smile for Ian, but my mind was still a blur from Saturday's outcome. Sitting numbly in Ms. Howell's class the following Monday, I couldn't ignore the nagging sensation that I had somehow failed again. Thankfully, nobody else believed it. Several students approached me after the event, saying we should have won. Even Mom thought we were robbed. Still, my confidence had taken a hit, and I wondered how we would move on to Nationals when we couldn't even get a first-place win at Regionals.

The bell rang. I slowly began gathering my things. Ian zipped his backpack and offered another sympathetic grin. "We're going to State! We need to stay focused. The competition is only three weeks away, and I'll be damned if we don't crush Jake and Dylan."

I laughed. "I'm sorry. Did Ian Gibson tell *me* to stay focused?"

"We're in the upside down," Ian said with a smile. "That's why I need you to snap out of this funk. I'm not supposed to be the responsible one, remember?"

"Ms. Fernández, Mr. Gibson—I'd like to talk to you."

Ms. Howell stared at us from the front of the class.

"Are we in trouble?" Ian whispered. With a slight chuckle, I grabbed my bag and followed him to Ms. Howell's desk.

Ms. Howell folded her arms and leaned forward. "So, one of the judges from Saturday's competition is an old friend."

"Wait? You're friends with one of the judges?" Ian perked up. "Which one: Mr. Nasal Voice, Mr. Pudgy, Ms. Hairspray, or Ms. Caffeine?"

"I have nothing to do with those names," I said, tossing my hands.

Ms. Howell furrowed her brow at Ian. "Mr. Pudgy?" I swear she was suppressing a laugh. "His name is Mr. *Williams*. We taught together at Red Mountain High a few years ago." She shuffled some paper on her desk, muttering under her breath. "But yes, Mr. Pudgy is more accurate."

Ian laughed.

"Anyway, as I was saying—" Ms. Howell shook her head. "I talked to Mr. Williams because I don't think the other team should have beat you, and I wanted to understand how the judges made their final decision." She pulled out a manila envelope from her desk drawer. "It took a little arm twisting, but he gave me your scorecards."

My chest tightened. The last time I viewed the judges' scorecards for TechEd, I was left with a lasting mantra that still haunts me. *Technology is lacking.* I took a deep breath, reminding myself that any feedback was good.

"What's interesting," Ms. Howell said, "is that both he and Ms. Jenkins—or Ms. Caffeine, I'm assuming?" She winked at Ian. He laughed. "Well, they both ranked you higher than the other two judges who didn't go inside *The Garden*. There's something to be said about experiencing the virtual world vs. viewing it on the projector."

"Okay, that is an easy fix," Ian said. "I can get two more headsets before State."

"Great, that will help. But there is another thing." Ms. Howell pointed to the scorecards. "All four judges worried that the culture you created wasn't an accurate enough representation of real life. They weren't convinced it would be an effective tool for teaching cultural anthropology."

Ian threw his arms in the air. "What? Our culture was *way* more accurate than that third-grade rendition of the solar system those Interactive Projector jerks presented."

"I agree," Ms. Howell said.

I read over the scorecard before handing it back to Ms. Howell. "Wait. What do they mean—*not accurate enough*? They were practically drooling over the details of the world."

"Williams said they debated for a long time about your project. Ultimately, they thought there were too many critical elements missing. The fact that there is no generational change —no birth, aging, death—made them wonder if the program was a realistic substitute for fieldwork. As you know, those things influence culture."

I rolled my eyes. "Why does it feel like they're judging us at a higher standard than the other teams?"

"Honestly? Because they are," Ms. Howell said. "You've built a reputation, Lucy. And so their expectations are high."

"Don't worry," Ian said, trying to pacify my obvious annoyance with the inequality. "We already planned on adding those things. I've been working on the code for a while, and it should be ready in time to test it before State."

Ms. Howell nodded slowly, placing scorecards back in their folder.

"There's something else, isn't there?" I said.

"Yes." Ms. Howell sighed. "The generational thing is important. But the judges also believed that the world was too idyllic. In real life, there is a struggle to survive. Our basic needs aren't magically met. Humans have to deal with a changing and sometimes dangerous environment. Life for the Simples was too safe. That was the biggest complaint the judges had."

"So this is my fault." My stomach churned as my worst fears were realized. It wasn't the tech that was keeping me from my goals. This time it was the educational component that was lacking. I was the reason we lost.

Ms. Howell shook her head. "No, it's my fault. As the anthropology expert and faculty mentor, I should have caught the issue. But I was so impressed with what you built that I think I got swept up in the magic of it all."

Ian scoffed. "Both of you need to relax. This is an easy fix! Give me a couple of hours, and I can update the code to mimic all sorts of things. What do you want? A flood? Locust? Earthquakes?" He pressed me for a response, but I was having a hard time processing everything. Were these my only options? Floods and locusts or say goodbye to MIT? Ian carried on. "If this is what's kept us from winning, you have nothing to worry about, Luce."

But I had a million things to worry about. I was desperate to win, and I was also attached to Evie and her people. Raining down a myriad of cataclysmic events horrified me. No matter how often I told myself they weren't real, I couldn't do it.

"I don't think you need to go all apocalyptic on them," Ms. Howell laughed. "Start simple and then fast-forward a few years to track the results. Do a little research on the scope and frequency of different natural events and try to make it as authentic as possible."

Hearing Ms. Howell give the order somehow made it easier. I'm a sucker for authority, I guess. I sighed and stared out the window at the desert landscape. The prickly pear across the street gave me an idea.

"How about a drought?" I said. "A mild one—something that forces the Simples to think differently about their resources and food."

"That sounds perfect," Ms. Howell said. "Ian, can you do a drought?"

"Easy," he said with a cocky smile.

"Alright, let's start there." Ms. Howell stood up. "Program a couple of dry seasons and see what happens. Let's meet again next week to discuss any other preparations for State. How does that sound?"

"Sounds good," I said, trying to force a smile. With a decision made, a spark of hope pricked my heart. The past few days had been emotionally taxing. It was nice to have a solid plan moving forward. Better than swimming through a million possibilities, at least.

Ian cocked his head and smiled. "Time to change the world."

"Finish the code yet?" I plopped my bag on Ian's bed. It had been four days since we decided to program a drought for the Simples.

He swiveled in his chair to face me. "Hello to you, too."

"Sorry." I plastered a fake smile across my face. "Hello, Ian. How's it going?"

He scoffed. "No time for small talk, Luce. We've got a drought to inflict!"

I looked over at Ian's monitor and saw Evie in the left-hand corner of the screen. "Have you been watching them? Anything interesting going on?"

"Not really," Ian said. "Most of the Simples are still blissfully enjoying the good life. Except for Evie, who always looks burdened with some sort of bigger purpose. She spent like two hours working on something inside her home."

"Working on what?" I leaned in for a closer look, brushing my shoulder against Ian.

Ian turned his head, and our eyes locked for a moment. "Uh," he stammered before quickly turning his attention to the computer. "I'm—I'm not sure. Doodling on paper, I think." He cleared his throat. "The Simples have developed their own symbols and lettering, so I can't be certain."

There was a distinct shift in the room's energy—a certain unspoken tension in the air. Carefully backing away, I sat back down on his bed. "That's Evie for you. She's quite an enigma, isn't she?"

"Mmm-hmm," Ian said, watching me from the corner of his eye.

"So, about that code? Are you ready to add a little drought to the mix?"

"Uh, yeah." Ian shifted in his seat. "I've calculated a change in rainfall that will significantly impact their growing season without totally wiping out their food supply. We should move them forward about seven years to evaluate the full effect."

"Awesome. Great work, as usual." I stood up. "Do you mind if I go in and talk to Evie for a minute before we jump ahead with the update? I'm curious what she's been up to."

Ian handed me a headset. "Go for it," he said with a smile. His eyes locked on me as if he wanted to say something. I strapped on the goggles and pressed the power button.

As I entered *The Garden*, my shoulders relaxed. More than anything, I wanted to settle in for a long nap on the sandy beach and let the sound of the ocean engulf me. Instead, I turned around and pressed forward toward the village. "Everything is so green and alive here. I'm struggling a bit with the idea of the drought. This place has been a haven, and I don't want to change it."

"I understand," Ian said. "But here's the thing, Luce, we can easily reset everything once the competition is over."

Reset everything? That was worse. I kept trying to remind myself that the Simples weren't real. But after all the emotional labor of creating and witnessing their growth, everything inside me resisted the idea of deleting it all.

"When all the craziness is done, this can be our little piece of heaven again," Ian said. "Doesn't that sound nice?"

I grabbed my necklace.

"Luce?"

"Shh... I see Evie." I walked toward a small brick home, the same one Ian had been watching from his desktop. There was a large window in front that perfectly framed Evie inside. Sitting at a desk and intensely focused, she continued to write until she heard me approaching. Jumping out of her seat, she ran to meet me.

"Lucy! You've returned!"

"Hey, Evie, how have you been?"

"I've been... okay." Evie's shoulders and face sank a bit.

"You sure?"

She slowly inhaled and then let all the air out in a satisfying sigh. "Yeah, I missed you. Things have changed a lot since you were last here. But I haven't ventured away from the village. Not even once—even though I wanted to. I've done as the Voice commanded."

"I'm proud of you." The words betrayed my guilt. I had caged Evie's spirit, and I hated it.

"Where's Steve?" I asked, sitting on a bench outside her home. "Have you guys enjoyed your time together?"

Evie sat next to me. "Steve is great. He sees the best in everyone and everything. I wish I could be more like him. I'm afraid I'm constantly letting him down."

"I doubt that."

"He really loves me. He makes me food, holds my hand, and wants to spend all his time with me." Evie turned her head, hiding her expression. But the sound of her voice told a story of regret. "He's sometimes sad because I don't always want to be with him. I like being alone. None of the other Fredenians are like me." She turned toward me. Her eyes welled with tears. "Why can't I be satisfied like the others? Why am I so different?"

Tears fell down her cheek, and I leaned in for a hug, hoping to comfort her. "I don't know why, Evie. But being different is not a bad thing."

"Everyone thinks I'm strange. They don't even think the Voice in the Sky is real anymore. Do you remember that celebration we had? The one many, many cycles ago?"

I stifled a laugh. For me, it had only been a few weeks. "I do."

Evie perked up as she brushed away her tears. "You heard the Voice, right? You remember how he told us to love each other and be happy with the companionship he designed for us?"

"Yes, I remember. You're not crazy, Evie. It really happened."

Evie sunk back into her seat. "The problem is that while I enjoy having Steve as a partner, I still ache to explore beyond our borders. I want to see where you live and meet other people." She hunched over, resting her head in her hands.

"I'm so sorry," was all I could think to say.

We sat still for several minutes. The sun warmed my face as a breeze rustled the leaves of the trees. I found it incredibly ironic that while Evie was desperate to leave, I was eager to stay. I loved the simplicity of *The Garden*—its pace and rhythm. Everything inside the village was the opposite of my high-demand reality.

Evie stood up. "I want to show you something." She walked into her home and came back with a piece of parchment in her hands. "I made this," she said, handing it to me.

"What is it?" I recognized the mystery document she had been working on.

"A map. Not a very accurate one, since I can't leave the village. But I've spent many days on rocks or perched in trees. I've drawn what I can see beyond our borders. I hoped I would find your village, but it must be too far away."

"Wow, this is... *impressive*." I handed the map back to Evie. "You have the heart of an explorer, don't you?"

Evie focused on her drawings, tracing the paths with her finger. "Yeah, that is my problem." She crumpled the paper in her hands, tossed it on the ground, and began crying again.

Unsure how to respond, I reached over and rubbed Evie's back, trying to offer comfort. Had this been real life, I would be Evie's greatest champion. I would tell her to follow her passions, break the mold, and throw rigid rules out the window. I would help Evie be courageous and adventurous—two things I wished for myself. But this wasn't real life. There was nothing for Evie beyond *The Garden.* So instead, I had to encourage the thing I knew best: Obedience.

"I understand, Evie. I do. But the Voice must have a reason to keep you here. Maybe if you tried a little harder—or perhaps if you spent more time with Steve—you'd find living here isn't so bad. You might even learn to love it. Good things are coming your way. Trust me."

Evie wrestled to keep her tears in check, brushing the last ones from her cheek. She smiled. "Well, if you say so, it must be true."

For a second, a weight lifted. Then I heard Ian's voice in my ear.

"What are you doing?" he whispered. "We're about to launch a drought, and you're telling her good things are coming?"

My heart stopped. I wish I could rewind time, but I couldn't. I had already given Evie my pep talk despite our plan. Flustered, I prepared my escape.

"I have to go, Evie." I hated that I was leaving after that horrible setup. My mind was racing for something meaningful to say before bailing. "I know I'm always leaving. But I will be back. Please, hang in there."

"You always go too soon, my friend. I'll miss you and wait for your return." Evie ran up and hugged me again.

"Here, save this." I bent over and picked up the crinkled map. I smoothed out the paper and handed it back to her. "You should be proud of what you've created. Besides, you never know when it will come in handy."

Evie hugged the map close to her body. "Thank you."

"And one more thing." I searched her eyes, hoping the right words would come to me. "Remember, even if things don't go the way you want, they can still take you where you need to go. The best lessons in life sometimes require the biggest sacrifices."

CHAPTER 15

IAN'S TEST

"Do it," I said.

At the edge of the village, Lucy hid behind some trees. Her hand gripped the time dial, marked for seven years. But for whatever reason, she wasn't letting go. She closed her eyes and slowly exhaled.

"Is the code uploaded into the system?" she asked.

"All ready to go, Luce. You need to let go and let things run their course."

Lucy didn't want to initiate the drought. But it was vital to produce a more realistic world for the Simples—and win State. I offered to fast-forward time from my computer, but Lucy felt like she needed to be the one to pull the trigger. She had said her parting words to Evie, and now her hesitation made me wonder if she had a change of heart.

I tried to be patient. "It will be fine, Luce. Do it." But that patience was wearing thin as my mom continued yelling at me to come down for dinner. "*Let go of the dial.*"

Lucy released her hand and stepped back as the world morphed before her eyes. Unlike the other jumps, this was a much smaller push into the future. From my desk, the world zoomed past as it had before, but with less velocity. If I concentrated hard enough, I could even follow the actions of a single person for a moment before they vanished into their homes. But after a minute, the whirlwind of activity made me dizzy. I turned my chair around. Lucy stood in the middle of my room.

I didn't usually view her from this angle. It was weird looking at her all strapped in and motionless instead of interacting with the Simples. I preferred watching from my screen as if protecting her on this new adventure—an adventure I had created.

Lucy took off her headset. "It's done." She braced herself against the wall before looking at me. "I guess we wait it out. Should we check back tomorrow to assess the damage?"

"Why don't you stay for dinner?" I stood up and put Lucy's headset on my desk. "We can pop in after to check on them. My dad ordered pizza. We always have extra."

Lucy scrunched her nose. "You sure your parents won't mind?"

"Not if yours don't."

She shook her head. "Dad's flying for another day and Mom's working late, so pizza sounds better than another PB&J. Sure, why not?"

We raced down the stairs and made our way to the kitchen table. Mom forced a half-smile as Lucy sat down next to me. She could never fully erase the exhaustion from her face. "Lucy! Are you joining us tonight?"

"I hope you don't mind. Ian invited me."

Mom grabbed another plate from the cupboard. "You're always welcome, hun."

After years of struggling with their business, my parents finally made decent money. But that didn't stop them from fighting about finances. Plus, my youngest brother had been dealing with respiratory issues since birth. His doctor's appointments and my sisters' dance classes consumed their time. I think they loved that I was a hopeless recluse. They didn't mind throwing a little cash my way anytime I needed a new computer or supplies for my gadgets as long as I didn't demand too much of their attention. Their energy was running on empty—always.

Lucy asked my sisters how they were doing and smiled at my Dad, who was half-watching a football game. Lucy used to love coming to my house as a kid. She'd always talk about how much she wanted a brother or sister—but not this time. There was no ease in her manner tonight. Her polite but restrained posture made me uncomfortable. She ate as fast as possible, avoiding small talk or requests from my sister to play another round of Twenty Questions.

"Your family is great," Lucy said as we left the dining room. "Thanks for having me over."

I smiled, wishing rather than believing she was sincere. "They have their moments."

As we got to the bottom of the stairs, she stopped to face me as if she had something important to reveal. I tried to read her thoughts. Her eyes were intense, and I found myself drowning in them. But before I could fully submerge in her quiet focus, she switched to the task at hand.

"Ready for the results of the drought?" She walked a little quicker up the stairs.

As we entered the bedroom, Lucy went straight for the VR goggles. I was still thinking about her eyes. Reluctantly, I sat down at my seat and powered up *The Garden.* Lucy plugged in.

"Whoa, this is... *different*," Lucy said. I bounced through a handful of views while she walked toward the village. She pointed toward the once lush forest. "Look at those trees! They used to be so full, and now they're basically tall twigs." Along the beach was an invasion of marshy, saltwater vegetation crawling along the shore. There were fewer signs of wildlife, making the world a little quieter.

"Isn't it amazing what too little freshwater does to an island's ecosystem? Things are definitely out of balance," I said.

Lucy marched toward the village, the tension in her body rising. "I've got a bad feeling about this."

"Remember, none of this is real. We need the Simples to experience challenges. That is the whole point of this project."

With a deep exhale, Lucy pressed on. She reached the edge of the village and gasped as she approached the dusty town. Wooden barrels stood tall against each house, most likely to collect rainwater. Animal hides were hanging along a stretched rope, and bows and arrows rested against several front doors. Many artistic flourishes that once highlighted the town were faded and neglected.

"I... I can't believe how much everything has changed," Lucy whispered.

My mouth dropped as I surveyed the entire town. My utopia was gone. "Crazy, isn't it? For more than two hundred years, the village maintained a certain personality. This looks like a whole different place."

Lucy walked through the center of the village, shaking her head. "Do you think the Simples have changed as drastically as the environment?"

The town was eerily quiet. As Lucy neared the furthest corner, I heard the faint sound of footsteps and chanting in the distance. I thought about changing views to better look at what was out there, but my instincts told me to stay focused on Lucy. Protect her. Gradually the noise grew louder until a crowd of Simples marching back toward the town came into view on my screen. I zoomed in on them. The group leader was wrapped in animal fur and carrying a large spear. She raised her arm high, yelling victoriously. I zoomed in again. It was Evie.

"What the hell?" I was as annoyed as I was surprised. "So much for staying inside the borders. What are they all doing?"

"It looks like some sort of hunting party," Lucy said. "I'm

guessing they got desperate for food. Good thing you didn't fix that glitch."

Hiding behind a boulder, Lucy waited for the group to pass. Steve walked slightly behind Evie. He cheered louder than anyone. As the crowd made it to the center of the village, he kissed Evie on the cheek and headed toward the other end of town. Lucy followed Evie, maneuvering her way through the bushes to ensure nobody saw her until she got to Evie's house.

"Hi, Evie." Lucy slowly walked out from behind a pile of chopped wood.

"Lucy?" Evie's countenance was stoic as she stood tall, still carrying a couple of dead rabbits in one hand. Her muscles were well-defined, her shoulders broad. "You're back. I didn't think you'd return." She walked past Lucy into her home. Of all the changes, Evie was the most startling. I had watched her greet Lucy countless times. There was always hugging and enthusiasm involved. But now, she was cold and distant.

Lucy followed her inside. "What happened here? Everything looks so different."

With a loud *thud*, Evie dropped the animal carcasses on the table. There was a bite to her voice. "A lot has happened, Lucy. The world changed while you were gone."

"I'm sorry to hear that, Evie." The pain on Lucy's face was all too easy to read. She was gutted—heartbroken. And I know she felt responsible. I probably should have, too. But unlike Lucy, I didn't struggle to remember what the Simples were: Lines of code—nothing else.

Evie sighed, and her hardened exterior cracked ever so slightly. "No, I'm sorry. You're not at fault. I'm tired, and I wish you could have been here. You could've helped us." Evie slumped down in a chair. "Honestly, I should probably thank you."

Lucy sat across from her. "Thank me? For what?"

Evie tipped her head upward, pointing toward a map on the

wall. It was larger and more detailed than the one she had drawn before the drought.

"You told me my map may come in handy. And it did." She kicked off her leather sandals and slowly rubbed her feet. "Understanding the land and tracking the different plants and animals has kept us alive. So, thanks for that."

Lucy leaned forward. "Can you tell me what happened?"

Evie shook her head and stared at the lifeless rabbits on the table. With a heavy sigh, she locked eyes with Lucy.

"Some time ago, the rain stopped." Evie's gaze waxed over—her face seemed weathered and stern. "For hundreds of cycles, the trees and bushes produced more than enough food for us to thrive. Then everything dried up. Now and then, the rain would come back. We'd dance and celebrate, but it never stayed long. Each cycle, things got worse. The plants changed. The world was thirsty. And then—" she sighed. "The fruit stopped growing."

"So, what did you do?" Lucy asked.

"I didn't know what to do. But everyone expected me to have answers. They were hungry and miserable, and for some reason, they believed I would have a solution. But I didn't. I was as scared as they were."

"I bet." Lucy reached over and rested her hand on Evie's. "But it looks like they were right. You've managed to help them work through it. You're an exceptional leader."

"Only because I broke my promise." Evie pulled away. "I left the village. I tried to find food—to find you. I searched for days, foraging for whatever little bits I could find. And I tracked everything. But no matter how far I traveled, it all led to a watery void."

Lucy placed her hand over her mouth like she was afraid to speak.

Evie leaned forward as if trying to read Lucy's thoughts. "What about you, Lucy? Did the rain stop where you live?"

Lucy shifted in her seat.

·"Where are you from? Why can't we go there?" Evie pounded the table and stood up. "I have searched everywhere, Lucy. *Everywhere*. There is nothing out there. *Nothing.* Even after I showed the others how to sneak out of the village, I couldn't find you. Everyone searched with me. We have walked every inch of ground on this island." She leaned over the table. Her face was inches away from Lucy's. "Where are your people, Lucy? Where is *your* food?"

Cemented in her chair, Lucy struggled to find a worthy explanation. Evie dropped her head and silently scoffed. I could sense Lucy's heartache. Her pain was enough to make me want to intervene.

"I sent Lucy."

The two women jumped out of their seats, surprised by my loud interruption.

"Voice in the Sky?" Evie stretched her neck heavenward. Her expression transitioned through multiple emotions—relieved, scared, happy, and angry. "You sent her? I thought you had abandoned us."

"I did not abandon you. I am testing you."

For once, Lucy relaxed at the sound of my omniscient outburst. I saved her from coming up with a response. Perhaps a little magic from above would infuse enough meaning for Evie or, at the very least, relieve some pressure.

"Teaching us?" Evie's voice wavered as she choked back tears. She paced back and forth as if running through internal dialogue. I could hear her muttering under her breath, unsure if she was upset or relieved to have some semblance of an answer.

"Some test," Evie said, staring out the window. A few Simples were roasting meat over a fire pit. "It has been hard, but we have grown as a people. We learned how to hunt, forage, and store food. We've come together—sharing what we have with one another. I dare say we've learned more about our resilience in these few cycles than we did all the time before it."

She got it. I only hoped Lucy was convinced our experiment was working. The Simple's struggle was necessary for growth. And I was pretty proud of myself. Spinning their trauma as a test was brilliant.

But then Evie pointed toward the sky. I swear she could see through the monitor straight at me. A hint of rage tinged her voice. "But was it necessary? Was there no other way to help us learn?"

I froze. For a split-second, I saw Evie the way Lucy did, and I doubted everything we had done. I spun around in my chair, watching Lucy stand helplessly next to my bed, reminding myself what was real and what was not. Everything on the screen was simulated.

I turned back toward the monitor, grabbed the microphone, and focused on Evie's penetrating eyes. "These are important lessons that will help you in the future. And perhaps now you are more grateful for what you had before it was taken away."

Evie threw her arms up. "Grateful? Grateful!" She scoffed, trying to choke back her emotions, but the tears came. Falling to her knees, she lowered her head as if letting my words soak into her bones. Lucy sat at the edge of her seat, still silent. Evie's hardened heart softened before our eyes. It was almost like a rebirth. A new Evie was there, pushing her way to the surface. "You're right," Evie said. "I haven't been grateful. I've always wanted more. And now, this struggle has shown me how good we had it before. This home is everything."

Damn, I was good. I was high on a power that was new and enticing. Watching Evie humble herself gave me a rush of adrenaline I'll never forget.

With a reverent submission, she pleaded from her knees. "Now that we've had these lessons, can we go back to how things used to be? Perhaps now you will permit the rain to fall again freely." She dropped her head to the ground.

I pulled up the menu from my computer, making my way

into the source code. Working as quickly as I could, I tapped out a few lines before returning to the scene on my screen. The room in Evie's house grew darker. Thick clouds swept across the sky. Thunder boomed. Lightning cracked.

Evie snapped to attention. She ran out the door as a downpour soaked the ground. "Lucy! You did it! You brought the rain!" She twirled in the muddy puddles, laughing with delight.

Lucy stood dry under the doorway. "This wasn't me."

Right answer, Luce. It wasn't you. This was all me, and it bugged me that Evie didn't understand that. I grabbed the microphone and spoke one final time. "Enjoy the rain for now. But there are more lessons for you to learn." Another rumble of thunder rippled through the town.

Evie's face dropped. "What does that mean?"

The thunder continued to roll. One by one, the Simples vacated their homes and danced in the rain. Neighbors cried and hugged one another as several people dropped to their knees, praising the sky—thanking *me*.

Evie turned toward Lucy, her expression flat. "What did the Voice mean by that? What other lessons?"

Lucy shrugged her shoulders. I'm sure she was as terrified by my words as Evie was. She hated spoiling this beautiful garden, and a part of me did, too. After all, this was my world—my paradise. But significant, scary changes were coming, and it wouldn't be long before the Simples would learn how harsh life can sometimes be.

It was for their own good.

MESSAGE FROM MOM

WED, OCT 12

Hey, hun. I'm slammed at work and won't be home in time for dinner. There are leftovers in the fridge. Eat some veggies!

> Thanks. But I am seventeen and don't need reminders to eat my vegetables like a toddler.

I'm only looking out for you. Speaking of... State is ten days away. Are you ready? Need any help?

> Yes, I'm ready. No, I don't need help. I appreciate the offer, but I'm good. You can relax.

Sweetie, I'm a mom. I haven't relaxed since the day you were born.

CHAPTER 16
A NEW GENERATION

I STARED at the shelves across from my bed as I snuggled under my blankets. The bookcase was full of awards and ribbons I had earned over the years. If things worked out at State next week, Ian and I would add another trophy to the collection.

While the drought produced some fantastic—albeit emotionally taxing—results, Ms. Howell was still pressing us to add the death update. Yesterday, Ian said he was close to finishing. But I never knew what he meant when he said things like "close" or "almost ready." He worked at a different pace than me. Deadlines didn't haunt him. I was a little jealous of it, honestly.

My phone dinged. I grabbed it off the nightstand to read Ian's message: *The code is ready.*

It was only 7:43 in the morning. I tapped out a reply: *What are you doing up this early on a Saturday?*

I pulled the covers over my head. There was no way Ian was working over the weekend. My phone dinged again: *I'm coming over.*

With a rush of adrenaline, I hopped out of bed and checked out my reflection in the mirror. My eyes were puffy from another restless night. I quickly changed my clothes and swept my tangled hair into a ponytail. There was a knock on the door.

"Luce? Can I come in," Ian said.

After haphazardly straightening the covers of my bed, I sat down at its foot. "Uh, yeah, come in."

Ian walked in, noticing the pajamas on the floor. "Did you just wake up or something? I've never seen anything on your floor before. Is this a bad time?"

"No." I quickly grabbed the PJs and tossed them in the hamper. "What about you? Isn't it a little early for you to be up and working?"

Ian sat down on my bed and pulled out his laptop. "I didn't wake up early. I haven't been to bed yet."

"Uh, sleep is important."

"Sleep is for the weak." Ian smiled, but his eyes were glazed over. "Besides, I finished it. The updates are done. I know. I'm amazing, and you're welcome." He flipped open his laptop and opened the backend to the program, showcasing an endless stream of code.

I scooted next to him, looking everything over. "Wow. This is fantastic. But what do you mean by *updates*? Is there more than one?"

Ian yawned and nodded. "I've made three separate updates. Each one is a foundation for the next: The aging update, a birth update, and the infamous death update."

"And what exactly does the death update do?"

"Oh, it randomly kills people. A new death every day," Ian said, rubbing his eyes. Even half-asleep, his sarcasm was on full alert.

"You're morbid." I chuckled, taking the laptop from him. "So, how does it work?"

"It works a lot like real life. If one of the Simples falls off a cliff, goes too long without food or water, gets a blow to the head, then—*kheehkg*—" Ian slid his finger across his neck. "—Dead."

"Lovely." I rolled my eyes.

"Basically, any trauma to the body can kill 'em. For everyone else, the aging program will *slowly* degrade their physical abilities starting around age 30. Based on a randomized setting, they will die between the ages of 75 and 99."

"And I'm guessing the aging program isn't retroactive. That 75 years started the moment you added the update?"

"I marked the current generation as being in the twenty-something range. They'll have another five to ten years before they start to feel any effects of the update, giving them another 50 to 75 years left of life."

Ian checked the clock. "As of 42 minutes ago, the Simples are no longer immortal."

Crazy. I couldn't stop thinking about Evie. The idea of a ticking clock attached to her life made me hesitant to jump forward in time again. I was terrified of saying goodbye.

Ian laid back on my bed and closed his eyes. "Man, I'm tired."

"Gee, I wonder why." I continued analyzing the new code. "So what about the birth update? How does that work?"

"Are you asking me how babies are made?" Ian chuckled, his eyes still closed.

I shook my head. "Ha, ha. And—*yes*. How do the Simples make their babies? Graphic details aren't necessary."

Ian slowly sat up, his eyes half-open. "Sadly, for them, getting pregnant is a little more like the stork story than it is a romp in the bed. The program randomly selects a woman to impregnate —with a new person selected every couple of weeks or so, then nine months until delivery. Although, I did hand-select the first person to test it on."

"You did? Who did you choose?"

"Who do you think? Evie, of course. She's the de facto group leader, so I thought she'd make a good example of motherhood for the rest of the Simples."

I stood up, rattled. "So, you're telling me Evie is pregnant. Like, right now?"

"Yep." Ian yawned again. "And I fast-forwarded time a smidgen. So, the baby will be here soon." He crashed back down on my bed. "Tell you what. Why don't you spend some time observing from the laptop while I take a short nap? I'm so comfy right now." His breathing slowed. "When I wake up, you can go check things out in person." He drifted off to sleep.

Anxious, I took Ian's laptop and moved to my desk. I clicked through a few camera angles, looking for Evie. Once I found her outside her home, I plugged in my headphones and turned up the sound.

A small group of people surrounded her and Steve. Evie rubbed her rounded belly. "I've been concerned about the changes in my body. I was afraid I was being punished for leaving the village borders again." She reached for Steve's hand, whose smile spread across his whole face. "Well, the Voice spoke to us today."

Steve interlaced his fingers with Evie's as he snuggled closer to her. "And he said Evie was chosen to bring new life to the village! A baby is growing inside. Can you believe it?" He leaned down and kissed Evie's belly. "It's so amazing. Evie is going to be a mother."

"And you'll be a father," Evie said, squeezing his hand.

I scribbled notes. Evie's evolution was fascinating. Her experience with the drought was hard to witness. But now, she appeared grounded—more confident in herself. Her intense passion that colored her personality in the past had tempered into a radiant glow.

The Simples congratulated and celebrated Evie and Steve for the next two hours. The idea of adding death to *The Garden* had stressed me out for a long time. But I was reminded that death made room for new growth. The Simples were finally learning about the cycle of life, and I was beginning to realize how vital struggle could be.

"Dude! Wake up!" I gently tapped Ian's shoulder.

"Wha—what are you doing?"

"Evie is in labor, and she's freaking out. We need to go."

Ian sat up, rubbing his eyes. "What am I doing in your room?"

"You came over this morning, remember? You fell asleep on my bed over three hours ago. I've been watching the Simples. Evie is about to have a baby. We need to go to your house and help her. Hurry!"

Ian dragged his body into an upright position. "Alright, I'm up. Mostly."

I grabbed his laptop and opened the door. "Come on, man. Chop chop."

We ran across the street and bolted through his bedroom door. Ian was still yawning as I strapped on the headset. "I'm ready when you are. Power on."

Ian held up his hands. "Powering on in ten, nine, eight—"

I shot Ian an annoyed look. "Now!"

"—two, one." With an emphatic *tap,* Ian connected me to *The Garden.*

The moment my eyes met the ocean horizon, I sprinted across the shore toward the village. When I reached the edge of town, it suddenly hit me that I had no idea how to deliver a baby.

"I don't know what I'm doing," I said as I power-walked through the town. "This was a bad idea."

"Don't sweat it. I've got your back," Ian said.

"What does *that* mean?" I lowered my voice as I walked past a couple of Simples in the street. "Why aren't you freaking out?"

"Don't worry about it."

"Ian? Ian! What are you doing?" Damn that kid and his sudden ideas.

I focused on Evie's house, a couple of blocks away. As my mind calculated my pathway through the crowd of Simples, there was a jolt. The scene in front of me shifted. It was as if *The Garden* had momentarily lost its internet connection. Everyone paused and then jumped out of place. The couple walking in front of me disappeared. A flock of birds blipped out of focus and reappeared, nesting in distant trees.

"Was that a glitch?" I asked.

"Nope, it was a teeny tiny hop into the future."

"But why?" I froze as I heard the sound of a baby cry from inside Evie's house.

"Hear that?" Ian asked. "*That's* why. Because why should we suffer through the trauma—or mess—of birth if I have the power to skip past it?"

I was unwilling to dignify Ian's statement with a response. Instead, I ran toward the house and barrelled through the door. In the corner were Evie, Steve, and a portly woman. Once the unfamiliar woman moved to the side, I saw two swaddled newborns nestled in Evie's arms.

My mouth dropped. "Twins?"

Evie's face beaded with sweat. The exhaustion from the delivery was apparent, but the smile on her face made me believe it was all worth it.

"I can't believe it," she said softly. "My precious, darling sons are here!" Tears streamed down her face as she kissed the heads of two beautiful baby boys.

Steve ran and picked me off my feet as he spun me around. "Isn't this the most amazing thing ever? I'm a dad!" He put me down and ran back to Evie as he gushed over his new little family.

The portly woman gathered some linens, washcloths, and a wooden bowl full of water. "I'll leave you guys for a bit. But I'll be back to check on Evie and the babies later. Congrats, you two." She smiled as she walked past me.

"Who is that?" I whispered under her breath.

"I programmed a midwife," Ian said. "I'm not a total barbarian."

I slowly walked toward Evie's bed. A swell of emotion clogged my throat. The pure joy that shined from Steve and Evie's faces hit me hard. It was all too perfect. Evie reached out her hand, and I grabbed it. "They're beautiful," I said softly.

Over the next two days, the Simples welcomed their newest additions. Steve named the boys Cade and Ash. After collecting data on all the changes, Ian persuaded me to jump ahead for one year—and then another. Little pushes in time helped us track patterns without fast-forwarding my friends into oblivion.

It was incredible to see how much was changing now that a new generation was starting to form. The needs of the individual made way for the needs of a community as more babies were born. I monitored the changes, enchanted by the speed at which rituals were created. Still, every time we inched forward on the timeline, year by year, a pang of sadness pricked my heart as the original generation showed their first glimmers of aging.

With everything considered, I was confident about the work we had done. After weeks of feeling stressed and overwhelmed, I was finally excited. I couldn't wait to share our project with everyone at TechEd. The changes made the Simples more like an actual civilization. The environment challenged them, better reflecting real-life circumstances. And a new generation was growing, giving the older generation a chance to teach and establish values.

All of it gave me hope for a win at State. But even more, it gave me a unique perspective of life, knowing full well that it wouldn't be long until the Simples would face their greatest challenge yet—dealing with death.

IAN'S NOTES

FRIDAY, OCT. 21

State is tomorrow. I'm impressed by how far the Simples have come these past few weeks. After so many attempts at creating realistic AI, Lucy cracked the code. My software wasn't the problem. The people needed time to figure out themselves so they could figure out how to deal with each other.

Strangely, my journey has been the opposite. Learning how to deal with the Simples has helped me figure out myself. They've given me a new kind of confidence. After years of believing I wasn't good around people, I just needed the proper role to find my place.

It turns out I was born to lead.

CHAPTER 17
HIGHS AND LOWS

I STOOD in awe as the audience jumped to their feet. The roar of applause was deafening. Ms. Howell stood a couple of rows behind the judges. The Gibsons were next to Mom and Dad. They all beamed with pride. Having nailed our presentation for State, my adrenaline was at an all-time high. Ian smiled, equally enchanted, and grabbed my hand as we headed toward the stage wing.

"Luce! That was amazing!" Ian wrapped his arms around me. "Getting all four judges inside *The Garden* was such a smart move."

I was dizzy as I continued to process the last fifteen minutes of my life. Was I excited? Nervous? Relieved? I couldn't tell. But Ian's huge smile helped ground me a little. "Did you hear their remarks as they walked through the village?" I asked. "They were gushing, Ian. *Gushing.*"

Ian leaned in closer. "Yeah, they were—almost as much as they gushed over your concluding remarks. Did you see the looks on their faces? You nailed it, Luce. You convinced everyone that this kind of resource isn't just cool technology but a tool to understand humanity better. If we win, it is because of you."

That made the hair on my arms stand to attention. A swell of emotion choked my words. "I couldn't have done this without you." The next team began their presentation. "We should probably leave," I whispered, and we headed out the backstage door.

Ms. Howell ran through the hallway. She offered enthusiastic high-fives when she approached us. "You guys! That was amazing! You should hear what people are saying. I feel bad for anyone who has to follow you."

Ian smiled at me.

"Speaking of which," I said, checking the time on my phone. "How many more teams do we have until this thing is over?"

Ms. Howell glanced down at the schedule in her hand. "We still have an hour or two before we're done. And then another hour while the judges deliberate."

I took a deep breath, trying to bring my energy down. "I can't watch any other projects. My nerves are frayed."

"Don't worry about it." Ms. Howell said as the three of us walked down the hallway. "I'll be your eyes and ears. Why don't you guys find some food? Relax a bit. You've earned it." She shot us a thumbs up and went back into the auditorium.

Ian and I walked toward the cafeteria of Tucson High. The area was a flutter of activity. Teams dotted the room, practicing their presentations while parents and teachers rushed by offering support.

"Sheesh, it's busy out here," Ian said.

"Seriously, I wish we had a quiet place to chill for a bit."

Ian smiled. "I have an idea. Follow me." He guided me around a corner and found an empty classroom. "Wait here," he said, opening the door. "I'll be right back."

I walked around what appeared to be an art room. Paintings lined the walls while half-finished projects cluttered the counters. One drawing of a woman caught my attention. The pencil outline of the face was nothing more than a few graphite strokes on paper. But the eyes had been shaded to perfection with an almost photo-like quality. I couldn't help but think of Evie. The sketch was nothing more than a facsimile, but the expressive details of the eyes made me believe this person on paper saw things nobody else could.

The door opened, and Ian walked in, holding two VR headsets.

"Did someone order some peace and quiet?" Ian sat the headsets on a table and pulled out his laptop. "I thought a little relaxing on the beach would be nice."

"Brilliant." I moved a few tables out of the way and strapped on the goggles. "Ready?"

"Ready," he said as he punched a key on the computer.

The moon glowed above the horizon, casting a beautiful reflection onto the ocean. A low tide made for calm waters. The only sound was the gentle push and pull of the waves as they rippled in and out, mimicking the sound of my breath. As I exhaled, my shoulders dripped down while a smile lifted on my face. "Oh, man, I've missed this."

Ian's handsome avatar appeared next to me. "Me, too," he said, leaning back. "I haven't been inside *The Garden* for weeks."

I gave Ian's character the once over, wishing to share this moment with my actual friend. "You know, as much as I love this chiseled persona you've created, I'd love to see the *real* you sitting next to me."

Ian scoffed. "Yeah, right."

"Seriously, I want to share this moment with the brilliant genius who created this magical place."

"If you insist." His avatar disappeared. I could hear him tapping on his keyboard from within the classroom. Suddenly Ian was sitting next to me. His wild curls and lanky body silhouetted against the moonlight. "You think this is better?"

"I do. Thank you."

We smiled at each other before I turned my attention toward the horizon again. "Man, what an exhausting day."

"I think you mean *days*." Ian chuckled. "After hearing how stressful this competition was, I never thought I'd be here joining you in the craziness."

I leaned back, tucking my arms under my head, admiring the stars. "Well, I'm glad you did." Ian followed my example, lying down next to me. I turned to face him. "None of this would be possible without you. I'm right at the doorway of my dreams— MIT. I can feel it. And I don't know how I'll ever repay you."

"Stop it. I'm the one who is in debt to you."

I scoffed.

Ian leaned in closer. "No, really. If we win this thing, I've got a future. I've slacked off so much, believing my own lies that college was a waste of time." His eyes locked on mine. "Remember the first day of school? When you were freaking out, worried about *the plan*?"

I laughed, embarrassed at the memory of it. "That doesn't sound like me at all."

Ian smiled. "Well, I still remember sitting next to you. Right here on this beach. And I knew you'd be heading off to some big important school after graduation, and I'd be stuck here."

"You're far too smart to be stuck anywhere, Ian." I wasn't used to him being this vulnerable, and I couldn't quite define how I felt about it.

"Well, my grades certainly aren't enough to follow you to MIT. Or any decent school for that matter."

Follow me to MIT? I tried to ignore that statement. "Grades aren't everything, Ian."

"Why do you think I'm competing? I'm ready to take my future seriously. So, I'm the one who is indebted to you, Luce. You've carved a path for me, and I'll forever be grateful."

The tension in my heart was confusing. I cared about Ian and wanted him to be happy. But I was increasingly uncomfortable with how he kept looking at me. I closed my eyes. My mind was a flurry of questions and concerns. For the next hour, I tried to focus on the sound of the waves, syncing my breath to its continuous flow. In and out. In and out.

***

"Before we announce today's winners, we want to give everyone a huge round of applause for their work at this year's Arizona's TechEd Tournament." The principal of Tucson High stood tall as the audience cheered. "The great state of Arizona will be well represented, no matter who wins. Now, I'd like to turn the time over to Ms. Crawford, one of tonight's esteemed judges, to announce our winners."

The crowd applauded as Ms. Crawford walked on stage. Her no-nonsense demeanor perfectly mirrored her squinty eyes and thin lips. The cheers died down as she picked up the microphone.

"Thank you, Principal Wilson. This was not an easy decision. There were countless projects worthy of representing our state. As you all know, first and second-place teams will be awarded airfare and accommodations for Nationals in Orlando, which takes place in three weeks."

I forced a smile for Ian, crossing my fingers. He smiled back.

"Before we announce the top two teams, we would like to recognize our fifth and fourth place winners—as well as our third-place team who will be the first alternate should the first or second-place team be unable to attend Nationals."

Fiddling with my necklace, I anxiously listened to the results. Fifth place went to a team from Flagstaff who created an online collaborative classroom. Fourth place was a specialized 3-D printer designed for special needs students.

"And our third-place winner is..." Ms. Crawford read her notes.

I wondered if everyone could hear my heart as it thumped against my rib cage. My cheeks were getting hotter as I hung onto every word. *Please don't say my name. Don't say my name!* The fear of repeating history nearly knocked me over.

"Jeremy Hanks and Kadeem Mosely of Canyon View with their Digital Literacy Assessment Tool!"

A sigh of relief washed over me. As the two teens walked up on stage, I recognized the conflicted expression on their faces—simultaneously happy and deflated, having barely missed the mark. I closed my eyes and exhaled deeply. I wouldn't be leaving with another almost win. This year was going to be different.

But the respite was brief. The crowd erupted again as the judge announced the second-place team. A few rows over, Jake was staring at me, and I realized he and Dylan still hadn't placed. What if they win again? My brain froze as I imagined the worst-case scenario.

We may not place at all.

I leaned over in my chair, trying to slow down my breath. My mind raced through every little mistake we had made, convincing me that there was no way we could win. Ian gently rubbed my back. "Luce, you okay?"

I sat up, shooting him a terrified look. "I failed."

Confused, Ian leaned in closer. "What are you talking about?"

The auditorium filled with a roar of applause as Ms. Howell nudged me. "You guys, that's you! Get up there!"

My eyes darted toward the stage. "What?"

Ian hopped to his feet, pulling me up with him. "We won, Luce! We won!"

The next few minutes were a blur as we accepted our trophy and returned to our seats. All I could sense were the shapes and muffled sounds of everyone around me. Dozens of people came to congratulate us, including Jake. Everyone was happy for us. Photos were taken. Hugs and high fives were non-stop. Through it all, I kept wondering if it was really happening. Slowly the weight of everything settled into my bones, and I felt rooted. We had crossed the finish line.

I was heading to Nationals.

"Looks like you guys did it," Mom said as we got ready to leave. "I guess trusting Ian paid off after all."

"I told you he wouldn't let me down." The smile on my face had not budged in the twenty minutes since I found out we won.

"Well, don't get too confident yet, dear. Nationals won't be a breeze."

I sighed. "Can't you just be happy for me, Mom? For one second?"

She wrapped her arms around me. "Of course, I'm happy for you. I'm proud."

"Me, too, mijita!" Dad swooped in, wrapping his arms around both me and Mom. I melted into their embrace, thirsty for their affection. Dad was gone so often, and it was easy to forget how supportive his actual presence was—how much I needed *him* and not just his texts. Plus, he had a way of softening Mom's edges. He pulled us in with his loving magnetism, reducing the sometimes cold distance between Mom and me. But Mom's joy which radiated after tonight's results, made me wonder if her tough love was worth it. At the very least, it worked.

As the celebrations settled, Ian and I made our way to the parking lot. We packed our gear into the Gibsons' SUV, ready for the two-hour drive back to Scottsdale.

"You sure you don't want to ride with us?" Ian asked.

"Nah, my parents are guilting me to go with them. We don't often have a weekend together."

"Yeah, I haven't seen your dad in a while." Ian glanced over my shoulder and waved to my parents, chuckling. "He's such a fun guy, but your mom still looks as scary as ever."

I smiled as I handed him the box of VR headsets. Looking up at the stars, I thought back to our peaceful moment on the beach earlier. This was even better. "Is this for real?"

"What?" Ian asked.

"This—this victory. This moment in time. It feels too good. I'm worried we're still inside *The Garden* somehow, and we're going to come out and realize none of this is happening."

Ian smiled. His eyes were wide and hopeful. "Very real."

I threw my arms around his neck. "We're going to Nationals!"

"We're going to Nationals," Ian said, hugging me tightly. He let go and stepped back. Shifting his weight to one foot, he cleared his throat. "Uh, so... Luce, I wanted to ask you something."

"Oh yeah? What's that?"

Ian pulled on his jacket. "I was wondering if you'd go to Fall Ball with me."

"Oh." My heart sank. "I'm sorry. I already told Jake I would go with him," I said, tripping over my words as my awkwardness increased.

Ian's tone turned cold. "Jake? Wittingham?"

"Yeah, he asked me a few weeks ago." The hurt in Ian's eyes pierced me, and I tried to lighten the mood. "Besides, since when do you go to school dances?" Unlike Ian, sarcasm wasn't my thing. It certainly wasn't the best choice right then.

"I guess I don't," he said softly, shaking his head. "Okay. Well, uh, goodnight. Congrats on your win." He turned around and got into his parents' car.

"Ian, wait. Can we—" I stepped forward as the door slammed.

CHAPTER 18
IAN'S SCORN

ARE YOU MAD?

Can we talk about it?

Will you at least call me tomorrow?

The string of messages from Lucy lit up my phone as my parents drove home from the competition. I didn't respond. I got home, threw my backpack in the corner, and crashed onto my bed. It was nearly midnight, but my mind wouldn't turn off. I was mad. I felt stupid. Was Lucy really going to Fall Ball with Jake Wittingham? Jake? How could she say yes to that asshole?

I wish I could be happy with our win and move on. I should have let it go, gone to bed, and put the matter to rest. In the morning, I would have realized I was overreacting. Instead, I logged into *The Garden*, anxious for a distraction.

That was my first mistake of the night.

It was daytime inside the village. I tapped through a few camera angles until I found a group of Simples dancing near the pond. Two dozen or so bodies swayed and bounced to exuberant melodies while others stood conversing around them. In the middle was Evie. Her usual intensity had given way to a blissful state as she swayed her hips side to side. A carefree moment like this was rare for a woman who questioned everything. Evie's smile reminded me of Lucy's face when they announced our win a few hours earlier. It was as if Evie was connected to Lucy—like they shared each other's joy.

Where was *my* joy?

Jake got Lucy. Lucy got her win. And the Simples had everything. *The Garden* was supposed to be *my* haven—my escape from the shitty life I was given. So why was I the one left hurting and alone?

As I said, I should have gone to bed. But as I stared at the Simples' smiling faces while they enjoyed the fruits of my brilliance, I lost it. I was envious of what they had.

I never considered myself a jealous person. All my life, I was surrounded by people determined to make me small in some pathetic attempt to make themselves feel bigger. But it didn't bother me because even though I often felt invisible, I've never felt small. Not with ideas as big as mine.

So why did I envy the Simples? The smallest of all. They weren't even real and totally of my own making. Why did I enjoy teasing and testing them? Why did I enjoy watching them squirm under the authority of my voice? Maybe it is because Lucy saw my simulation as something bigger than life—bigger than me. She didn't care that the Simples weren't real. She loved them anyway while dismissing me. And for that, I want them to learn how small they really were.

I reached for the microphone, unsure what I would say but determined to put the Simples in their place. Then an idea formed, and I grabbed a VR headset instead.

That was my second mistake of the night.

Before strapping in, I pulled up my avatar's profile and made a few quick changes. I put the goggles on and plugged in.

. . .

The sky darkened as ominous clouds formed above. A crash of thunder followed a bolt of lightning, jolting the Simples to attention as I hovered above them. A long, white robe replaced my t-shirt and jeans, blowing in the strong winds.

"You ungrateful children!" My voice boomed louder than the thunder. Everyone screamed, dropping to their knees—everyone except Evie. She stood stoic as she tried to understand the situation.

"Who are you? What do you want?" Evie yelled from the ground.

"Silence! On your knees!" I wasn't about to let some bundle of code get the best of me. My threatening tone worked as Evie quickly stumbled to the ground. I flew over the group, allowing my penetrating eyes to latch on to anyone who dared look at me. "Why are you so ungrateful? Don't you know I created you? I gave you this world, and I can take it away."

The more I spoke, the more I wanted to punish the Simples. It wasn't their fault Lucy had said yes to Jake. They weren't responsible for my crappy life. They had never made jokes at my expense. If anything, the Simples were the only people to give me a semblance of respect. To them, I was the Voice in the Sky.

And that's why I did it.

Being the Voice in the Sky gave me the control I never had in real life. The power I had over their world meant nobody could shove me down or say no to my desires. In *The Garden*, I was better than Jake Wittingham. I was everything—the beginning and the end.

Evie kept her eyes cast to the ground, speaking loud enough to be heard while the others crouched below my feet. "Are you the Voice in the Sky?" Her words were weak and timid as if she didn't want the answer. It was the only time the truth seemed to terrify her.

"Yes, I am." A whimper rippled out from the group at my

bold declaration. "I am your creator. I have been your protector. But I can also be your destruction."

Several Simples wept openly. A voice in my head told me to stop, but I was too intoxicated by the power as they waited on bated breath for my next command.

"We don't want to be destroyed!" Evie yelled. Nobody else dared move, so she continued to step up as their leader. She was courageous. I'll give her that.

"Then prove it," I said.

The Simples exchanged worried looks, unsure what I was asking.

"Prove your gratitude. Show me you appreciate this world I've created. Gather your greatest gifts and convince me that you deserve to live this life I've provided." Another crack of lightning echoed through the sky before I vanished before their eyes.

I ripped off the headset and sat back down at my computer. The adrenaline in my veins was pulsating. I smirked as the Simples frantically came to terms with this new reality. For a moment, vengeance boiled in my blood. But slowly, the potency faded, leaving me merely amused. I laughed, realizing this was all a game with no real consequences.

Over the next few minutes, the Simples frantically made plans for their offering. They scurried into their huts like cockroaches scattering at the first hint of light. Ten minutes later, they gathered with an assortment of items in hand. Evie led a long band of Simples, carrying a small rabbit hide. Steve was behind her with a basket of fruit. Some had jewelry—others, polished rocks. The line of people stretched long as they made their way toward the altar.

"Dear Voice in the Sky," Evie shouted after making her way to the top of the structure. "We have brought you an offering of gifts—our very best in hopes of pleasing you. We do not wish to be destroyed."

I chuckled. This was fun. My smile grew as every Simple took a turn climbing the stairs. One by one, they placed their object on the altar and bowed their heads before letting the next person go.

Like a kid with a magnifying glass and nothing better to do, the Simples were ants at my feet—easy targets I could provoke to pass the time. I grabbed the microphone, broadcasting my voice again. "You call this your best?" My biting intensity made the villagers tremble. The Simples fell to their knees. "I am not pleased with these gifts. Perhaps you are not truly grateful for all I have given you."

My phone dinged.

Annoyed at the sudden interruption, I read Lucy's message: *What the hell are you doing?*

Shit. Lucy must have been watching from her laptop. My instinct was to lie—make up a story and ask for forgiveness. I wasn't sure how much she had witnessed, but she had to be fuming. I began typing out an explanation but deleted the words.

What was I apologizing for?

The Simples stayed prostrated near the ground, nervously waiting for another declaration from the sky. Their fear was unmistakable.

I texted Lucy: *I'm blowing off a little steam. Don't worry about it.*

All the Simples peeked from behind their bowed heads, looking toward Evie for guidance. Evie closed her eyes and slowly stood up.

"We're sorry you are not pleased with our gifts," she said. "Perhaps you'll give us another chance to prove ourselves. We are so grateful for all you have provided."

Lucy texted me again: *Don't you think you're overreacting?*

You're going to ruin our chances at Nationals. Stop playing god with these people!

Why couldn't Lucy get it in her head that the Simples weren't people? They were stupid lines of code. Why did she care more about them than me?

The Simples had formed a circle around the altar, chanting. "We are grateful. We are grateful."

With a heavy sigh, I grabbed the microphone one last time. "You have done enough. I am pleased."

The Simples collectively exhaled and hugged one another. A wave of affirmations rippled through the crowd as they rang out songs of gratitude.

But here's the thing—I *was* pleased. While everything about my life sucked, at least the Simples understood my value. And I only wondered what it would take for the real world to recognize it, too.

I picked up my phone and typed out a final message: *Remember, Luce. They're not real. But I am. I AM.*

It was my last mistake of the night.

I heard a knock the next day, and I knew my mistakes had caught up with me as soon as my mom answered the door.

"Lucy! Already back at it, huh?" Mom said.

"Hi, Mrs. Gibson."

My heart jumped at the sound of Lucy's voice. A reckoning was coming, and I was trapped in my kitchen. My worn-out pajamas and bloodshot eyes didn't help. I sniffed my pits to ensure my smell wasn't too offensive before running my fingers through my matted hair. I held my breath, listening to the conversation happening in the entryway.

"I gotta say, yesterday was amazing," Mom said. "I'm so

impressed with what you guys did. It means so much that you let Ian tag along for the ride."

"Ian was way more than a tagalong," Lucy said. "But with Nationals coming up, we got a lot of work. Is he around?"

"He's finishing breakfast. I tell you, that kid sleeps in till noon whenever he can."

Five seconds later, Lucy was in the kitchen. Our eyes locked. My head dropped.

"Oh, Luce, I'm so sorry. I was a complete jerk yesterday." Swirling my spoon through my cereal, I looked up with my most pathetic puppy dog eyes. "Forgive me?"

With a heavy exhale, Lucy plopped down across from me. "What even happened? I mean... I just... What *was* that? After everything that happened—after *winning State*—how could something as silly as the Fall Ball rile you up?

"You don't get it, Luce." I placed my spoon next to my bowl and sighed. "I don't like Jake. I think he's a slimeball who weasels his way into any opportunity that suits him. And that includes getting together with you. And it kills me to think of you with him."

Lucy rolled her eyes. "I'm not *with* him. I'm going to one stupid high school dance with the guy. That can't be what this is really about."

I rubbed my forehead, trying to find the right words. My stomach was doing origami while my heart performed jumping jacks. I wondered if there was any way to stop the words from moving up my throat. But my mouth was running faster than my brain, and before I could stop myself, everything spilled out.

"Come on, Luce. You gotta know how I feel about you."

She stiffened with fear as if someone had grabbed her from the throat. Her reaction told me everything I didn't want to know. I wished I could run away, hide, and never come back. But I was in too deep to back out now. So, I buried my gaze into my cereal, not brave enough to meet her eyes, and continued my confession.

"Since the day we met, you've been it for me. There is nobody else I want to be with. After working together these past couple of months, I thought you felt the same way."

My chest tightened. I was putting it all out there. And for a brief second, I believed all it would take to make her see we belonged together was to say it out loud. My sister's music boomed from the second floor. Blake was crying in the next room. Still, the only sound I heard was the beat of my heart as I waited for her response.

"I—I'm not sure what to say," Lucy finally muttered. "You're my friend. I care about you so much. I think you deserve every good thing. But—"

My defense system kicked in. "—But you like Jake."

"No, I don't like Jake—not like *that*. If I did, this would be a lot easier. All I know is I don't want to lose you as my friend. And I don't want something silly like one date to ruin everything we've built together."

I stood up and put my bowl in the sink. My mouth pressed on even while my brain said shut up. "So why do you keep him around? Why lead him on by going to the dance if you don't like him? It doesn't make sense."

"Again, I'm not marrying the dude. We're going to one stupid dance! Why do you care?" Lucy bit her lip, looking ashamed that she had raised her voice.

"Because I think he's garbage, Luce. He's no good for you. He's playing you because you're popular and because people expect you two to hook up. And no matter how much you deny liking him, you will always keep him around because people like Jake are an asset to your reputation, and I'm a liability. I can't compete with the Jake Wittinghams of the world."

"Oh, please, what does Jake have that you don't?"

"Charm. Big muscles. Smoldering eyes. Clear skin." I locked eyes with her. "You."

Lucy shook her head, blinking back tears. "He doesn't have me, Ian."

I crossed my arms and shrugged. "Sure, if you say so."

The sound of the kitchen clock ticked away the seconds. I focused on the bird feeder outside the window, trying to diffuse my rage. Lucy spoke quietly. "Can we focus on Nationals for the next three weeks? Please?"

"Sure," I said with a sigh. "Gotta stick to *the plan*, right?" It came out more heartless than I intended, but it was too late to take it back. I sighed. "You coming?"

She reluctantly followed. An awkward silence filled the room as I booted up my computer. I kept replaying the conversation from the kitchen in my head, wishing it had never happened.

"So, I have to ask," Lucy said timidly. She paused as if afraid she was pulling on a string that could unravel everything. "What exactly did you do last night?"

"Oh yeah—*that*." I had almost forgotten about last night. I sighed, gearing up for another awkward conversation. "Uh, well... I was feeling a lot of things last night—feeling sorry for myself, mostly. And when I got home, I decided to check on the Simples. Hoping for a distraction."

Lucy chuckled softly. "Great minds, I guess. That is why I hopped on, too." She cleared her throat. "I saw the Simples making their way to the altar. Evie said something about not wanting to be destroyed? What was that about?"

If Lucy had only caught the tail end of things, I could fix this. She didn't know I had shown myself to the Simples. Perhaps I could spin this as a small, simple mistake. With a deep inhale, I began weaving my story.

"As I said, it was stupid. I noticed how happy the Simples were. They were so pleased with their life I gave them. And I was feeling pretty crummy, knowing that the things I want are always out of reach." I attempted my best puppy-dog expression, hoping to earn some sympathy from Lucy. My gut twisted tighter.

Lucy blushed and walked toward my window. "So, what did you do?"

I shook my head, still not fully believing my actions. "I sorta lost it. It was like another person had taken over. I was drunk with anger and jealousy, and the Simples were oblivious to how good they had it—so ungrateful for their blissful existence."

"Uh, we nearly destroyed everything with a major drought not too long ago," Lucy said. "You remember that, right? It hasn't been all sunshine and sparkles for them."

"But all I could see last night was their joy. And I wanted them to hurt as I did. I guess that whole *misery loves company* thing is true."

Lucy's eyes met mine. Ashamed, it was my turn to look away.

"So, I told them they needed to prove their gratitude. Show me they appreciated all I gave them, or I would—" I sighed heavily. "—or I would destroy them."

Lucy's face fell.

"I'm sorry, Luce. Really, I am." My voice was weak.

Lucy faced the window again. "Is that *all* you did?"

I vowed to bury the rest of the story deep within.

"Ian?"

My eyes met hers as I forced a smile. "Yep."

She sighed. "Well, let's hope your tantrum doesn't come back to bite us in the ass. Now, Nationals are in three weeks. What do we need to do next?"

LUCY'S NOTES

SUNDAY, OCT. 23

I hate that Ian is hurting, but he crossed a line. All those times he interfered with the Simples before were problematic, but this 'love me or be destroyed' business is on a whole other level. Ian is right. He is a liability—but not just to my reputation. He's a risk to his own creation.

Despite the glaring red flag waving in my mind, I'm choosing to move on. We won State. Nationals are three weeks away. MIT is within reach. That is what I need to focus on, not this drama.

CHAPTER 19
OPTIONS

Ms. Howell was unusually chipper when the bell rang for class on Monday. "Good afternoon, students! Before we begin, I want to congratulate Ms. Fernández and Mr. Gibson for taking first at the Arizona TechEd Tournament this weekend. They'll be heading to Orlando to represent our school—and state—at the national competition."

I shot Ian a smile as the class applauded. He seemed entirely disinterested.

"You okay?" I whispered.

He half-nodded before resting his head on his desk.

Meandering through the classroom, Ms. Howell began her lecture. "As we've discussed before, anthropology aims to understand humans better and view the world through new eyes, no matter how different someone's way of life may be. Unfortunately, as history has shown, many people don't approach new cultures with the intention of understanding. Instead, fear, power, and exploitation often drive these interactions."

Ms. Howell grabbed a marker and wrote the word *dehumanization* on the whiteboard. She turned and faced the class. "Who can tell me what this word means?"

Zarine raised her hand. "When people dehumanize others, they think of them as something other than human."

"Correct, Ms. Rashid. Thank you." Ms. Howell continued. "Think about the crusade of the Holy Roman Empire. It was a period of bloody campaigns that lasted over six centuries. It was built on the dehumanization of the other. It's the same with Columbus and his violence toward Native Americans. Slavery, the Rwandan genocides, and even in our daily interactions—when we call others pigs, snakes, or scum, we strip people of their humanity."

With a tap on the whiteboard, Ms. Howell drove home her point. "When we dehumanize others, it enables us to treat them in ways that would otherwise be considered morally reprehensible."

My gut sank.

"Most people won't spend their careers studying different cultures, but everyone must adopt the mindset of an anthropologist," Ms. Howell said. "The world needs more curious observers and less exploitative conquerors."

She carried on with her lecture until the bell rang. Every word out of her mouth made me think of the Simples and what Ian had done. It no longer was like an experiment fueled by curiosity. I was afraid Ian enjoyed the role of conqueror better.

The bell rang, waking Ian from his midday nap. He slipped out of class before I could talk to him. His empty seat made me uneasy. I couldn't help but relive our awkward conversation from Sunday. Slowly gathering my things, I waited for the last few students to vacate the classroom. All the while, the word *dehumanization* on the whiteboard stared back at me.

"Ms. Howell? Do you have a minute?" I asked.

"Of course! What's on your mind?"

"Your lecture today is sitting weird with me."

Ms. Howell leaned back in her seat. "Oh? How so?"

"Maybe I'm being crazy." I chuckled softly. "I tend to overthink things, but while you were talking about the awful things people have done to other cultures—" I wrung my hands, trying to find the right words. "I couldn't help but wonder if what we're doing to the Simples is wrong."

"Hmm..." Ms. Howell pressed her lips together, slowly nodding. "That's quite the question, isn't it?" She leaned forward, placing her elbows on her desk. "Well, first of all—I don't think you're crazy."

I smiled. Ms. Howell had obviously never been inside my head.

"Second, I want you to remember the Simple's growth that came from the drought. Struggle is a part of life, so I don't think you need to worry about being some ruthless invader on the wrong side of history because you give them challenges."

I slowly nodded my head, thinking about what she didn't know.

She continued. "The fact that you're even worried about this tells me a lot about who you are." Ms. Howell leaned back in her chair, tapping her finger to her mouth as if pondering the question longer.

I took advantage of the silence and summoned my courage. "I guess what I'm asking, Ms. Howell, is whether *you* think the Simples are real."

Ms. Howell laughed. "Shoot. You're heading into some deep philosophical territory there, which is not my forte. So, let me turn the question back on you. What do you think makes something real? What makes a person alive?"

I thought for a moment. "I think if someone can feel emotions. If they have a sense of their own identity, maybe? If they grow and adapt to their environment. Someone who fears death."

"That's a pretty decent list. Do you think the Simples meet that criteria?"

"Well, yeah. I mean, they adapted to the drought. The Simples have shown all kinds of emotions. They're even aging now and having babies. And..." I stopped. My stomach churned as I thought about Ian's latest antics.

"What is it?" Ms. Howell asked, sensing my hesitation.

"They're afraid to die."

Ms. Howell pulled back, surprised. "I didn't think the Simples had experienced death yet?"

"They haven't, but Ian threatened to destroy them on Saturday." I exhaled heavily, relieved to share the secret with her. "And the look of fear on their faces—" I closed my eyes, shaking my head as I imagined it. "It was awful, Ms. Howell. Awful."

"Oh, I see." She was quiet. I waited, listening to the muffled noise coming from the hallway.

When Ms. Howell didn't offer an immediate response, I swallowed hard and vocalized the internal debate I had been having for weeks.

"They're just computer code, right? The Simples don't have flesh or bones or blood. And Ian keeps telling me they're not real."

"Mmm-hmm." Ms. Howell nodded. She tilted her head ever so slightly with tender concern. After a moment, she finally lifted her shoulders and exhaled loudly. "I wish I had an answer for you. Like most situations, it is not black or white. I think the work you've done is phenomenal. And I believe *The Garden* can have a major impact on the field of anthropology—not to mention government, history, climate studies, and so much more."

Ms. Howell stood up and walked toward me, sitting on the edge of her desk. "But I understand where you're coming from. As the world's designers, you two have a lot of power over the people. And as the saying goes: More power. More responsibility."

"Yeah."

"So, imagine if you were in the Simples' place. What if you were the one being programmed—manipulated, even—by some force bigger than you. What would you want?"

My eyes grew wide as if the answer was so obvious I couldn't believe I hadn't considered it before. "That's it, Ms. Howell! Yes, thank you. That helps a lot. I need to go talk to Ian."

"Wait, wait, wait... hold on!" Ms. Howell smiled as I turned around, already halfway out the door. "You're not going to share your epiphany with me?".

"As you said," I replied, "I need to imagine myself in their situation. The answer is obvious when I do that."

Are you home? Can we talk?

My feet pounded the pavement as I sped down the street toward the Gibsons' house. Every few seconds, I glanced back at my phone, hoping for a reply from Ian. No luck. By the time I reached his front door, I was beginning to worry. Ian had barely talked to me all day. He insisted he had to retake a test during lunch and slept through most of Ms. Howell's class. At first, I didn't mind, as I wasn't in the mood to talk to him either. But his silent treatment made me wonder if there was something else going on.

Mr. Gibson answered the door as his usual, distracted self. At least his parents were unaware of whatever was happening between Ian and me.

"Hi, Lucy! I'm sorry, but Ian isn't home."

"Oh, okay, do you know where he is?"

"He said he was going to the store. He needed some supplies to fix one of the Amplifier Chips before Nationals." Mr. Gibson cocked his head to the side. "Were you two supposed to be working today? Did he forget?"

"Oh, no." I lied. "I remember now. He told me. But he said I could work on the project from his computer until he got back —*if* you're okay with that."

"Of course. We'd swap you for Ian in a heartbeat." Mr. Gibson winked. "Come on in. Make yourself at home."

I made my way upstairs, nervous about entering Ian's room without permission. But I was eager to check in on the Simples. And while I could watch them from my house, I needed to go inside the program to check things out. Besides, I wanted to go to Ian's room and look for any red flags.

As I opened his door, everything appeared the same. I rummaged through some notes on his desk—journal entries of some kind. After glancing out the window, I checked my phone one more time. With no sign of Ian, I strapped on the headset and logged in.

As soon as I entered *The Garden,* I walked toward the village. Past the dunes, hidden mostly by foliage, a bit of carved stone popped above the tree line. That was new. I picked up my pace and cut through some bushes for a closer look. As I pushed back a few branches, I finally came face to face with the massive structure nearly two stories high. My eyes almost popped out of my head. Mouth dropped.

The Simples had created a statue of Ian's avatar.

Unable to move, I stared at the figure in disbelief. Standing at around fifteen feet and made of stone, there was no way the thing could have been built in the last day or two. Did Ian fast-forward time again? Or did he code it himself?

"Lucy? Is that you?"

I turned to see Evie walking from behind the structure.

"Evie! What is this thing?" I pointed to the stone figure, unable to hide my shocked face. "Did you build it? When?"

Evie sat down on a rock near the statue. "The others and I

built it together. We've been working on it for many moons. It is our gift to the Voice in the Sky—our attempt to please him so he'll preserve our people and let us stay here in Fredena." Her shoulders dropped as she wiped the sweat from her forehead. She closed her eyes as tears gently ran down her cheeks.

"What's wrong? Are you okay?" I knelt in front of her.

Evie began to cry. "Oh, Lucy, I'm so scared. What if the Voice doesn't like it? What if it's not good enough?" She wrung her dirt-covered hands.

"I still don't understand. Did the Voice tell you to build it?"

"Not exactly. He said we were ungrateful. The sky raged with anger as he told us our gifts weren't enough. But then he said they were acceptable. We were so confused—so worried. We wanted to prove our gratitude. So we built this."

I struggled to piece together the timeline of events. Ian must have fast-forwarded things since Sunday. But was it before or after I had talked to him? And why didn't he tell me about it? There was something else that worried me even more. I took Evie's hands, trying to comfort her.

"Evie, how did you know what the Voice looks like?"

"He revealed himself to us. Amidst the thunder and lightning, he floated high in the sky."

Evie closed her eyes, shaking her head. Her face winced. It was as if the very act of remembering the events caused her pain. "He said if we don't do better, he will destroy our whole village. He told us we would all die." She dropped to her knees, throwing her face into her hands. Her body shook as she sobbed uncontrollably. "Everyone is so afraid. What can we do?"

I placed my hand on Evie's shoulder. "I'm so sorry. This must be hard, but I promise everything will be okay."

Evie shook her head, brushing away tears, making room for more to fall. "How? He's so powerful."

"Do you trust me?"

"Of course."

I inhaled slowly, looking up at the statue and shaking my head. "You've done more than enough to show your gratitude. The Voice will be pleased with your gift, and he will leave you alone. Believe me. Now, please, enjoy your life. Don't waste any more of it worrying about this stuff. Try to be happy."

"I'll try. If you say we'll be okay, I'll try." Evie rubbed her eyes, her breath still sporadic.

I stood, brushing the dirt off my dress. "Good. And tell the others. Tell them not to worry."

Evie hugged me tightly. "Thank you, friend. I'm always so happy when you come to visit." She ran to tell the others.

As I pulled off the headset, the tension in my jaw hardened. I don't think I've ever been so angry. My mind jumped from one thought to the next. How could Ian be so cruel? What would the judges think of this insane statue? How dare he jump time ahead without telling me.

My mental tirade was interrupted by the chirp of my phone. It was Ian: *I'll be home in fifteen minutes if you still want to talk.*

Panic flooded my body. Looking around, I was desperate to take back control of the situation—somehow. I frantically pulled my backup hard drive out from my bag and connected it to Ian's computer. While I had a viewer-only version of *The Garden* on my laptop, what I really needed was the source code if I was to understand what was going on inside. Looking over my shoulder, hoping nobody would barge into the room, I began copying the program onto my device.

While it was uploading, I contemplated taking one of the headsets on Ian's desk, but I'm sure he would notice it missing. I peeked inside his closet and found the box with the extra VR goggles and Reality Amplifier Chips we used at the competition on Saturday. Grabbing one of each, I stuffed them into my bag. My heart was racing as I checked the time. Ian would arrive any minute. As soon as the program finished uploading, I unplugged and rushed out.

"Leaving already?" Mr. Gibson asked from the family room as I came down the stairs.

My hands were shaking as I grabbed the doorknob. "Yep, I decided to work from home. I'll talk to Ian later. Thanks!" But as I bolted out the door, I nearly slammed into Ian.

"Whoa, watch out!" he yelled.

I froze. "Ian! Sorry, I wasn't paying attention."

He laughed. "Obviously. Where are you going? I thought we were going to talk."

Forcing a smile, I tried to act relaxed. "Yeah, of course. I came over earlier and waited for a bit but then decided to head home when you didn't show."

"Didn't you get my text?" Ian squinted his eyes as if my story wasn't adding up.

"Text?" I took out my phone. "Oh, yep, must have missed it."

"So, do you want to talk or not?"

My pulse pressed against my skin. "Uh, can we talk tomorrow? I remembered I have an assignment for chemistry that I need to finish. Sorry."

"No problem, boss." Ian moved out of the way to let me pass. He lifted one eyebrow. "Are you sure you're okay?"

I stopped, took a deep breath, and turned around. "I could ask you the same thing. You seemed distracted at school."

Ian rocked back on his heels. "Yeah, sorry, I got a lot on my mind, I guess."

We stood silent for a moment, refusing to look the other in the eye.

"Maybe an afternoon off is what we need," I finally said. "Let's connect at lunch tomorrow, okay?"

"Sure, yeah."

Turning to walk away, I closed my eyes, breathing slowly out my mouth. I wasn't sure what my next move was, but with Ian's technology stuffed inside my backpack, at least now I had options.

MESSAGE FROM JAKE

TUE, OCT 25

Okay, I admit it. You're the TechEd champion! I bow before you. But even though you crushed me last week doesn't mean you have to avoid me at lunch. Our table isn't the same without you.

Ha, ha. I'm not avoiding you. Lunch is the best time to work. Nationals are coming up. Lots to do. How have you been?

Can't complain. Other than trying to deal with my raging jealousy toward Ian. Kidding. But promise me, when Nationals are over, you'll put the universe back in place and eat lunch with us again, okay? The two of you hanging out isn't natural.

CHAPTER 20
FRACTURED FRIENDSHIP

"CAN WE REWIND THINGS?" Ian said as he arrived at the lunchroom on Thursday.

It had been a few days since I had swiped Ian's tech. Nearly a week since Ian's power trip inside *The Garden*. While we continued to work on the final touches for Nationals, neither of us ventured to talk about what happened after State. It was like a verbal game of chicken. We both waited for the other to swallow their pride and clear the air first.

"Time doesn't work like that," I said with an uncomfortable chuckle.

"Yeah, I wish we could go back to the moment we won. It was perfect. And then I ruined it all." He forced a weak but tender grin and pulled a sandwich out of his bag.

I sat quiet, unsure how to act around him—not confident I could trust him. But I still needed him. The TechEd National Tournament was two weeks away, and without his support, my chances of getting into MIT were not great. Seeing him take the first step toward reconciliation gave me hope.

"If you want, we can pretend it didn't happen," I said with a smile, trying to convince Ian *and* myself that the past week was nothing more than a minor hiccup.

"I'd like that," Ian said. "Although, I need to tell you something first."

I cocked my head. "What's that?"

"Well, I sorta did some stuff inside *The Garden* you probably aren't going to be too happy about." Ian scrunched his face as if trying to hide from my gaze.

I assumed—or at least hoped—he was finally coming clean about everything, including showing himself to the Simples and the giant statue they had erected. I tried to act surprised as I waited for his confession. "Oh yeah? What kind of stuff?"

"Well, remember how I told the Simples they'd be destroyed if they didn't prove their gratitude to me?"

"Yeah," I said carefully.

"What I didn't tell you was that I sorta... *definitely* revealed myself to them while saying those things."

"Revealed yourself—*how*?"

"I, uh..." Ian closed his eyes and sighed. "I showed up as my avatar—floating above their heads, draped in robes, surrounded by a lot of thunder and lightning for extra dramatic flair."

I smacked my lips. It sounded so much worse hearing it from him. "Wow. Uh, okay, that isn't good."

Ian slowly sighed. "There's more."

"More?"

"Yeah. On Sunday, after you left my house, I logged back in to check on the damage my little tantrum created. And I saw the Simples building something." Ian nervously tapped his fingers on the table as he talked. "I couldn't tell what they were making, so I skipped ahead a few days—and then a few days more. And some more—until nearly a year's worth of days had passed. By then, I finally realized what the Simples had constructed."

"What did they build?" I leaned in closer.

He slumped over, banging his head on the table. "They built a giant statue of me."

"They did what?"

Ian sat tall, his eyes wide with sorrow. "I'm so sorry, Luce. It was stupid and arrogant and—" He paused, swallowing hard. "—I let you down."

I rubbed my head, thinking about the best way to respond. On the one hand, I was glad Ian had confessed. It restored a little of the trust I had lost in him. Of course, that didn't change his horrible actions. Then again, I had done my own terrible things when I stole his code and devices. My guilt rang in my mind as I reminded myself that I hadn't used anything I had taken. But I worried I might still need them to safeguard against further outbursts. So, while Ian confessed, I chose to keep my secrets safe.

"Thank you for telling me," I said quietly.

Ian sighed with relief. "Do you still think we can pretend this miserable week didn't happen?"

"No."

"Why not?"

I sat up tall and cleared my throat. "You can't keep playing god with these people, Ian. We can't keep treating the Simples like they're our playthings."

Ian rolled his eyes. "I told you. They're not people, Luce. Nor have we treated them like playthings. They aren't toys. They are part of an educational experiment, remember? An experiment that won us first place at State. An experiment that will be the reason *you* get into MIT."

Like a toddler with a hand stuck in the cookie jar, I was caught. Ian knew how to rein me in. *The plan* was like a magnet, pulling me toward it—no matter the cost.

"I do remember, of course." I fiddled with my necklace. "But I can't shake the thought that we're doing something wrong with the Simples."

"Luce, that is the beauty of *The Garden*. It gives us a chance to put the struggles of life under a telescope. We can do things to the Simples that we couldn't do in real life, allowing us to learn and grow. Think of it like an incredible game of *What If?*—without any real consequences."

Ms. Howell's words rose to the surface of my mind. *Imagine you were in their place.* I pictured myself in the village—trying to see the world through Evie's eyes. I remembered the panicked worry on her face when confronted with her own destruction. For the Simples, their world wasn't some game with zero ramifications. It was real to them: Consequences and all.

I leaned in toward Ian. "How do you know *you're* not in a simulation?"

"What are you talking about?" Ian leaned back and laughed as if I were joking.

I cocked my head. "Well?"

Ian huffed as he pinched my arm. "Do you feel that?" He pounded his chest. "Look at this body of flesh and bone."

"If you ask the Simples, they'd say their bodies are real, too."

Ian scoffed. "Hate to break it to you, Luce. It is not even close to the same thing. I can trace my family history back for centuries. I have visited countries all over the globe. If you cut me, I bleed. Tickle me, I laugh. I am real, and the Simples are not."

"Who's to say some smarter version of you is creating *this* life for us?" I folded my arms, letting the question hang in the air for a moment. "Perhaps our world is more advanced than the one you've built for the Simples because someone has been working on it longer—or has better technology."

My eyes narrowed in, punctuating my words. "Honestly, it doesn't matter if we are real or part of a simulation. What matters is that we *believe* we are real. And the Simples believe *they* are real. They love, grow, and adapt just like us."

"But it's not the same—"

"—why not?" My defenses were on alert. "Why isn't it the same, Ian? How would you react if someone was treating you the way you've been treating the Simples?"

I could see Ian's mind at work, carefully processing everything. He slowly began putting away his half-eaten lunch. "Well, if they are real, they should be grateful I gave them life."

I wasn't expecting that response. "Are you serious right now?"

"Absolutely. For hundreds of years, they got to live a worry-free existence. I gave them food, shelter, and companionship. They thrived under my protection."

"Protection?" I scoffed. "Instilling them with fear and forcing them to worship you? You call that protection?"

Ian stood up.

I hopped out of my chair. "Where are you going? We have to resolve this."

"No—not now. You're all bent out of shape because I have been the key to this project. You hate that I'm the one in control. Yet as much as you want to point fingers at me for playing the puppet master inside *The Garden,* you're the one who's been pulling my strings for years." Ian shoved his chair under the table and turned to storm away.

I called after him. "Ian, wait. Please, let's talk about this."

He waved his hand, walking away. "I said, *not now.*"

Ian bolted from anthropology class as soon as the final bell rang. He hadn't spoken to me since lunchtime. But his words continued to echo in my head.

You hate that I'm the one in control.

Ian was right about one thing—I craved control. I liked rules, deadlines, and expectations because they helped me manage my life. But I didn't want power. And I certainly wasn't looking to manipulate Ian.

Still, there was a hold on Ian's heart. He had tethered it to me, giving me a power I never desired. Even if I wasn't eager to be Ian's puppet master, he had willingly handed me the strings. When I pointed my finger at him for what he was doing, three pointed back at me for the same thing.

"Everything okay?" Ms. Howell asked as I lingered at my desk.

"That's debatable," I said with a faint smile.

"Still worked up about your philosophical struggles with *The Garden?*"

"Sorta. Unfortunately, Ian and I aren't on the same page."

Ms. Howell shook her head. "That's tough. I'm sorry."

"Yeah, it has been a rough few days. But at least we're trying to clear the air. After a little breathing space, I hope we can come back and push through this drama. Don't worry. I promise we'll be ready for Nationals next week."

Ms. Howell folded her arms. "I'm not worried about that. If anything, situations like this remind me there is more to life than awards and schoolwork."

I chuckled. "Tell that to my mom." I waved goodbye to Ms. Howell and walked out of the classroom.

"Hey, Lucy! Wait up."

Jake ran down the hallway. My stomach tightened. We hadn't been alone since the day he kissed me. I didn't have the energy for another awkward conversation—not now.

"What's up, Jake?" I forced a smile as I turned to open my locker.

Jake leaned against the wall of lockers next to mine. "We haven't talked in a while. You're not avoiding me, are you?"

"Of course not. The past few weeks have been crazy."

"Yeah, sure. Congrats again. Even though I wanted to crush you guys, you deserved the win."

"I'm sorry you guys didn't place. It would have been fun to hit up Orlando together."

"Eh, don't worry about it. I've got several schools eager for me to play for them next year. I'll be fine."

"I never doubted it." I placed my final book in my locker and zipped my backpack. Jake hesitated like he wanted to say something else. "You alright?"

He sighed, casting his eyes down. "Yeah, I wanted to apologize again for what happened in Ian's room. You know? The kiss." As he lifted his head, his brown eyes melted into mine. "I'm sorry if I crossed a line, and I hope I can make it up to you. I've got some big plans to make Fall Ball amazing."

I smiled. "I'm looking forward to it, and I appreciate you talking to me. We're all good. Promise."

"Alright then, I'll catch you later." Jake noticed another football player rushing toward practice. "I gotta run before Coach gets on me for being late again." He gently squeezed my shoulder as he zoomed away.

I closed my locker door, startled to find Ian standing on the other side.

"Ian! Sheesh, you scared me."

He furrowed his brows. "What was that all about?"

"What do you mean?"

"With Jake—he said something about kissing in my bedroom. What's going on?"

I turned and started walking down the hall. "It's not what you think, Ian. Nothing happened."

Ian's voice got louder as he followed me. "What was Jake Wittingham doing in my bedroom? Tell me now!"

I had never witnessed his rage like this before. As much as I tried to be unfazed by it, I was terrified. "Calm down. He came to my house while you were on vacation and kept me company while I watered the plants for your parents. Seriously, that's it."

"If that's it, why did he mention a kiss?"

I sighed. "He kissed me, okay? He kissed me, and I told him to leave. And we haven't talked since. Why do you care?"

Ian slammed the wall of lockers. "I care because *we're* supposed to be together, Luce—you and me. Why can't you see that?"

Recoiling from the loud *bang*, I stepped back. Students in the hallway eyed Ian's outburst and kept their distance. I tried to hide the tremble in my voice. "What happened to my friend? Where's the guy who promised he'd never let me down?"

Ian dropped his head. "I'm trying to keep you from making a huge mistake with the douchiest guy in school."

"What's your problem with Jake? He's nice." I picked up my pace, wanting nothing more than to go home.

Ian sped up, one step behind me. "Nice, sure. As long as he gets what he wants."

"Go home, Ian."

"He's not good enough for you, Luce. You're only interested in him because everyone expects you guys to be together, but you deserve better."

Digging my heels into the ground, I spun around. Ian nearly bulldozed into me. "For the last time, we're not together. But if I had to choose between him and this person standing in front of me—who I barely recognize—I'd choose him. In a heartbeat."

We stared at one another, our faces inches apart. I refused to look away first, even though my stomach was in knots, urging me to throw up. Finally, Ian stepped back, glancing at the crowd that had formed around us.

"I think we both need to cool off," I said softly, embarrassed beyond belief. "I'm going home to prepare for Nationals. Tell my friend—wherever he might be—that I miss him. And when he's ready to talk, give me a call."

DEAR DIARY

LUCY, AGE 13

Today we found out Abuelita has cancer. Both Mom and Dad told me not to worry. They say she'll get better. But I can tell they're lying. They are scared.

I went to talk to Lita because I knew she'd tell me the truth. She says she doesn't know if she'll get better or not. She didn't seem afraid, though. I asked her how she could be so happy when her body was sick. She said now she knows how precious each day was.

Comforting lies cloud your vision, she said. But the truth lets you see clearly.

CHAPTER 21
HARD TRUTHS

BEEP. Beep. Beep.

I grabbed my phone—it was 4:30 in the morning. I turned off the alarm and yawned loudly. After a long night trying to decide what to do about the whole Ian situation, I needed to assess *The Garden* from the inside. Before bed, I spent a couple of hours analyzing the program's code and installing it on my laptop to enter via the headset. I was ready to go solo with my stolen Amplifier Chip—hoping Ian would still be asleep as I ventured into the village. I powered on my computer and clicked through a few camera angles to ensure it was safe to enter. With no sign of Ian, I strapped on the goggles and plugged in.

Basking in the rising sun's glow, I stretched my arms above my head. The familiar serenity of the virtual world was heightened by the fact that Ian wasn't watching me from above. That thought filled me with courage as I walked toward the village.

Except for the quiet chirp of birds and the rustle of leaves in the trees, everything was quiet as I neared the town. The sun poked over the horizon, hitting the rooftops of the homes inside the village. Everyone was probably still asleep. I needed to fast-forward an hour or two if I wanted to talk to someone.

I tapped the space in front of me and pulled up the time dial. As I was about to set the timer, I heard a noise coming from Evie and Steve's home. Carefully making my way to their front door, I leaned my ear against it and listened to Steve as he spoke.

"I understand," he said. "I don't want to do it either, but we have no choice. We have to do what's best for everyone."

"We *do* have a choice," Evie said emphatically. It sounded like she had been crying. "We can do the right thing or the easy thing."

I crouched down and got closer to the window. Steve faced the bed where Evie sat. Evie's eyes were red and puffy.

"The easy thing? You think this is easy?" Steve said as he burst into tears. "Can't you see what this is doing to me?"

Steve slumped down on the bed next to Evie, dropping his head into his hands. His torso shook as he sobbed. Evie leaned over and embraced him as they both continued to cry. Both were inconsolable. After what felt like an eternity, Steve finally blinked away a few more tears and somberly spoke. "You need to tell me where you've hidden him."

Evie stood up, firm and resolute. "Never."

I had no idea what was going on, but something was very off. I quickly darted behind a tree as Evie walked out of the house. Back inside, Steve continued crying, talking to himself as he shook his head. "What can we do? What can we do?"

A wave of emotions nearly knocked me over as I tried to figure out the situation. I had never seen them so worked up before. Desperate for answers, I snuck around the outskirts of the village, tailing Evie as she made her way to the far corner of town. She carefully peered over her shoulder as she squeezed through the invisible crack. Ian's glitch still gave her access to the rest of *The Garden*. I quietly followed her as she headed toward the beach.

"Everything okay?"

Evie turned around, startled. As soon as she recognized me, she ran and threw her arms around my body. "Lucy! I'm so glad you're here."

I held her tightly as she cried. "Oh, Evie, what's wrong?"

"Everything is wrong, Lucy. Everything is absolutely awful." Evie could barely speak.

"Shh... shh, it's okay. I'm here. And I promise I will do whatever I can." I held Evie's arm as we sat down in the sand. A cool breeze tousled her curls. After a few deep breaths, she finally opened her eyes.

"Yesterday, the Voice visited us again."

"What? He did?" *Dammit, Ian.* I was afraid he would do something stupid after our argument at school. I hated that my suspicions were confirmed.

"Yes, he came. And he was outraged. He said we didn't love him. He said we were nothing without him." Evie's voice broke as more tears streamed down her cheek. "He threatened to destroy us again."

I rubbed Evie's back. My heart raced as I hung on to her words. "I'm so sorry, Evie."

Evie closed her eyes, shaking her head. "Everyone was trembling. The Voice was so angry. They all turned to me, waiting for a response, even though I was just as terrified."

"So, what did you do?"

Evie slowly exhaled out her mouth, her breath still jumpy from crying so hard. "I stood up. I told the Voice we were grateful—that we have always been grateful. And then... and then—" Evie burst into tears again.

"—and then what?"

Evie's eyes were red with grief. "He said we needed to prove our love by sacrificing my child. He demanded the blood of Ash if we wanted to save everyone else."

I was paralyzed. My eyes bounced back and forth while my

body stood still. Nothing made sense—nothing. I leaned over, trying to fill my lungs with air. I was reeling with anger—overwhelmed by heartbreak. This couldn't be real. This was too much.

Evie sobbed softly, resting her head on my shoulder. Dumbfounded, we both sat as the ocean waves rippled forward and retreated. After a long time, I finally ventured a question. "So what happened?"

"I did the only thing I could do," Evie said. "While the others made preparations for the ritual, I hid Ash. I hid him far away—where nobody could find him. I'd rather die than give him up willingly."

Even amid a traumatic heartbreak, Evie's integrity was firm. Her moral resolve added fuel to my raging emotional blaze. I didn't care if Evie was technically real or not—she was real enough for me to defend. She deserved the truth.

I stood up. "You did the right thing." I pulled Evie to her feet as a rush of urgency swept over me. "Listen. You do not need to sacrifice Ash. You don't. And I promise the Voice won't destroy you either."

Evie shook her head, "How can you be sure?"

I sighed. "Because I'll talk to him. I will make this right."

"You know the Voice?" Evie's face dropped, her eyes wide with disbelief. "How?"

"I'll try to explain." I closed my eyes, not even sure where to start.

For the next twenty minutes, I told Evie everything. I told her about the simulation, TechEd, and Ian and me—all of it. Parts went over her head, but the majority sunk heavily in her heart. The color in Evie's face drained, and her eyes glazed over in disbelief.

"I don't understand," Evie said quietly. "I mean, I always wondered why you were different—why I could never find your home. But this can't be true."

"It is. Believe me."

"Why should I believe you?" Evie roared. Her eyes were still swollen from crying, but now they were filled with indignation. "You're telling me my whole life has been a lie. You're saying I'm not real. I'm some experiment—a temporary ruse for someone else's agenda!"

Evie began pacing in the sand, shaking her head. "No, no, no —this can't be true. This can't be true." She ran her fingers through her hair and snapped back at me. "So what do you have to say for yourself? Huh? Say something!"

"Like what?" I said weakly. This was not the reaction I expected. I knew the truth would be hard to accept, but I hadn't anticipated so much anger. "I'm sorry, Evie. I never intended to hurt anyone, especially not you."

"Sorry?" Evie yelled. "All I've wanted from the moment I met you was to understand this world and my purpose in it. And this whole time, you've been feeding me lies to keep me complacent. You forced me into a relationship—into motherhood! The drought you created endangered the village. You've traumatized us by making us believe in some all-knowing being in the sky." Evie towered over me before turning away. "I—I can't even look at you right now."

She took a few steps and then fell to her knees. Her body slumped over in the sand as she began crying again. I knelt beside her, resting my hand on her shoulder. Overwhelmed with guilt and shame, I sobbed right along with her.

"I'm so sorry. I never expected any of this to happen." Tears streamed down my cheeks. "And I never imagined Ian could be so cruel."

Evie sat up. Her eyes drilled into mine. "Cruelty comes in many forms," she said coldly. "You think Ian is the only one who has been cruel? Your cruelty has taken away everything from me."

"But, I'm not taking anything away from you. I told you—I'll talk to Ian. Ash will be safe. Nobody will be destroyed. Trust me."

"Trust you?" Evie scoffed as she wiped away a tear. She stood up. "If what you're saying is true, my entire existence has been nothing more than one long deception. Everything I thought I knew has vanished like a puff of smoke. What even am I? I am nothing. Nothing!" Her voice cracked, and she began sobbing again.

I hugged Evie, trying to steady her. "Shh... it's okay. Everything will be okay."

We embraced for a few minutes as Evie let her tears flow. Her rage simmered into grief, wrapped up in fear. "I don't want to die. I don't want this life to end. What will happen to me—to all of us—when your experiment is over?"

"I told you. I won't let Ian shut you down. I will protect you."

Evie stepped back. "For how long? And at what point do you move on from this game and turn us all off? You don't understand what it is like to know your world will end someday. To realize your life is meaningless."

"But I do." I searched her eyes. "My life is just as fragile. I could die tomorrow. But that doesn't mean my life doesn't have value now. Life is only as meaningful as you decide to make it. If anything, the truth will help you find your purpose—not take it away."

"I don't understand," Evie said. "Right now, everything feels pretty meaningless."

I sighed. "More meaningless than a life spent trying to please some voice in the sky? Yes, Ian created you. But there is something uniquely *you* that neither of us can account for. You are special, Evie. And now you are free to find your own purpose. You're free to do the things that make *you* come alive instead of cowering at the foot of someone driven solely by their ego."

Evie sat down again. Her expression was numb. "But the Voice did create me. Maybe I owe it to him to do as he says?"

"Really?" I sat down next to her. "Think about your children. Do you want Ash and Cade to worship you? Do you demand gifts or sacrifices for them to prove their love to you?"

"No, of course not."

"And do you lead your people with love or fear?"

"Love," Evie said with a smile. "So much love."

I smiled back. "Exactly." I sighed. "Listen, Evie. I don't have all the answers, but I know you're a good person. You lead with your heart. And your curiosity keeps you from blindly following a crowd. To me, that makes you more alive than anyone I've met. You're real. You love, grow, and yearn. So, even if the story you used to believe has changed, you now get to decide how to write the next chapter."

Evie closed her eyes, breathing in the salty air. With a deep exhale, she planted her feet and pulled herself up.

"So now what?" Evie said, reaching for my hand to help me up. "I can't keep this information from the others. But I'm not sure they'll believe any of it."

I stared off into the ocean. "We should tell them, and we will. But first, I need to deal with Ian." I turned my head toward Evie. "For now, go to Ash and comfort him. I promise I'll be back soon to ensure this mess gets cleaned up."

CHAPTER 22
STRINGS ATTACHED

"Knock, knock," I said as I tapped on Ms. Howell's door.

She looked up from her book. "Lucy? School doesn't start for another hour. What are you doing here?"

"Do you have a minute?"

"I've got a little time." Ms. Howell closed her book and gestured to the chair in front of her desk. "What's up?"

Fidgeting with my necklace, I tried to find the right words. I was still in shock from everything I had learned earlier that morning. Ian's demented demands shocked me. But I was also ashamed, knowing I caused Evie pain by telling her the truth. My heart was heavy as I took a seat.

"I want to talk about *The Garden*..." I cleared my throat. "And Ian. I'm worried he's taking things too far with the Simples. But I'm also nervous to say anything because it only makes things worse each time I do."

Ms. Howell furrowed her brows. "Can you tell me what he's been doing?"

"He's threatening the people—demanding their loyalty." I sighed, avoiding the disturbing details. "Everyone in the village is freaking out, and I'm worried what it could do for our chances at Nationals."

"And you've tried talking to him?"

"Yeah, he's apologized twice for his actions. But then something will trigger him again, and he takes things even further."

"I don't understand," Ms. Howell said. "What's getting him so riled up?"

My cheeks turn red and closed my eyes.

"Ah, I bet I can guess," Ms. Howell said, nodding her head. "Teenage emotions can be tough to navigate, but surely Ian is smart enough not to let that ruin this opportunity."

"Ian has never cared about grades or achievements. Still, he promised he wouldn't let me down. Of course, that was before —" I shook my head. "—before I rejected him or whatever he thinks I did."

Ms. Howell frowned at me sympathetically.

My tears pushed toward the surface. "This is so stupid. He's blown everything out of proportion. I don't even know him anymore." I blinked a few times, trying to maintain my composure. "He's supposed to be my friend. Why is he doing this?"

Ms. Howell leaned forward. "I don't know, Lucy. I really don't. But generally, I think communication is the key to any relationship."

My stomach was in knots. Talking things out with Ian would mean having to come clean about my own covert activities. He would be furious about me swiping his code and devices.

"I'm not sure Ian is in the right mindset to talk things through," I said.

"Well, in that case..." Ms. Howell sighed. "Maybe you can distract him with tasks outside of *The Garden*—at least until Nationals are over. Stay focused on the presentation. You guys have worked so hard for this, and I'd hate for it to slip away from you."

"That might work." I thought it over, nodding my head.

"Keep Ian preoccupied—away from the Simples. That doesn't necessarily solve the problem, but it gives me time to figure out a solution until after Nationals." I nodded at Ms. Howell. "Thank you. I always appreciate your help."

"Not sure how helpful I've been." Ms. Howell chuckled. "Life is sometimes a little messy."

"That's for sure." I threw my bag over my shoulder. "I'll see you in class later today." I walked out, deep in thought.

"Luce!" a voice rang from the hallway.

I froze at the sound of Ian's voice. What was he doing at school so early? I turned around as he marched toward me. The hair on my arms stood tall. A million thoughts rushed into my mind, each colliding with the others. Does he know I talked to Evie? Did he hear me talking to Ms. Howell? Has he done something else to the Simples?

"Ian! What—what are you doing?" I rubbed my sweaty palms on my pants. "School doesn't start for a while."

"I went to your house, and your mom said you had already left." Ian was out of breath, fidgeting with his jacket.

"Is something wrong?" I already knew the answer. Everything was wrong. Not only had Ian gone back into *The Garden* without telling me, but he had demanded a child sacrifice to appease his broken ego! I still couldn't wrap my mind around it.

"I'm sorry about losing my temper yesterday. I overreacted, and I wanted to apologize. I thought I'd catch you first thing in the morning, but I should have known you'd be up and at 'em early." He forced a smile.

I began walking to my locker, too anxious and upset to respond.

Ian shoved his hands into his pockets and followed me. "Anyway, I'm sorry. Again. I think the stress of everything is getting to me—TechEd, the presentation, showing up for class every day. It's a lot for a slacker like me." His sarcasm could barely squeak through his nerves. "I didn't realize how much pressure came with this over-achiever world of yours."

"Yep, it can be a lot if you're not used to it."

"So, do you forgive me?"

I sighed. "I want to."

Ian slowly nodded his head. "*Want* to? What does that mean?"

At my locker, I focused on the combination lock. My anger was overwhelming. But if we didn't find a resolution to this mess, I was terrified we'd ruin our chances for TechEd.

"You keep apologizing. At what point do you stop saying sorry and start changing?"

"How can I make it up to you, Luce? I want to set things right."

I wasn't sure I'd ever fully trust Ian again. But whether he was sincere or not, I wanted to turn this around. Perhaps I could persuade him to stay away from the Simples—at least until Nationals.

After taking out a couple of books, I slammed my locker door, looking Ian in the eyes. "For starters, you need to stop flipping out every time things don't go your way. And I need you to focus on preparing for TechEd."

"Absolutely," Ian said.

"And it might be smart if we take a break from visiting *The Garden*. Leave the Simples alone. Let's spend our time and energy nailing the presentation."

Ian sighed in relief. "I was thinking the same thing."

"Really?"

"Yeah, I think *The Garden* affects both of us. It stresses you out and turns me into a—"

"—narcissistic overlord?"

Ian smiled. "I was going to say drama queen, but sure."

"So we agree. We'll give the Simples some breathing room while we polish our presentation. Deal?" I shot out my hand.

Ian reached his arm out, mimicking Steve from our first day in *The Garden*. I forced a laugh and moved my arm up and down.

"Deal," he said.

For the rest of the day, things were normal. We spent lunch reviewing the judges' notes and discussing potential changes to our presentation. Ian was back to his sarcastic, carefree self. He cracked jokes, praised me, and flashed a smile as often as possible. But I refused to let my guard down. Every time the old version of Ian popped to the surface, all I could think about was the fear in Evie's eyes after being told she had to sacrifice her son.

The Garden had changed Ian. And it changed the way I saw him.

Still, I was relieved to put a pause on the drama. I hoped Ian was sincere in his promise to stay out. But I couldn't stop wondering if he was playing me the same way I was trying to play him. Maybe his resolution had nothing to do with preparing for Nationals. Perhaps it was merely a guise to keep me away from whatever he was planning to do with the Simples next.

After spending the afternoon at Ian's house practicing our presentation, I went home. I made myself a peanut butter sandwich and headed to my room. Plopping down on my bed, I grabbed my laptop—my mouse hovering over the icon that would open *The Garden*. I was nervous logging on—nervous and feeling a little guilty. To ease my conscience, I told myself that I wasn't going *into* the program. I was merely checking things out —making sure Ian hadn't broken his promise.

Reluctantly I clicked.

As I scanned the town limits, things had settled down. There were no apparent signs of turmoil or change. Then I switched camera angles, looking at the altar near the pond. My heart rate spiked. A hoard of Simples was carrying a small body toward the giant structure. Sitting up, I turned the volume up and leaned in. I squinted my eyes, trying to make out who was being hoisted up by the crowd.

It was Ash, and he was screaming.

"Dammit." I zoomed in, trying to find Evie or Steve among the group. Steve was near the front, sobbing as he led the others toward the shrine. But Evie was nowhere. What have they done with her? My heart stopped as the mob placed Ash's body on the altar.

Hopping off my bed, I frantically threw on a pair of shoes. Promise or not, I wasn't about to let Ian go through with this demented plan. As I was about to open my door, I heard Ian's voice ringing from the laptop.

"Stop!" Ian yelled.

I ran back to the computer. Ian's avatar floated in the sky a couple of feet above Steve, who was holding a knife in his raised arm. "You have proven your loyalty. Spare your son," Ian said resolutely.

The crowd of Simples broke out in celebratory cheers. My shoulders relaxed as I exhaled slowly. Steve sobbed as he threw his body over his child, hugging him.

"Thank you! Thank you!" Steve cried.

One by one, the Simples dropped to their knees, offering their gratitude. A twisted sense of pride and pleasure spread across Ian's face. *He loved this.* The idea only made my stomach sink deeper. While I was relieved that Ian had stopped the sacrifice in the nick of time, the satisfaction he felt devastated me.

I tapped the keyboard arrows, switching camera angles to find Evie. Finally, I saw her—bound and gagged in the corner of her home. Evie struggled to break free, tears streaming down her face. The fear in her eyes broke my heart. I had promised things would be okay. It had turned into another lie.

Looking over at the VR headset on my desk, I debated whether I could sneak in to help Evie without Ian knowing. But before I even had a chance, a bright light filled Evie's room. I watched in disbelief as Ian's avatar formed out of thin air, addressing Evie.

"Why do you defy me?" Ian asked.

The bands around Evie's arms released, and the gag dropped from her mouth. Her voice was loud and firm. "Where is my son?"

More than anything, I wanted to transport myself inside that room. Helpless watching from the outside, I had no clue what Ian would do next—or Evie, for that matter.

"Your son is safe," Ian said. "Because of everyone else's faith —they passed my test and saved your son. But you?" Ian moved closer to Evie, who scooted back against the wall. "You displease me."

The rage burned from Evie's eyes. Now that she knew the truth, there was no telling what would happen next. Would Evie yell at Ian? Would he kill her? Not willing to wait to find out, I frantically grabbed my phone and dialed Ian's home number. His mom answered.

"Hey, Mrs. Gibson, it's Lucy. Sorry to bother you." My hand nervously tapped against my leg as my eyes locked on the scene unfolding on my computer.

"Oh, no bother," Ian's mom said. "How's it goi—"

I cut in. "I've been trying to reach Ian, but he's not answering his phone. I think I left a book in his room. Would you mind taking a look?"

"Of course," Mrs. Gibson said. "Give me one second."

I held my breath as I was put on hold. *Come on, come on.* Evie stood up and took a step toward Ian. *Hurry up.* I needed Mrs. Gibson to stop Ian before he or Evie did anything rash.

"I displease *you*?" Evie said with a snarl.

Suddenly, Ian's avatar disappeared from the screen. With a

confused look, Evie turned around, scanning the room as I heard Ian's voice on the other end of the phone.

"Luce! What's this about a missing book?" he said.

"Uh…" I stuttered, unable to comprehend the instant shift in his personality. He sounded so casual, so normal—nothing like the maniac I had been watching for the past couple of minutes. I tried to match his tone. "Yes, my book." My voice was still shaking. "I think I left my chemistry book at your house this afternoon."

"I'm looking all around, but I don't see it. Sorry."

I pressed down on my leg, trying to stop my jittery foot. "No prob, I probably left it in my locker." I searched my brain, looking for something to say to keep Ian distracted longer. "I, uh—I hope I'm not interrupting anything."

"Nope, just finishing some biology homework."

Liar. Closing my eyes, I pushed down the rage building inside. I couldn't believe Ian was lying to me—again. I worried about what his next move might be. If Ian found out Evie knew the truth about *The Garden,* that could be the end of the Simples —of TechEd. He already seemed focused on punishing Evie for not complying with his ridiculous commands. What the hell could I do?

Out of all other options, I realized I still had one card left to play—one power move up my sleeve. Ian had handed me the strings to his heart a long time ago. And for the first time, I was willing to pull them.

I swallowed hard and spoke as sweetly as I could. "I was thinking of watching a movie. Want to come over?"

MESSAGE FROM DAD

THU, NOV 10

Mijita! Good luck at Nationals this weekend! I can't believe I won't be there to cheer you on in person.

Thanks, Dad. Mom said you tried to get work off. Bummed it didn't work out. Can't believe it is finally happening. I'm excited but nervous.

You'll do great. Win or lose. I'm so proud of you. I hope you are, too.

Honestly, I'm not sure the competition has brought out the best in me.

Nonsense. You're a girl who knows what she wants and does what it takes to get it, just like your mom. You've got this.

CHAPTER 23
IAN'S REVELATION

THE PILOT'S voice woke me from my nap.

"Ladies and gentlemen, welcome to Orlando. Local time is 4:12, and the temperature is 76 degrees. Please remain seated with your seat belt fastened until the Captain turns off the 'Fasten Seat Belt' sign."

I stretched my long legs in the cramped space of my seat, eyeing Lucy, who was transfixed by the clouds outside the window. While she was most likely thinking about tomorrow's tournament, I couldn't stop reliving the past two weeks. It was all a blur—exhausting but surprising. Sure, we spent most of our time getting everything ready for Nationals. Lucy was a taskmaster, determined to perfect every last detail. But amidst the preparations, I noticed a change within her—an undeniable shift.

While still laser-focused on winning, Lucy was surprisingly eager to spend time together outside the project. I tried not to get my hopes up, but I couldn't ignore the signs. She was more attentive, inviting me to watch movies and go out to eat. We even played video games at my house a couple of times.

But more than that, Lucy was finally interested in me—in what I was doing and thinking at all times. She was eager to be with me, making me believe we were finally on the same page. Staying out of *The Garden* was the best move. With her focus off the Simples, it was like she finally saw me—all of me. And that small change made the real world much more enticing.

I do regret the things I did to the Simples. After overreacting the way I did, I wasn't sure Lucy would forgive me. Thankfully, it seems she has. And now, with TechEd almost over, we were ready for a new beginning.

Everything was coming together.

"Man, that was a long flight," I said.

Lucy finally faced me and smiled politely. She picked up her phone and turned off airplane mode. I tried not to peek at the string of notifications as they flashed over her screen. I pulled out my phone. Big surprise—not a single message. Her smile grew as she read through a dozen texts. There was at least one from Jake, which I tried to brush off. Besides, who was the one sitting next to Lucy now? It wasn't Jake Wittingham.

By the time we got to our hotel, it was already dark outside. We dropped our bags off at our rooms, and I suggested a quick dip in the pool before dinner.

"I'm exhausted and want to crash," Lucy said. "Can we just get some food and take it easy tonight? We've got a big day tomorrow."

"Come on, Luce! We're in Florida with no parents. You gotta live a little."

She rolled her eyes. "We're not here on vacation, remember? We're here to win TechEd." Her shoulders were tenser than usual, but that was only natural. This was a huge moment for her—for us. I could be patient. One more day and this whole TechEd business would finally be over.

"Fair enough," I said. "Can I at least buy you dinner? You don't even have to leave the hotel. The restaurant downstairs looks pretty good."

"Sure." She smiled weakly. "That sounds nice."

After a quick change of clothes, we made our way to the hotel lobby. There was a twenty-minute wait before we could be seated, so we wandered the hallways.

"Hey, look!" I pointed to a set of doors adjacent to the restaurant. "They're setting up for tomorrow's event."

Lucy cracked the door to peek inside the empty conference room. A couple of workers were hanging a massive banner. In bright red and gold letters, it read: *TechEd National Tournament.* A huge smile crept across her face. Suddenly, the door pushed back as a man opened it, nearly knocking Lucy over.

"Oops! Sorry, ma'am."

"No, it's my fault," Lucy said as she quickly moved out of his way.

The man held several large poster boards that he began placing on giant easels outside the conference entrance. We stood back and smiled as we realized the posters featured students from the competition. As soon as the man finished setting them up, we searched for our photo.

"There we are," I said, pointing to our photo.

Lucy leaned over, beaming as she read our names out loud. I couldn't help but notice a shift in her energy. Animated and relaxed, her happiness at reaching this finish line was palpable.

"This is crazy," she said. "What if we win it all?"

"We're totally going to win. We've built something incredible."

"Yeah, but so has everyone else."

My eyes scanned the photos of the other contestants. Under each participant's name was a line of text describing their project. I read through a couple dozen of them. While many sounded impressive, nothing stood out as a real threat. Lucy was reading right next to me.

"We can do this," she said quietly to herself.

Buzz. Buzz. Buzz.

I pulled the pager out of my pocket. "Looks like they are ready to seat us. Shall we?" I held out my arm for Lucy to grab.

Lucy smiled and hooked hers around mine. "Ready."

I guided her into the restaurant, where we were seated next to a large window.

"The stars are pretty tonight," Lucy said as she gazed up at the night sky.

"They sure are." But I wasn't staring at the stars—only Lucy. She briefly caught my eyes before looking away. She looked nervous. I know I was. I had been waiting for a night like this for a long time. This was going to be one of those defining moments. Like the beginning of our friendship, tonight would be significant. Every cell in my body knew it.

Lucy grabbed the menu, clearing her throat. "So, what are you thinking?"

I briefly considered my options and placed the menu down. "Chicken tenders."

She laughed. "You came all the way to Orlando and are getting the chicken tenders?"

"Hey! Don't food shame me. Chicken tenders are a perfectly respectable choice." I flashed my cheesiest grin. I ordered my chicken while Lucy went for the salmon tacos. We laughed as we talked about the time I ate an entire bag of Oreos during health class in seventh grade, which turned into a twenty-minute review of all the crazy things I had done throughout the years. Finally, our food arrived.

"You've always done your own thing, haven't you?" Lucy poured the dressing over her salad.

"Yep, sure beats taking orders from anyone else."

She nodded her head. I couldn't tell if she envied my independence or was terrified by it. "Do you ever worry about what other people think?"

I shrugged. "Not usually. Why?"

"I wonder what it's like," Lucy said. "I've spent so much energy stressing over the expectations of others."

I laughed as I dipped my chicken in some honey mustard. "That's an understatement."

Lucy chuckled, gently picking through her salad with her fork. She took a few careful bites before looking at me. "Ian, do you think I'm a coward?"

I paused, taken back by the sudden shift in Lucy's mood. "A coward? Definitely not." I tossed a french fry in my mouth and continued talking while chewing. "A perfectionist? Yes. A pain in the ass? Sometimes. But a coward? No way."

Lucy smiled.

I leaned forward. "I mean, let's review the first day we met. Would a coward shove Garret Floyd—a kid twice your size—to the ground to stick up for the awkward new kid? You risked your whole cool-girl street cred on some boy with apple red underwear."

"Yeah," Lucy said with a slight giggle. "It's funny. Standing up for you was one of the few times I felt—" She sighed. "—alive." She shook her head while taking another bite. "My mom was so mad. I got in so much trouble, but I was proud of what I had done."

Lucy's eyes sparkled when she talked about that first day we met. I was putty in her hands, willing to do or be anything she wanted. She could mold me to her will, and I would happily adapt.

But then the sparkle vanished. Lucy focused on her plate, somehow triggered by an afterthought of the memory. "I know everyone thinks I'm some sort of control freak. But honestly, I'm not the one calling the shots, just obeying them."

I reached over and touched her hand. She pulled it back.

"You okay, Luce? What's this all about?"

"Oh, nothing." Lucy smiled faintly. "Just thinking out loud, I guess. Hoping I haven't wasted too much of my life pursuing someone else's dream."

"Are you saying TechEd isn't your dream? Or MIT?"

"No, of course not. I'm thrilled we're here. I love the work, but—" Lucy paused, searching for the right words.

"But what?" I had no idea where she was going with this, but my heart was growing bigger by the moment. I wanted to be near her—to be with her.

Lucy sighed. "When I reach the end of my life, I want to be happy with my choices. I want to do things because I want to, not because people expect it. I mean, look at you. You don't care what people say about you or if you have a perfect GPA or awards plastered to your wall. You're a genius and don't have to prove anything to anyone."

I slowly nodded my head as I leaned back in my seat. "Sure, but don't be fooled. Even if my actions aren't based on other people's expectations, it doesn't mean I'm always happy with my decisions."

Lucy gazed out the window again. "I was happy the day I shoved Garret Floyd to the ground. I knew I'd get in trouble for breaking a rule, but I also knew what I did was *right*." Her eyes narrowed in on me with a determined look. "I'm beginning to think there are more Garret Floyd situations in life—a lot more gray in what I thought was a black and white world. And I wonder if my rigid loyalty to the rules isn't because I'm a good person but a scared one."

I shook my head, trying to figure out where all this was coming from. "I have no idea how you function with that overactive conscience of yours, but trust me. You're a good person. I wouldn't stress too much about it."

"Yeah, well... the stress comes with the territory." She smiled faintly.

For a brief moment, I believed I was the most important

person to her. She was confiding in me, sharing her fears. You don't do that without some deep level of trust.

As we finished dinner, the conversation became more casual until I finally paid the bill, and we headed to our rooms. After sharing her vulnerability during dinner, it was time for me to open up.

"Promise me you'll go to bed soon," Lucy said as we walked off the elevator. "I need you refreshed and ready to go tomorrow."

"Whatever you say, boss." I smiled, trying to ignore my nerves. "You don't need to worry about me. I told you I won't let you down." We walked outside our neighboring rooms. Lucy opened her purse, trying to find her room key. "Hey, Luce?" My heart was beating so fast I was worried she could hear it drumming. My stomach turned.

"Yeah?" she said, still fiddling through her bag.

"I've enjoyed these past few weeks," I said. Lucy's face went flush. I leaned in closer, locking onto her eyes. "Things got a little rough, but after spending so much time together, it is nice to be back in sync."

I grabbed her hand. She opened her mouth, but nothing came out. Every moment she remained speechless, I grew more confident. I leaned in to kiss her.

"Wait," Lucy said, pulling back.

I stopped as I realized what was happening. "Are you kidding me?" I whispered.

"Ian, I'm sorry. I think you've misread the situation."

"But—" I closed my eyes, shaking my head. "—you were the one who initiated everything. The movies, the late-night snack runs, the flirting."

"It wasn't flirting. I thought we were hanging out as friends."

"But that's it—we never hung out like that before. For six years, you ignored me. Are you telling me you felt *nothing* these past two weeks?"

The ground caved from under my feet. Lightheaded and nauseous, I fought the emotions that were trying to escape. Lucy knew I loved her. She wasn't stupid. Why did she spend all that time with me if she didn't feel anything? What was she thinking?

"I'm so, so sorry." Her words were small and meaningless.

My expression turn cold, but a piece of me was still grasping for understanding. "Sorry about what? About leading me on? Choosing Jake over me? What is it? And why spend all that time with me if you weren't interested? I know your school schedule, Luce. You had other things to do. Why all the effort?"

She shifted her weight from one foot to the other as she fumbled over her words. "I thought you needed a break from *The Garden*. I was trying to help."

The world stopped spinning. The clarity of the situation snapped to attention. Everything made sense. The past two weeks were a diversion—a ruse to keep me away from the Simples.

"You thought I would do something bad to them. Didn't you?" My words were sharp.

"Well, you do have a track record." I could tell she regretted the words as soon as they escaped her mouth.

I pursed my lips and crossed my arms. "So the whole time I thought we were connecting, you were, what—babysitting me? Distracting me?"

"No, of course not," Lucy said weakly. "I was trying to do what's best for the competition. I didn't want our hard work to go to waste."

I was right. Tonight was a defining moment.

Your entire world can change with one piece of information. My eyes were open. The person who had stolen my heart eight years ago was suddenly a thief I was desperate to take down.

"I should have known. Anything for the win, right? And here I thought you actually cared about *me*. What a joke." I shook my head, banging the wall with my fist.

Lucy jumped back. "Ian, please, let me explain."

"I think you've said enough." I grabbed my keycard out of my pocket, turned around, and disappeared into my room. I kicked the wall before my eyes settled on my laptop charging in the corner. One minute later, I could hear the muffled sound of Lucy sobbing next door. *Good.*

IAN'S NOTES

FRIDAY, NOV. 11

In the beginning, there was only me.

Of course, that changed with time. And that was my biggest mistake—sharing my world with others. I should have known better. As a kid, I learned there was safety in isolation. I practiced pulling inward, creating distance to protect me.

Lucy changed things. Letting her in forced me to deal with people. Sure, I can go back to my invisible life in the real world. But inside The Garden, I have the power to make sure nobody ever forgets who I am.

CHAPTER 24
SHATTERED DREAMS

"HE'LL BE HERE any moment, I promise." I tried to convey confidence as I spoke to the wiry woman wearing a TechEd Staff lanyard, but I was on the verge of collapse.

"You guys are on in ten minutes. If your partner doesn't show, you'll need to present yourself," the woman said.

"I understand." Grabbing my phone, I scrolled through the fourteen unread texts I had sent Ian. I quickly tapped out message number fifteen: *Seriously, I need you!*

Beads of sweat dripped from my forehead. I tried calling him again, but he still wasn't answering. An hour earlier, I had spent nearly ten minutes banging on his door. And while several other hotel guests yelled profanities at me for making so much noise— Ian was committed to the silent treatment.

Where the hell was he?

"Surprise!"

I recognized the voice and turned around. "Mom! Wh—what are you doing here? I thought you couldn't make it." I glanced over at the 'Tournament Participants Only' sign that hung from the rope separating the student section from the rest of the audience.

"I gave Sandra my case and took the red-eye. Being married to a pilot has its perks." Mom wrapped her arms around me. "You didn't think I would miss your big day, did you? We've been working twelve years for this."

"Glad you're here," I said, still trapped in her embrace. "But now's not a good time. We're about to go on. Besides, you're not supposed to be back here. "

"I know, I know. I just wanted to wish you two luck." Mom reached over and straightened my shirt collar. "Where's Ian?" she said, looking around.

"Uh, he went to the bathroom." I lied. "He'll be back soon."

Mom flashed a concerned look. "What's going on, Lucy?"

"Seriously, Mom, everything is good. Now, grab a seat, and I'll talk to you when we're done." I grabbed Mom's shoulders, turned her toward the exit, and gently pushed her away.

On the verge of an emotional breakdown, I couldn't calm my nerves. My hands were clammy. My cheeks were flush. This wasn't how I envisioned the day going at all. Time was running out, and all my equipment was locked in Ian's hotel room. I needed to improvise. At least I had the spare headset I had stolen in my bag, but I couldn't find the Amplifier Chip. It was probably still in my bedroom at home.

Today was supposed to culminate three months of hard work. After tweaking and polishing our presentation, I couldn't believe I'd have to wing it. The judges wouldn't go inside *The Garden*. There was no Amplifier Chip to show off. My partner was MIA. Epic failure was imminent, and I was crushed.

Standing on the sidelines, I panicked as a pair of students from Vermont nailed their presentation. A roar of applause rang throughout the crowded conference room. It was time to present, and Ian was still missing. Using every ounce of strength, I tried maintaining my composure as I walked on stage. My hands shook as I connected my laptop to the projector. With a deep breath, I began.

"What would our world be like if people had never ventured beyond their own borders?" My voice trembled. I took another deep breath—my millionth attempt to calm my nerves. "What foods, beliefs, and traditions would be missing from our lives if we didn't step outside our own homes?"

Like I had done at both Regionals and State, I clicked through a series of images. "Cultural anthropology is like a window to unknown worlds. It gives us the chance to study human existence—providing the tools to question our assumptions while discovering new ideas."

"Discover new ideas? Or exploit them," Ian said as he hopped onto the stage.

I was stunned. Quiet murmurings rippled through the audience. I thought I would have been happy to see Ian. Relieved, at least. But the snide determination on his face instantly told me this wouldn't end well.

"Where have you been?" I whispered.

Ian ignored me and continued addressing the audience. "History shows humans' track record of exploiting new cultures—taking their best ideas and making them their own."

What was he doing? This wasn't the script. I glanced over at my mom, recognizing her concerned face. Ian walked over and grabbed the headset out of my hands. The blood rush out of my face. My heart sank.

He knew.

Holding up the VR goggles, Ian faced the audience. "Say, for example, you found someone who had built a piece of incredible technology. Something that allows you to create, visit, and learn from different civilizations. A piece of technology so advanced that you don't just see the world around you—you *experience* it."

With a cynical chuckle, Ian shot me a nasty look. "My partner and I came here today to present a piece of tech that can do all that and more. This program has every promise to change the way we teach and learn."

Desperate to regain control, I leaned into Ian and whispered. "What are you doing?"

Ian walked over to my laptop and powered on *The Garden*. The world appeared on the giant projector above the stage. The audience gasped, and my mouth dropped. I couldn't believe my eyes. The once idyllic haven was now a world in chaos. Houses had collapsed. Mud and dirt caked the few still standing buildings. Several parts of town were fully flooded. In other places, the ground had split—forming large cliffs along fault lines.

But that wasn't the worst part. Scattered along the deformed terrain were dozens of unresponsive bodies lying face down in the dirt.

"Oh, my g—" I buried my face in my hands. I couldn't face the devastation in front of me. I was on the verge of hyperventilating. This couldn't be real.

"You might not believe this used to be a peaceful landscape a couple of months ago," Ian said. "When we first introduced the Simples to our virtual garden, they were happy. They had everything they needed. They were a vision of the future—an example of a better way to live."

He turned and pointed at me. "But my partner here wanted to create something *realistic*. She took my technology and corrupted it to give herself an edge in this stupid competition."

Hushed reactions murmured from the audience. I stood frozen, still stunned by what was happening.

"I was the one who built the system and programmed the people," Ian said. "I was the one who developed the Reality Amplifier. I was the one who figured out how to fast-forward time. Lucy would have nothing without me. And no matter what I gave her, she always needed to be the one in charge of the project."

Ian clicked through a few more camera angles of the program. There were signs of destruction everywhere. Even without the sound, the Simple's pain echoed in my mind. I could tell they were howling with grief, consumed by terror. As Ian changed the view one last time, my heart choked. There was Evie—kneeling in the mud. She held Steve's lifeless body as she rocked back and forth, sobbing.

Barely able to speak, I muttered under my breath. "Ian—what did you do?"

"This is what you wanted, right? To make them more *real.* Well, is this real enough for you, Luce?"

Ian turned back to the crowd. "Lucy exploited my idea. All she's ever cared about is winning this competition—making sure she could impress the decision-makers from all those big fancy schools." He snapped back at me. "You accused me of manipulating the Simples. But this whole time, you've been manipulating me. You used me. Lied to me. And I won't stand for it."

The crowd was buzzing with noise. The judges, stern-faced, whispered to one another. One gestured toward a staff member.

My eyes caught my mom sitting in the crowd. Embarrassment dripped from her face as she slowly stood up and exited the conference room. It was like the greatest "I told you so" in history. And I was left alone with the reverberation of her disappointment. Except I wasn't alone. I was the center of attention. Dozens of phones lifted high, recording every unthinkable moment. Fear that this instance would live forever online, I thought about Ms. Howell, Jake, and everyone at the school who would witness my fall. Helpless, my future shattered into a million pieces right in front of my eyes.

"I—I, uh..." My voice trembled. The audience judged my every move. I turned to face Ian. My eyes filled with tears. "Why are you doing this?"

Ian moved in closer, waving the headset in my face. "I checked the logs, Lucy. I know you've been watching me inside *The Garden.* I know you stole my tech." He pointed to Evie on the screen, shaking his head. "You care more about these digital nobodies than you do me."

A conference staff member walked toward us. "It's time for you two to leave the stage," he said.

As tears started streaming down my face, I pleaded with the man. "Please, give me another chance. This is not how this was supposed to go."

"I'm sorry. You're done." He escorted us away.

"No, you don't understand!"

"How's that plan of yours turning out, Luce?" Ian said smugly. He sneered as he walked past me and stormed his way through a side door.

I slowly turned around. Every eyeball was on me. I could only imagine what sort of hideous things they were thinking. Another staff worker handed me my laptop. As I walked out of the conference room, my face went numb. The world moved in slow motion as I made my way back to my room, wondering if the wave of shame would sweep me away.

Slumping down in a corner, I opened the laptop. On the screen, Evie continued grieving the loss of Steve.

"Oh, Evie, I'm so sorry," I whispered.

My heart continued to fracture as she wailed. I was desperate to turn back time—to make things right. And even though I couldn't, I had to at least talk to her.

I began poking around the control settings, looking for the button to broadcast to the whole village. The small microphone icon in the corner had to be it. I clicked it, not sure what I would say. But it didn't matter. As soon as I opened my mouth, the screen froze. A red error message flashed across the screen: ACCESS DENIED.

"No. No, no, no!!" I banged on the keyboard, trying to get the program back online. I shook my head, looking for any way to reboot the system and log back in. "Dammit."

Ian had kicked me out of the program.

And for the second day in a row, in the dusty corner of my hotel room, I dropped my head and cried.

MESSAGE TO DAD

I blew it, Dad. I ruined everything.

I heard what happened. I'm so sorry. I wish I were there to hug you. I meant what I said before. Win or lose. I'm still proud of you.

Except I didn't even have a chance to lose. There's absolutely nothing about what I did to be proud of.

Oh, mijita. I wish you could see yourself the way I see you.

CHAPTER 25
CLOUDED VISION

IT WAS like pushing through a dense fog as I walked the halls of Orchard High the following Monday. Everything was fuzzy and tinted with an air of danger. While I couldn't know for sure what the sideways glances or hushed whispers were about as I passed my classmates, one thing was certain. Even if no one was talking *about* me, they sure weren't talking *to* me.

The same could be said for my mom. She left the tournament before I could even say goodbye on Saturday. Other than one sideways remark about the inconvenience of finding an earlier flight home, she hasn't said a word about what happened. I get it, I guess. Mom cares too much about order and rules. She doesn't handle messes well. What happened on Saturday was messy, and I was left alone to clean it up.

But I didn't expect the silent treatment at school. At first, I tried to convince myself that it was all in my head. Why would anyone care how I did at TechEd? But then Misty Wright hand her phone to Trevor Holt before English started. They laughed, looking back at me as they pointed to the video on the screen. My face went bright red as I watched the replay of Ian's bold accusations and my now-famous meltdown. The video had nearly two thousand views and counting.

The first half of school lasted a lifetime. As whispers turned to taunts, I no longer had to wonder whether they were talking about me. Everywhere I went, someone was discussing what happened. It wasn't long before the story was spread throughout the entire school.

The speed at which my classmates turned from fan to foe was mind-boggling. It was like they had been waiting for me to stumble, eager to dethrone me from the ranks of popularity. Even more concerning was the realization of how few true friends I had. Like a chameleon, I had spent years blending in with whatever crowd I was around. Until now, I never knew how shallow those relationships were. Ian had been the exception, and then Evie. Both were now gone. I had no roots—no support.

As I made my way to the cafeteria for lunch, I wanted to disappear. The table in the far corner—Ian's former sanctuary—had become a place where I could escape the facade of high school life and be myself. Now, it reminded me I was an outcast. I thought about returning to my regular table with Jake and the others, but my so-called friends were passing around the video of me. I was too numb to care. So I sat in the corner alone. Reluctantly, I pulled out my lunch and began eating.

"Hi, Lucy," Jake said softly. I was surprised he pulled out the seat across from me and sat down.

"Jake? How's it going?" I had never been so relieved to see a friendly face.

Looking uncomfortable, he shifted in his chair. "I heard about the competition. I'm sorry. That must have sucked."

I smiled weakly. "It wasn't the best day."

Jake ran his fingers through his hair while looking down at his feet. "I, uh—" he cleared his throat. "—I wanted to talk to you about Fall Ball."

"This Saturday, right?" Reading the expression on Jake's face, I braced myself for what was coming next.

"I hate to do this, but I think I'm going to go with someone else. Sorry."

"Oh." Embarrassed, angry, and sad—I felt it all and then nothing. "Sure, don't worry about it."

"It's nothing personal."

I stared at my sandwich.

Jake leaned in, whispering. "Hey, forget those people who blame you for what happened. Ian is the obvious ass in this situation."

"They're blaming me?" I blinked back tears. "What are they saying?"

"I dunno. Dumb stuff."

"Like what?"

"Come on, Lucy. It's stupid gossip."

"Please tell me."

Jake sighed. "Some people are saying you used Ian. That you aren't as smart as all the teachers think you are. They think you had it coming—being called out and all that."

My voice cracked. "Wow, okay. Is that what you think?"

"No! What Ian did was inexcusable."

"So then, why are you ditching me for Fall Ball?"

Jake's shoulders dropped. "I think it would be easier. People are starting to drag me into the drama, which isn't fair. I had nothing to do with it."

"Nothing about this is fair." My anger rose to the surface. Sure, I had made mistakes, but I didn't deserve to be cut down like this.

Jake crossed his arms. "What would you do if you were in my shoes? You're not the only one with a reputation to uphold. People expect me to go with a certain type of girl."

"And what type of girl is that?" My voice was rising.

"Come on, don't make a scene. You're taking this the wrong way. Besides, this whole thing will blow over soon enough."

"Answer the question, Jake. What type of girl?"

Jake swallowed hard, looking down at his hand. "I dunno. Someone who isn't at the butt of every joke. I mean, you didn't do anything so terrible, but other people are talking. And I don't want to deal with it. You understand, right?"

I tossed my lunch into my bag and stood up. "I get it, Jake. I do. We're all playing the same game, aren't we? We each have a part to play." I flung my backpack over my shoulder and walked out.

"Ms. Fernández, do you have a minute?"

I was startled to find Ms. Howell hovering over my desk. A couple of kids snickered as they got up to leave. I had no idea how long school had been over. Trying to snap out of my daze, I dragged my body and sat across from Ms. Howell. The expression on her face crushed me.

"Ms. Howell, I know what you're thinking," I said, shaking my head. I tried to maintain my composure but couldn't keep the tears from flowing after fighting my emotions all day. "I'm so, so sorry. I let you down. After all your help, I ruined it all. And I wish I could fix things." I buried my face in my hands and cried.

"Oh, Lucy, no," Ms. Howell said gently. "I'm not disappointed in you. I wanted to make sure you're okay. You seemed distracted during class, and I was worried after hearing about what happened on Saturday." She walked over and placed her hand on my shoulder as she leaned against her desk. "It's a crappy situation. And if you need to cry, by all means. Let it out."

So for the next few minutes, I sobbed as Ms. Howell patiently stood by my side. The relief of letting it out only lasted until the embarrassment returned in full force. "How did this happen?" I finally said, my eyes swollen and red.

Ms. Howell sighed as she sat back down in her seat. "After teaching high school for almost ten years, I wish I could tell you this was the first time a situation got out of hand. People can be unkind."

"I should have been honest with Ian. I should *not* have snuck behind his back. You told me communication was the answer, but I was too scared."

"Scared of what?"

"I'm not sure. Scared he'd flip out. Scared of hurting the Simples." I closed my eyes. "But I guess I was most afraid of losing."

"Would losing be so bad?" Ms. Howell said.

"It shouldn't be. Losing is a part of life. I understand that, logically." I shook my head. "But I've spent years doing everything I can to be on the winning side of things because deep down, I know..." My voice trailed off.

"Deep down, you know—what?"

Tears streamed down my face. "Deep down, I know I'm a fraud. If you take away my awards, grades, and achievements—what's left? Nothing. A nobody." I reached for a tissue from Ms. Howell's desk and wiped my nose. "And today, everyone finally saw the real me."

"Lucy, you don't believe that, do you? You are more than the sum of your achievements. Your value doesn't come from grades or success."

"Then why hasn't my mom talked to me since Saturday? She can't even look at me. TechEd was supposed to be the finish line —the doorway to MIT. It was my chance to prove myself once and for all. And I ruined it."

Ms. Howell pushed the tissue box closer, and I pulled out a handful. She leaned back in her chair and sighed. "I flunked out of high school."

My tears stopped. I looked over at the framed diploma from Stanford University hanging on the wall and then back at my teacher. "You did?"

"Yep, high school dropout, right here. Like you, I had made a name for myself. I was the faithful screw-up," she said with a slight chuckle. "I did plenty of things I'm not proud of—spent lots of time in detention."

"But you're like the smartest, most level-headed person I've met."

"Thank you. I had plenty of hard lessons that forced me to grow up—most of which came from my own bad decisions. And while I hope my students don't have to spend a night in jail to learn what I did, I wouldn't change a thing."

My eyes grew wide. "You spent a night in jail?"

"That's a story for another time." Ms. Howell laughed. "But do you know why I am grateful for my mistakes?"

"Yeah, yeah. Because they made you the person you are today," I said with a hint of sarcasm. "I'm familiar with the cliché."

Ms. Howell laughed. "I mean, sure. But past failures only teach you something if you're willing to put in the work. When I was at my lowest, I finally asked myself *why* I kept doing so many dumb things. And guess what I learned?"

"What?"

"It was easier to create an identity made from bad choices than learn to be comfortable with the real me—flaws and all. I could justify my negative thoughts and give others a reason to be disappointed by purposely getting into trouble. It was a way to control how others perceived me."

My eyes were still puffy and red, but I was smiling for the first time since last week. "Wow. That's kinda messed up."

"You bet it is. But here's the thing, even though you have a different approach, I think you're doing the same thing. You're trying to define yourself by a long list of achievements—hiding under a shield of shiny gold stars, hoping nobody sees the real you. Why do you think that is?"

I grabbed my necklace as I thought about the question. When I finally spoke, my words were soft. "I'm not sure who the real me is."

"Well, that is an important realization in and of itself," Ms. Howell said. "And if you can come to terms with an answer, you might stop trying to measure your worth by some arbitrary checklist. Trust me. Your value isn't based on what you do."

"Then what is it based on?"

Ms. Howell smiled. "Do you remember the first time you came to talk to me? It was back when you were getting started for TechEd. You were stressing over what rules you should give the Simples."

I nodded. "Yeah, you told me that rules don't just happen. They're reflections of our values."

"And I told you to think about what you value. Remember that? Did you ever define your values for *The Garden?*"

Of course, I did. I always finished every assignment from a teacher, even the unofficial ones. I reached down, pulled my notebook out from my backpack, opened it to the second page, and began reading.

"As I think about how I want to influence this culture, the values important to me include: Courage, Kindness, Curiosity, Hard Work, Integrity, and Love." I closed the book.

"Nothing about obedience? Or perfection?" Ms. Howell smiled. "It sounds like you're being more generous to the Simples than yourself. Maybe you should define the values that will guide *your* life."

I silently read over my list again. "I think you're right."

Ms. Howell stood up and began gathering her things. "And to answer your question, I think a person's worth is determined by the values they hold—*and* how well they stick to them."

"Then I guess I've got some things to figure out."

"Writing your values down is a good practice, to be sure. But from what I can tell, you already live by some solid principles." Ms. Howell began walking toward the door. I followed her. "The real key is to keep your eyes open for any misalignment. When we betray our values, we feel the most fraudulent."

My heart sank. I must have drifted pretty far from my values to be feeling this crappy.

Ms. Howell smiled. "But here's the good news, Lucy: Those moments of betrayal are like a lighthouse on a foggy shore—showing the way back to yourself."

CHAPTER 26
BREAKING THE RULES

"We need to talk."

Mom swiveled her desk chair around as I stood in the doorway of her home office. "Well, that sounds serious. Is everything okay?"

I stepped forward. "You tell me. You've barely said two words to me since Saturday."

Mom leaned back, folding her arms. "What do you want me to say, honey? TechEd was a disaster that could have been avoided had you listened to me about working with Ian."

I wasn't surprised by her response. Still, it stung. I walked over to the oak bookcase that filled the entire west wall of her room. My mother's gaze followed my every move as I dragged my finger along the edges of several large, leather-bound books that lined the shelves. I paused and picked up a small framed photo. It was a picture of me with my parents at the circus.

"I remember this day," I said softly as my lips curled into a faint smile. "I was like what—Seven? Eight, maybe?"

"Something like that," Mom said.

I stared at the photo. "I remember being so mesmerized by

the trapeze artists. I begged you for days to sign me up for aerial arts lessons so that I could be in the circus one day."

My mom chuckled. "You were relentless. Every night you asked dad to hang a bar in your room. You even tried tying your sheets to the top of the banister and nearly broke your arm dangling over the stairs. The look on your face when I told you trapeze artist wasn't a real job—oh boy, you were so angry."

"Why *did* you tell me that?" I put the picture back in its place and turned to face her. "I mean, it's unconventional, sure, but that doesn't mean it is fake. Why lie?"

"Oh, come on, sweetie. Do you think I was about to let my bright little girl give up her future on some pipe dream of joining the circus? You were born for greatness."

"But what if the circus was my dream?"

Mom scoffed. "You're telling me your dream is to travel all year long with a bunch of circus freaks, spending your life in a giant tent?"

I rolled my eyes and sighed. "It might be a nice life, but that's not the point."

"So what is the point?"

I sighed. "Would you support me no matter what? Even if I had a dream other than MIT?"

Mom frowned. She stood up and straightened the photo. "What are you talking about? Your dream has always been MIT. What else have we worked toward all these years? Just because TechEd was a bust doesn't mean you have to give up on the bigger goal. Remember the plan."

I sat down in an overstuffed chair, hugging my legs close. For years, I dreamed of MIT. But I hated the nagging dread that always pricked my senses whenever we discussed *the plan*. And I was curious to figure out why.

"Do you love me?" I finally asked.

"Of course I do." Mom scrunched her face. "You're being so weird right now. Why would you even ask such a question?"

I shrugged my shoulders as I scanned the other photos perfectly positioned on Mom's bookcase. There was a picture of Dad and me in the cockpit of a plane. Another of the family on our trip to Cannon Beach. There were half a dozen snapshots of my childhood lined on the shelves. I couldn't help but notice that the joy in my eyes grew more subdued with each passing year.

"Would you still love me if I dropped out of school and joined the circus?"

Mom rolled her eyes. "Oh sheesh, you're not telling me you've been secretly crushed all these years because I wouldn't let you dangle from some hanging bar for a living?"

"That's not it, Mom. I just—I need to know you'd love me even if I didn't follow through with *the plan*."

She put her hands on her hips. "What is this really about?"

I closed my eyes and exhaled sharply. "What Ian did to me on Saturday was humiliating. When you left the conference room without a word—I couldn't help but think I had failed you." I wrung my hands together. "And when you abandoned me, I wondered if it was because you didn't love me anymore."

My mom slowly sank into her chair. Her voice was quiet. "You think that?"

I swallowed hard, summoning all the courage I could. "Since Saturday, you've done nothing but give me the cold shoulder—and it hurts, Mom. It really hurts."

She pursed her lips. I couldn't tell if she was angry or remorseful. "Hmm. Well, I'm sorry you feel that way. I didn't mean to hurt you. But did it ever occur to you that I was hurting, too?"

"Of course it did!" I didn't mean to say it so loud. "Everything about your reaction told me you were upset, which is the problem. If it was *my* dream that had been smashed, you should have been there to help me." I stood up and walked toward the window. "But I'm not sure it has ever been my dream. Maybe my whole life has been spent pursuing *your* dream."

Mom walked over, taking me gently by the shoulders. "If you mean giving you the best possible future, then you're right. That *is* my dream." She sighed. "You think I'm being unfair, but you'd be chasing all kinds of wild ideas that will lead you nowhere without me. Everything I do is for you. That's why I push so hard."

"It often feels like you're pushing me away," I said quietly.

"Well, what do you want me to do? Sit by and let you throw everything away—everything you've worked for?"

"No, I just..."

A single tear slid down my cheek. Why couldn't she tell how much I was hurting? My eyes met hers, pleading. "I needed my mom, and you weren't there." I took a deep breath, trying to calm my trembling voice. "I need your love even when I fail —*especially* when I fail."

Closing my eyes, I tried to push down the gnawing concern that Saturday's blowout might never have happened if I hadn't constantly chased my mom's approval. How many times had I drifted away from *my* values to conform to *hers*?

"Okay," Mom said. "I hear you, and I'll try to be better. But love comes in many forms. What you may read as strict is how I try to protect you. It is all rooted in love. You're capable of so much, and I won't let you waste your potential."

Lightheaded, I opened the window to let in some air. The faint sound of bass echoed across the street from Ian's house. I wondered if his parents had heard about TechEd and how it turned out. Were they angry? Disappointed? Indifferent? I had no idea.

"You're right," I said. "Your high expectations have produced some impressive results. And I love that you believe I'm capable of achieving so much. But when things fall apart, I need to know that I'm your priority. Not the damn plan." I stood up to leave.

"Hey, don't go. We're not finished." Mom walked toward me. "You said we need to deal with what happened. So, let's deal with it. What are you going to do? How are you going to fix this?"

"Fix what? The competition is over! They disqualified me, remember?"

Mom threw her arms up and plopped back down in her chair. "You never should have worked with Ian. I never trusted him." She sighed, glaring out the window at the Gibsons' house, clearly annoyed at the music booming from its direction. "Do you remember what happened the first day you met him? Remember how you were sent to the principal's office? I was so humiliated when the school called to tell me my angel child had shoved some kid to the ground. You never did that sort of thing before you met Ian."

"You mean the moment when I defended someone in need?"

Mom frowned. "Fighting is never okay, Lucy."

"Ian was being bullied."

"That's no excuse to break the rules."

"Sometimes, breaking the rules *is* necessary!" I paused, trying to calm myself. I was desperate for her to understand. "Sometimes, you've got to get messy to make things right."

Mom scoffed. "Things sure got messy on Saturday, didn't they? You'll excuse me if I prefer my way. Following the rules has given me a great life. And it gave you a great life, too—before Ian came and ruined everything."

I didn't want to keep fighting. I was done trying to change her mind. After spending the past two days daydreaming about how TechEd could have gone, I finally realized I couldn't change my mom any more than I could change the past. There was no rewind button, and imagining a make-believe future wouldn't help me make things right now.

Mom sat down and organized the papers on her desk. She took a long, slow breath. "Look, TechEd didn't go the way we wanted. But there is no reason to throw your future away. You still have an impressive track record. This little blip doesn't have to ruin your reputation forever. You can still make this dream come true."

It was like my mom was telling me the stove was hot, warning me to stay away lest I burn myself. And after seventeen years of believing her, I finally wanted to test it for myself. I wanted to reach out and touch it. Because whether I got burned or not, I'd never understand how painful or wonderful life could be until I started living it on my terms.

"Mom," I said calmly. "I think I have a new dream."

I'm not sure what surprised her more: The calmness of my presence or the audacity of my words. She lifted her eyebrows. "Oh? Giving up, are you?"

"No. But I am done trying to live a life for everyone else. That is what got me in this mess. And while it would be easier to sweep it under the rug and show up as the person everyone expects me to be, I think I'm going to try to build something new with the wreckage instead." I smiled. "Something *better*."

I walked over and hugged her, hoping she understood I wasn't trying to defy her. I just needed to find myself. Surprised by the gesture, her body stiffened for a second before she wrapped her arms around me, melting into the embrace.

"I love you, Lucy," she said tenderly.

"I love you, too." I let go and smiled. "By the way, the day I got sent to the principal's office was one of the happiest moments of my life. Because even though you think I did the wrong thing, I did it for the right reason. Some things are worth fighting for."

12:57 AM.

I stared at the clock, bleary-eyed and tired. After talking to my mom earlier, I realized I needed to realign with my values, even if it meant breaking a few rules. Stealing Ian's code and leading him on would have been inexcusable if it was only about winning TechEd. But there was a deeper reason for my actions. The Simples were being bullied, and now more than ever, they needed my help. They were my guiding light back to myself. My reputation be damned.

With a copy of the code on my backup hard drive, I was determined to find any vulnerability in Ian's program. There had to be *something* that I could use to hack his system. I needed a back door into *The Garden.*

I had to talk to Evie.

My phone kept buzzing as dozens of notifications popped on the screen. The video of Ian's rant had spread like wildfire. I was constantly being tagged—and I could only assume the comments and shares weren't very flattering. Unwilling to confirm those suspicions, I turned my phone off.

I hadn't stopped thinking about Evie since Saturday. I worried about how the Simples were dealing with the ramifications of Ian's rage-induced behavior. Was Steve actually dead? What about Ash and Cade? How many people were lost in the earthquakes and flooding?

I tried logging into *the Garden* several times over the weekend, but Ian had found a way to block me from the system permanently. Each attempt deflated my mood as my technological incompetence battled against his brilliance. I had been so anxious about helping the Simples I even tried reaching out to Ian to make amends—with no luck. I hadn't heard from him since he stormed off on Saturday.

Now, I was revved up. I had spent the last five hours trying to find a digital backdoor into the village. I was done playing second fiddle to Ian and ready to prove that I could make things right.

"I can do this," I said to myself. "I *will* do this."

Line by line, I scanned Ian's code. Occasionally, I had to stop and read up some details about the programming language. But slowly, it all started to make sense as the information translated inside my brain. My energy returned as the logic of everything finally came together. Unfortunately, my excitement came to a grinding halt when I realized how secure Ian had made *The Garden*.

"Oh, come on!" I yelled as I hit another dead end.

It was nearly 2:30 in the morning. I needed to sleep with a full day of school inching closer by the minute. I shut down the computer and collapsed onto my bed. As I began drifting off, my mind pulled up an image of Evie from the first day we met. Her passionate curiosity was carved deeply into my mind. I smiled, thinking about how often she ventured off to explore the world —Evie's persistence in trying to escape fueled my desire to find a way back in.

Ian's glitch!

I sat up tall. Any signs of sleepiness evaporated as a rush of energy filled my body. "That's it! The crack in the barrier that Evie found. The glitch—Ian never fixed it!" I ran to my desk and opened my laptop.

Whatever bug had allowed Evie to escape the village borders could be the answer to let me inside. All I needed was a minor vulnerability in Ian's programming. Even a tiny mistake could be enough. I searched carefully through the many lines of code, looking specifically for the invisible boundary Ian had created when he first introduced the Simples to the village. Once I finally found it, I scanned each section looking for any mistakes —line by line.

For the next twenty minutes, my eyes lasered in on the screen. Careful not to skip over anything, I combed through every character, hoping to find the glitch. *There.* My breathing sped up as I reread the line to be sure. With a big smile, I sat up tall.

"Gotcha."

TO LUCY

ON YOUR 15TH BIRTHDAY

¡Feliz quinceañera, mi nieta!

Lucy, I can't believe you're already fifteen years old. You make me so proud, and I hope you know how much I love you. I've been saving this special gift for you since the day you were born. This necklace was given to me by my abuela. The Mexican Sunflower is as strong as it is beautiful. It can tolerate drought, bringing beauty even in the harshest of environments.

Whenever life got hard, I'd press my thumb against this little charm and remember my strength. I hope it helps you remember your strength, too. No matter what life brings your way, you'll always be able to blossom.

Love always,

Abuelita Fernández

CHAPTER 27
BORN TO DIE

"Psst... Evie."

Evie jumped to her feet. She was all alone at the edge of town. "Who's there?" Her body went rigid as if ready to fight.

"It's me, Lucy. I need you to be very quiet and listen for a moment."

"Lucy!" Evie yelled. "I didn't think you—"

"Shh!" I interrupted her. "Please, don't speak. I'm not supposed to be talking to you. If Ian heard you speaking to me, it would be bad."

Evie slowly nodded her head. Her posture, which had always been poised, appeared on the verge of collapse. Her clothes were ratted and muddy. But it was Evie's grief-stricken expression that hit me the hardest. Her transformation was devastating.

It took me nearly two days to figure out how to manipulate the glitch in Ian's code and cloak my online presence. I was fairly confident I could interact with Evie without Ian knowing, especially since it was only four o'clock in the morning. He should be asleep. Still, my nerves were on fire as I surveyed *The Garden,* hoping to make contact without any problems.

"Evie, head back to your home." I spoke clearly into my

computer's microphone, needing her to follow my instructions precisely. "I've created a digital camouflage that should make it so Ian can't see you once you're inside. We'll be able to talk quietly and hopefully avoid detection."

Evie trekked her way through the town, jumping over crevasses and pushing through fallen branches. She passed a couple of people working hard to rebuild one of the many fallen structures. Everyone was silently mourning. Glazed, vacant expressions were the norm. Once Evie made it inside her home, she spun around. "Okay, where are you, Lucy? Show yourself."

"I'm right here."

"I can't see you,"

"Sorry, I meant I'm in my room, watching from a device. You won't be able to see me. Ian has kicked me out of the program. He's gone crazy."

"Uh, yeah." Evie gestured to her barely standing home. There was a large crack in the wall, all the furniture was turned over or broken, and her handmade map was torn in two. Still, Evie was luckier than most. At least she had a home.

"I'm so sorry about everything. How are you doing?" I asked. "I've been so worried. I've barely slept these past few days, trying to find a way to talk to you."

Evie smiled, barely. "It's nice to hear your voice. I was worried something might have happened to you." She leaned against a wall and sunk into a sitting position. Her rounded shoulders and long face proved she was losing a game with gravity. Everything about her was half-alive.

I took a deep breath, trying to stop my emotions from bubbling over. "Can you tell me what happened?"

Staring off into a void, Evie began recounting the events. "After you told me to stay with Ash, I thought things would be okay. We hadn't heard from the Voice—or Ian, I guess—for a few days." She inhaled deeply. "But the others found me."

Evie's voice broke, and tears streamed down her face. She

grabbed the end of her skirt, wiping her cheeks, leaving a smudge of dirt. I clicked a button and zoomed in, wanting to be closer to her.

"That must have been scary," I said.

Evie nodded. "They took Ash—tied him up, and hoisted him onto their shoulders. I tried to stop them, but they hit me with a rock or something. I was unconscious for a long time. When I came to, I found myself back here, bound and gagged."

"Oh, Evie, I can't believe—" I paused. Every word that came to my mind was too hollow. "I'm so sorry," was all I could mutter.

Evie continued. "Thankfully, Ian stopped Steve moments before he was about to..." Her voice trailed off as her gaze drifted out the window. Swallowing hard, she closed her eyes. "Anyway, he didn't go through with it. Then Ian came to visit me. He told me I wasn't faithful like the others—said I didn't pass his test. I was so angry. And even though I couldn't hurt him, I was ready to scream and yell and then..." Evie shrugged, blinking back tears. "He vanished."

I could picture the scene perfectly in my head. I remembered how I had used Ian's mom to prevent anything from happening that night.

Evie inhaled deeply. "Later, Steve told me about Ian's appearance at the altar and how he had stopped the sacrifice in the nick of time. Steve was so grateful that Ian had changed his mind. He was proud that he had passed Ian's test." Evie shook her head. "How psychotic is that? I couldn't bear to look at Steve. He was willing to kill my baby. He said he didn't want to, but he would have gone through with it if Ian hadn't stopped him."

"Unbelievable," I said.

Evie hopped to her feet and began pacing the floor with a fiery rage that revived her. "I told Steve I didn't want to see him again. I told him he was unfit to father our children." She paused, looking out the window. "For the next little while, things were better. I figured you had fixed it like you said you would since we didn't hear from Ian. My boys were safe. And then..." Evie's sudden resolve crumbled as she dropped to her knees and cried.

"What happened?" I asked gingerly.

"The earth caved in. The ground shook and split. Large waves crashed into the village, carrying people off into the ocean. Our homes fell. Trees were torn asunder. It was like the world was trying to devour us. Ian appeared in the sky, telling us how worthless we were without him. He said we didn't deserve his world—that we were being punished for not worshiping him with all our hearts."

Evie tried to catch her breath, but her emotions were too strong. "We had lived peacefully in this world for hundreds of cycles. And he destroyed it like we were nothing to him." Evie began to whimper before the flood of tears sprang from her eyes. Her body craved the release of so many emotions. But as soon as she regained composure, another wave would hit. Her eyes were drained, unable to summon another tear even though she was desperate to drown in them.

Afraid to ask, I spoke quietly. "How many people did you lose?"

"So many—more than half the village." Evie choked. " Including Steve." She wiped away her face again. "My last words to him were so cruel. And now? Now, he's gone forever." She wrung the edge of her skirt in her hands. "I never made things right with him."

"I feel terrible," I said softly. "I'm just—so sorry."

Evie sat quietly against the wall. Her chest gently rose and fell as her breathing slowed down and deepened. The wind blew, rustling the leaves outside Evie's window.

"I guess none of it matters," Evie said, shaking her head. "It

turns out I'm not even real. I'm some unhinged teenager's experiment. My world is going to end anyway. Why should it matter if
it's now or later?"

I pushed back a tear. "Don't say that."

"Why not? We're all made to end. And Ian doesn't care about
us. We're tools to satisfy his ego."

I searched for something meaningful to say. I picked up the
sunflower charm around my neck. Tears filled my eyes as I
thought about my abuela.

"My grandma died a little over a year ago," I said softly. "She
was the greatest human. She was a master in the kitchen. Always
made me smile. And she had the greenest thumb in the whole
world."

"Why was her thumb green?" Evie asked.

I chuckled as I wiped away a tear. "It's an expression. It
means she had a talent for making things grow. She used to live
down the street from me, and her garden was the most beautiful
thing—which is no small feat in our Arizona climate."

"She sounds amazing," Evie said.

"Her favorite flower was the Mexican Sunflower. It reminded
her of summer nights as a child in Cholula. She loved it when
the sun sank low toward the horizon, giving everything a golden
glow." I traced the charm draped around my neck with my
finger. "She gave me a sunflower necklace when I turned fifteen.
She hoped it would remind me of the beauty that survives the
droughts of life."

A thousand memories flashed through my mind. I could
smell the spicy aroma of Lita's perfume, taste her delicious mole,
and hear the sound of her singing in Spanish. "When she died, I
was so broken—like I was missing a piece of me. It was hard to
think of her not existing anymore. All her light, love, and
laughter were gone."

"I know what that feels like," Evie said quietly.

I pressed the charm between my finger and thumb. "Grief

can be overwhelming, Evie. The darkness from losing a loved one can swallow you whole. But even though my abuela's body isn't here with me anymore, her memory lives on. Her smile is forged in my mind. Her stories continue to teach me."

Evie slowly stood up and stared out the window. A small smile crept across her face. "Do you remember the way Steve praised everything and everyone? I mean, before things got bad. I could always count on him to see beauty everywhere. Everything was a miracle in his eyes."

I laughed. "I remember the first time I met him. He was drawing circles in the water. I asked him if he was bored, and the word was foreign to him. He loved his world and never took for granted the privilege of being alive."

"I could probably learn something from him," Evie said.

"Me, too." The wall across from my bed was full of awards and certificates—none of which mattered anymore. "My grandma was battling cancer, a horrible disease in my world, for almost three years. And I remember crying next to her hospital bed a few days before she died. I was so mad this vibrant woman was made frail by something we couldn't even see. It felt so unfair that she was dying. It made me question the whole purpose of life."

I wiped away another tear. "I remember arguing with her. Can you imagine some sixteen-year-old berating a dying old woman?" I shook my head. "But I was so mad she was dying. And asked her what the point of life is if we're all made to die." I picked up the framed photo of Lita and me on my desk. "She said something that stuck with me, but I don't think I fully understood it until now."

"What did she say?" Evie asked.

"It may be true that we are born to die, but more importantly —we are born to *live*." I closed my eyes, letting the tears drape over my cheeks.

"I like that," Evie said. "But I'm not sure it applies to me inside this simulation. Was I ever made to live? Or am I merely a machine designed for someone else's purpose?"

Wiping my cheeks, I watched Evie on my screen. Beautiful, strong, and curious—from the moment I first saw her, she beamed with life. "You decide what your purpose is, Evie—nobody else. Ian may have created you. He might have given you your start. But you are the creator of your life. You can make it what you want."

Evie exhaled as she took inventory of the ravaged village outside her window. "Well, if that is true, I'd like to fix this mess. I want to tell everyone the truth and help them take back control of their lives." She shook her head. "But how can I when Ian's grasp is so strong? Even after all the trauma, most still pray to him for protection. They believe he is a wise, all-powerful being they have to obey. So, how do I convince them otherwise?"

"You may not be able to convince them. I think you need to be prepared for pushback from some people. A lot of people. You can't tell others what to believe. All you can do is give them the facts and let them decide."

"Right. Okay." Evie began pacing again. "What do I even say? I'm so nervous they won't want to hear the truth. I can't stand the idea of anyone living under Ian's oppressive rules."

I nodded. "Hopefully, they'll believe you. But the truth can be hard. Remember how angry you were when I first told you?"

Evie laughed. "Oh, I remember. I was angry, confused, and heartbroken. Honestly, the emotions still catch me off guard, even now."

"Exactly. Sometimes we think a cage is safer than venturing into the unknown. Still, watching others choose bondage is painful when freedom is one choice away."

"And what if they do follow me? What's to stop Ian from ending us the moment we stop worshiping him?"

I sat up tall in my seat and took a deep breath. I glanced over at the pages of notes I had been making over the last few days.

"I'll figure that out. I'll fight for you to have the freedom you deserve. Leave Ian to me."

CHAPTER 28
THE DOORWAY

TAP, tap, tap.

"Be brave," I said under my breath as I knocked on the Gibsons' front door.

Ian had been absent from school all week, and Ms. Howell had asked me to drop off some classwork for him.

"Me?" I said to Ms. Howell. "Can't someone else do it? Ian isn't exactly talking to me right now."

"That's why I'm asking you. You two need to talk." Ms. Howell handed me a stack of papers. "Besides, the final project is due tomorrow. You guys are still working together, aren't you?"

"Honestly, I don't know."

Ms. Howell offered a sympathetic smile. "Time to figure it out."

Now, I was waiting outside Ian's house, wondering if he'd even open the door. I had no idea what to say or how he'd react. After standing on his porch for an uncomfortable amount of time, I was relieved I wouldn't have to worry about it. I slid the papers under his doormat and turned around. But I only made it two steps before the creak of the door paralyzed me.

"What do you want?" Ian's voice was sharp and unforgiving.

I turned around slowly. "Oh, hey, I wasn't sure anyone was home. Ms. Howell asked me to drop off your homework." I reached for the papers under the mat, brushed off some dirt, and handed them to him.

He snatched them out of my hands. Unmoved, his gaze pierced me. "Well? Is that all?" he said coldly.

"Yep." I slowly rocked back on my heels, stuffing my hands in my jacket pockets. My brain kept telling me to turn and leave, but something in my heart forced me to stay. "Actually, there is something. I—uh..." I sighed. "I wondered if you were still planning on presenting our final anthropology project together. It's due tomorrow. I've already got the presentation mostly outlined, and I'd be happy to include you."

"You're kidding, right?" Ian sneered. "After what you did to me? No." He shook his head emphatically. "No way."

I yelled inside my mind. *What I did to you? How about what you did to me?* I didn't understand how Ian could paint me as the only villain in this situation. At least I was trying to make things right.

I took a few deep breaths, not looking for a fight. "If you don't complete the project, you'll fail," I said calmly. "I'm trying to help you. Consider it an olive branch or something."

Ian took a step closer. "I don't want or need your help. I don't care if I fail since I don't plan on returning."

A little afraid, I stepped back. "Like ever? You're dropping out?"

"Why not? I have no reason to stay. I'll get my GED and move on with my life. End of story. And as a side bonus, I don't have to see you."

I bit my lip, trying to maintain a brave face. "Ian, are you sure about this? Things are a little rough right now, but this seems—"

"—what? Irresponsible? Well, at least I don't try and shove myself in some box to make others happy. I don't want to go back to Orchard High. End of story."

"Okay, fair enough." I tugged on my jacket, wishing I could warm the frigid tension between us. After everything we had been through and promising we wouldn't let each other down, my whole body was heavy with regret. I turned to walk home but stopped.

"For what it's worth, I'm sorry about what happened," I said. "I didn't deserve to be humiliated, but you didn't deserve to be misled. And I regret doing it. I hope someday you'll be able to forgive me."

I tried reading Ian's thoughts as I blinked back tears. For a brief moment, a hint of remorse bubbled to the surface. Behind the coldness were the eyes of the same scared boy I rescued in fourth grade. Ian was a kid trying to protect his heart by pretending he didn't care. At that second, I wanted to jump in and rescue him as I did before. Maybe there was still hope to save our friendship. I missed our lunches, the jokes, his witty banter. But before I could lock on to the innocence in his eyes, it vanished. And in its place was only rage.

"I gotta go," Ian said. "I'd wish you luck on the project tomorrow, but I can't imagine you'll do very well without the tech." He snickered quietly to himself. "I guess that perfect GPA of yours will nose dive the same way your TechEd presentation crashed. Oh, how the mighty have fallen." He turned around and shut the door.

I stood frozen, waiting for the familiar sting in my heart to take over. I should have been mad... or sad... or something? Instead, I felt free, and I wasn't sure why. Like being cut from a heavy chain, I was buoyant. Ian's decided departure was the last piece of my former world. Everything had slipped out from under my feet.

But instead of falling, I realized I could fly.

———

"Come on!" I yelled at my computer as I picked up my mug, only to find it empty. I put it down, annoyed. Caffeine was the only thing keeping me awake.

I had spent all week trying to find a permanent solution for the Simples. Evie was right. If she could convince the others about the truth of the simulation, they would still need protection against Ian. After talking to him earlier, I was worried he was about to do something drastic.

The goal was to transfer the Simples onto my server. I had already copied the entire virtual world on it, but copying the people was trickier. The Simples had evolved from their original coding. Their experiences and interactions had changed them. A simple copy and paste would delete everything they had learned over the past couple hundred years—killing who they had become. I needed to figure out how to switch them over without resetting them.

Delirious from staying up late and getting up early every day this week, I was close to an answer. I needed to figure out a doorway that could temporarily bridge Ian's server to mine.

That's it! The doorway!

Evie had first used the invisible crack in the village border to roam freely. It was the same glitch that allowed me to hack Ian's server. I wondered if it might also work as a conduit onto a new server. I pulled up the code for the hundredth time, knowing exactly where to find Ian's original mistake.

Buzz... Buzz....

A calendar reminder for my final presentation in Ms.

Howell's class popped up on my phone. Fighting the urge to cry, I dropped my head onto my desk. There was so much to do, and I still wasn't sure how to approach things now that Ian had ditched me entirely.

Switching gears for a moment, I pulled up the outline of my presentation. I had the key details required for the project. I remembered how excited I was to share The Garden with my classmates a few weeks ago. And now, I wondered what was left to show. The VR aspect was a bust. The village was still in ruins. More than half the people were dead. But at least I had access to the system again. Maybe I could improvise something and call it good.

It was 11:23 P.M. I decided to take five minutes for an emergency coffee break. It was going to be another long night. I hobbled down the stairs. My eyes were red from staring at the computer for six hours. They did not enjoy the sudden jolt of light as I flipped the switch on in the kitchen.

"What are you still doing awake, mijita?"

I nearly jumped out of my skin. "Dad! Jeez. You scared me."

"Sorry." He laughed. "Sorta."

I smiled as I turned on the coffee maker. "When did you even get home? I didn't think you'd be back until tomorrow."

"About twenty minutes ago. But the more important question is, what are you doing up? You should be in bed, not making coffee at midnight."

"I've got a big project I'm trying to finish for tomorrow. I don't do this often, promise."

Dad raised his mug. "Me either," he said. He took a slow sip. "Must be a big project for you to be working so late. Everything okay?"

"I hope so?" I said with a faint smile as the smell of coffee filled the room. "I was supposed to be presenting this project with Ian tomorrow, but he bailed on me."

"Ah," Dad said, taking another sip. "I'm guessing things still aren't great between you two after the whole TechEd mess."

"No." I sighed. "I tried making amends, but he's holding on to this grudge like The One Ring. I finally realize I can't control what he does or thinks." I leaned back against the counter and chuckled. "I'm learning I can't control most things, much to Mom's disappointment."

Dad smiled, putting his mug down on the counter. "You know, when you were born, your mom was a total basket case."

"Mom? Ms. Perfection herself?" I laughed. I couldn't even imagine it.

"Yep, she second-guessed every decision. She wanted the perfect life for you. I mean, we both did. But since I was often hopping around from airport to airport, your sweet mother was left with the lion's share of the work. And it took several years for her to find her groove. She spent a lot of nights sobbing on the floor, thinking she was failing you."

I poured myself a cup and drank slowly. Picturing Mom in such a vulnerable way was a new idea. "I guess we're all trying the best we can, huh?"

"That's always been my philosophy. Not that it's a reason to excuse bad behavior, of course. But believing everyone is doing their best is a great way to summon compassion for those going through a rough patch. And that includes ourselves."

"Good advice." I took another sip. "I'll try to keep that in mind as there are still a few rough patches ahead of me."

"You do that, sweetie." He rinsed his mug and put it in the dishwasher. "Now, go to work. But try to get to bed soon, okay? My other philosophy in life is that a good night's rest solves almost anything."

I smiled as I wrapped my robe tighter around my waist. I hugged Dad and went back upstairs. My mind ping-ponged back and forth as I decided what to work on next. The school project had the most pressing deadline and significantly impacted my grade. Last week, I wouldn't have dared to do anything else. But now, I wanted to ensure I was doing what was best—not for my reputation, but for the people I loved. And that meant finding a solution to help Evie.

"I can do this," I said as I pulled up the code again. "Let's make a doorway."

CHAPTER 29
IAN'S ASCENSION

I HATED TO ADMIT IT, but Lucy's visit rattled me. When I first saw her on my porch, a tiny piece of my heart called out for help. An echo of my fourth-grade self yearned to run back into her shadow, safely stitched to her forever. But I wasn't the same helpless kid anymore. Whatever pull she had on me had been severed. *The Garden* changed me. It showed me my strength, proving I didn't need a savior.

Then I realized Lucy wasn't there to save me.

In her eyes, I was now the bully, and the Simples were the ones she aimed to defend. After decimating their village last week, I left them alone to pick up the pieces. I didn't care if they survived because they were never alive—something I wish Lucy could remember. I figured I'd delete them soon enough and restore my digital paradise to its original glory, but I wasn't in any rush. I needed a break from anything that reminded me of Lucy.

Then she showed up on my doorstep, and it was clear the story wasn't over. It was a race to write the final chapters, and I was determined to finish what I had started. This was my world.

These were my people. If anyone decided how it would end, it sure as hell wouldn't be Lucy.

I would be the final word.

As soon as Lucy left, I went upstairs to evaluate the program. After two hours of searching, I couldn't detect any abnormal activity. The Simples continued to rebuild what I had destroyed in a pitiful display of hope amidst a hopeless cause. But there was no sign that Lucy had been inside *The Garden*. Still, I couldn't shake the thought she was up to something.

Around midnight, I noticed the light from Lucy's bedroom from my window. She rarely stayed up late, but she had been burning the midnight oil for the past few nights, spiking my suspicion.

Had she found a way back into the system?

I tried to convince myself she couldn't sneak past my firewall. Lucy was bright, but I was luminous. Still, my curiosity wouldn't let up. If I couldn't find signs of Lucy, there were most likely other clues of sabotage. If she was forging a plan, there was only one person she would trust to help her: Evie.

The thought disgusted me. I couldn't stand Evie's pestering curiosity or unrelenting questions. But mostly, I despised the way Lucy connected with her. It was like Lucy was compelled to understand Evie. That's all I've ever wanted. To be seen, understood, and loved by anyone—but especially by Lucy. I wanted to be more than the freaky genius across the street. I wanted her to believe I had what it took to improve the world. But Lucy preferred Evie's questions to my absolute truth. She couldn't see my vision of what life could be.

I logged back into the program and clicked around, changing camera views. Urgency fueled my rising anger as I searched for Evie and any sign of Lucy's influence. But Evie's barely standing house was empty. She was nowhere in the village. I investigated the beach and far beyond the borders—nothing.

"What have you done, Lucy, and where the hell is Evie?" My

curiosity turned into an obsession, desperate for answers. Suddenly Evie appeared, standing outside her front door. I didn't understand. When I checked her house seconds ago, it was empty. Where did she come from?

Tap, tap, tap. I zoomed in on Evie's face. The grief and exhaustion I saw from the other Simples were noticeably absent from her resolute expression. Her determined manner lingered in my mind as my gut grew weary.

"Dammit, Lucy, what did you do?"

Evie meandered through the town, stopping to talk with every Simple she met along the way. I turned up the volume to hear what she was saying, but her whispered words were difficult to decipher. Still, the expression on the people's faces as she spoke said enough. Uncertain of the details, it was clear Evie was spreading rumors—forbidden secrets that I'm sure Lucy had shared.

"There's a simple fix," I said smugly. I pulled up the backend and highlighted all the coding related to the Simples. My finger hovered over the delete key. "Say goodbye to your precious little people, Luce."

But I couldn't pull the trigger. Not because I cared whether the Simples existed or not. I wasn't ready to lose my place in their memory. I didn't want to give up being the Voice in the Sky. If I deleted them, I'd be killing the only version of myself I liked —my power along with it.

Deflated, I switched back to view the village. Evie walked away from a man dressed in a bright-colored coat. Joe, I think. He seemed more shaken than the other Simples who listened to Evie's words. I followed him as he made his way back home. A smile spread across my face as I waited for him to fall asleep.

I had an idea.

. . .

"Joe. Hello, Joe." I spoke calmly into my microphone, easing the man out of sleep.

"Who's there?" Joe said with his eyes half-shut.

"The Voice in the Sky."

He snapped to attention. His eyes widened while his breath raced. Stumbling out of bed, he fell to his knees, looking heavenward. "Oh, wise Voice in the Sky. Please do not hurt me!"

"Hurt you? I'd never harm you, my son."

Joe swallowed hard, looking around his room. "Am I dreaming?"

"Sure," I said. "Call it a vision, if you like. I have an important message for you, and I'll only say this once. So, pay attention."

"Is this about what Evie told me?" He gulped, shaking on his knees.

"What did she tell you?"

His face went pale as he choked on his words, afraid to speak.

I kindly prodded him to make his point. "Don't be afraid. You can tell me."

"She, uh..." Joe rubbed the back of his neck. "She said you have lied about who we are and why we are here. Says we need to stop listening to you and save ourselves." He ducked under his arms as if expecting me to strike him.

So that was Lucy's game, huh? She must have told Evie some version of the truth. But did Lucy talk to Evie before *or* after I kicked her out of the program? Was it possible she had found a way into the system undetected? I doubted it, but I wasn't going to take my chances.

"Joe, did Evie say anything else?"

Realizing his life wouldn't end immediately, Joe stood a little braver. "She said tomorrow she'll be heading somewhere safe, and anyone who wants to join her is welcome."

Somewhere safe? What could that mean?

"You did good, Joe," I said. He smiled at the compliment.

"You're a faithful servant, and you'll be rewarded for your obedience."

Joe lifted his head. His eyes revealed a mixture of fear and hope. "Evie's lying, right? I didn't believe her, of course."

"Yes, Evie is spreading lies. She has been deceived, but let's keep this between you and me for now. There will come a time when I'll need you to testify of what I've told you. For now, let it be."

I tapped a few buttons, putting Joe's character back into sleep mode. I didn't need him spilling the beans before I had a chance to set things right.

Outside my window, Lucy's light finally turned off. What did she have up her sleeve? And what was I going to do to ensure she never messed with my creation again? I pulled up the backend code, looking for any sign of Lucy's sabotage.

"I guess tripping you at TechEd wasn't enough," I said as I typed furiously. A smile crept over my face as a plan unfurled in my mind. It was clear what I needed to do. With a big swig of soda, I prepared myself for a long night. The first thing I did was pull up the avatar profiles. It was time to show the world the real Lucy.

"I'll make a pit so deep you'll never be able to ascend the fall."

CHAPTER 30
IMAGES OF REGRET

"WE WERE TOLD to make a fictional culture. At the time, it sounded easy enough."

I stood nervously at the front of Ms. Howell's class, trying to ignore the splitting headache from another nearly sleepless night.

"But in real life, you can't sit down and design a civilization from scratch. That's not how the world works. It is not how people work. A single choice by one person can change the course of life in countless ways. We can't predetermine anything."

I tapped a button on my keyboard, and images from the beginning days inside *The Garden* popped up on the screen. There was a picture of Steve daydreaming by the pond, one with Evie exploring the town, and dozens of other idyllic scenes painting a picture of ease and bliss.

"When we started this project, we thought we could approach the assignment like an architect. We talked about the types of rules, rituals, and traditions our culture could live by— as if the people had no free will of their own. But cultures aren't like houses. No matter how well you draw your blueprints, the result will always differ from what you intend."

I stepped away from the podium. "We thought we had planned the perfect world. It was beautiful, offering its inhabitants everything they needed. But when dealing with people who possess curiosity and intelligence—even the artificial type—you quickly discover the challenges of trying to play the roles of anthropologist *and* creator."

"Oh, come on," Skyler Ford said, abruptly interrupting me. "We've all seen the video of your epic fail. You guys weren't creators. You were destroyers."

Several students snickered while others shook their heads in agreement. Ms. Howell, who offered sympathy, wasn't about to jump in and rescue me. My teacher nodded her head as if urging me to continue. The knot in my stomach grew tighter as I swallowed hard.

With a deep breath, I tried to focus my mind. All I wanted to do was finish the presentation, return home, and transfer the Simples onto my server. After a long night of work, I finally cracked the code. Or at least, I hoped I had. I fell asleep at my desk before I had a chance to test it. There was enough time to throw everything into my backpack and make a mad dash to school when I woke up. Exhausted, I waited for school to end— eager to finish what I had started. This presentation was the only thing left standing in my way.

The clock ticked on. Everyone was staring at me, waiting for me to respond to Skyler's accusations.

"You're right," I said with a shrug. "We did more damage than good inside the program. We foolishly believed we had to give the people arbitrary rules. We thought we had to tell them how to live. But all they needed was time to figure things out for themselves." I tugged on my shirt. I felt guilty about the way things had turned out. "We interfered too much. And each time we did, the results were surprising at best—heartbreaking at worst."

Most of the class was unwilling to give me even a hint of sympathy, but a few kids showed some interest as I explained myself. Staring at the images on the screen, I shook my head.

"I would certainly do things differently if given a chance. But I did learn a lot from this assignment. I learned that culture takes time. It develops in both expected and unusual ways. Our way of life is influenced by the environment and by the limitations of physical laws." I smiled at Ms. Howell. "But mostly, culture is influenced by people—by their hopes, fears, curiosities, and values."

A picture of Evie leading the Simples back from a hunt during the drought popped on the screen. Courageous and unflappable, Evie stood out like a superhero, ready to do whatever it took to save her people. No matter what was going on inside *The Garden*, she never backed down from the challenges handed to her. I wanted to be more like her and hoped I was finally on the right path.

"Civilizations thrive when courageous, curious people lead the way. But when driven by power, ego, or fear—societies shrivel up." I looked at Skyler. "It was never my intention to hurt the people inside our world. But I now realize I was more interested in controlling the narrative instead of letting them lead. My drive for grades and accolades put them in harm's way. I was wrong."

With a heavy sigh, I continued to tap through the slideshow of images, providing a transparent look at the village's progression. The idyllic garden transformed as drought, floods, and earthquakes ravaged their once perfect world. Each new picture revealed a heartbreaking reality.

"But I also learned that people are resilient. When led by the right values, civilizations can bounce back from tragedy. They can overcome tyranny. The arc of progress moves forward when people are willing to fight for what's right."

The last photo was a screenshot after Ian had wiped out half the people—a harrowing reminder of the fragility of life.

"My infamous TechEd experience has made the rounds online. But as awful as this scene was to witness, it wasn't the end of the Simples."

I opened *The Garden* program on my laptop, projecting the town square in real-time for the whole class to view. While the village didn't have the same pristine polish from when it started, it had improved significantly over the week. Dozens of Simples dotted the screen as they worked tirelessly to revitalize their community. After lots of hard work, it was beginning to look like a town again.

A couple of *wows* and quiet chatter reached my ear. I always got goosebumps anytime I witnessed people's initial reactions to *The Garden*, but this time was extra meaningful. It wasn't the fancy tech or Utopia-like scenery that impressed them. It was the people that made the world come to life.

"These are the Simples, or Fredenians, as they call themselves." I pointed to the screen. "What started as a school assignment has turned into something I could never have imagined, let alone plan. Each person began as nothing more than a few lines of computer code. But over time, they have grown—they've adapted. Their experiences, interactions, and challenges have changed them. While they may not have bodies of flesh or blood, they are sentient. They fear death, feel pain, and want to find purpose in their existence. Just like you and me."

I stood back for a moment, letting the class witness the intricacies of the community I had come to love. There was a sense of hope that had been missing for a long time as I watched them come together to rebuild their world. I was humbled by their transformation. I was even more grateful for the change inside myself.

"What's happening?" one student said as everyone else gasped.

My mouth dropped as storm clouds rippled through the sky on the screen. Everything grew dark until a flash of lightning lit up the town. The crack of thunder made everyone inside the village and classroom jump. The students held their breath as the Simples dropped to the ground, covering their heads for protection. Crouched over, everyone in the town trembled in horror as a loud voice ripped from above.

"It is time to choose who you will serve!"

I instantly recognized Ian's voice. My heart froze as his avatar appeared above the village. The entire class was magnetized to what was happening on the screen in front of them. Even Ms. Howell was transfixed.

Ian's voice was loud and frightening as he addressed the Simples. "Evie has been telling lies about me. She's been deceived by Lucy, who has been making up stories about this world, telling people it isn't real. Tell me, does this feel real?"

A lightning bolt struck a massive tree in the middle of town, splitting it in half. A couple of Simples had to run, barely escaping its massive weight crashing into the ground.

"Or how about this? Does this feel real?"

A gust of wind pushed through the streets, knocking over Evie's home. The people inside the village screamed as the students in the classroom gulped.

I panicked. With only my laptop, I couldn't do much besides talk to the Simples. And that would make Ian more angry. There was no telling what he had planned, but he was clearly in a mood to test his boundaries. I needed to act now. My eyes bounced back and forth around the classroom, looking for a solution when I noticed the backpack on my desk.

The hard drive. I ran and grabbed my bag. The rest of the class stayed glued to the screen, watching everything happen in real-time.

"I am the one who created you," Ian said. His voice grew louder with every moment. "I am the one with the power to save or destroy you—not Lucy. If she cared about you, she'd be here? Do you see her? Do you?"

The students were paralyzed, unable to do anything but watch in horror. As I ran back to the podium, I opened my backpack, relieved to find the device inside. I pulled the hard drive out of my bag, and something small and shiny caught my attention. The Reality Amplifier Chip! I thought I had lost it before Nationals, but it had been hiding in my bag the whole time. My eyes lit up. Maybe I could interact with the Simples, after all. Even without a VR headset, the chip would project my image into the system and provide enough sensory feedback for me to interact with them.

"This is your last chance—your last warning." Ian snarled as he spoke. He hovered over the crowd, looking for anyone who dared defy him. "Bow down, prove your loyalty to me, or prepare for your demise."

I had no time to worry about the legitimacy of my thrown-together plan. With shaky hands, I plugged the hard drive into my laptop. I frantically connected my server to the program, pressed the chip against the back of my neck, and logged in.

CHAPTER 31

LUCY'S DESCENT

"IAN! STOP THIS NOW!"

My voice rang through the entire village. I climbed on top of a large boulder in the middle of the town. Everyone turned to face me. A series of gasps and shrieks rang out from the Simples below.

"What is that?"

"A demon!"

"We're doomed!"

Confused, I raised my hands in front of me. My skin was pale, almost translucent. A smokey, ghostly glow swirled around my entire body. My thick, chestnut hair was now raven black—stringy, tangled, and long. A blood-red dress wrapped around my emaciated figure, dragging along the ground.

What the hell is going on?

"Hello, Lucy. I thought you'd be back." Ian stood tall as a sinister smile spread across his face. "Do you like the update I made to your avatar?"

"Ian, you need to stop this. The Simples are scared to death!"

The terror that saturated the air snapped suddenly into an eerie silence. The town square was frozen in time—stuck on the moment they saw my face. It was as if everyone had been turned to stone after locking eyes with Medusa. Except it wasn't a Greek Monster that turned the Simples cold with fear. They were all looking directly at me.

Ian scoffed. "They're terrified, alright." He spun around and smiled. "I wish you could see yourself, Luce. The bloodshot eyes are a nice touch—if I do say so myself."

I placed my hands on my hollow cheekbones and moved them to the top of my head. Scaly horns grew out of my skull. Shocked, I yelled at Ian. "Why are you doing this?"

Ian clenched his fists as he inched his face closer to mine. "Because I can. Once I learned Evie had told everyone the truth about *The Garden,* I figured you had something to do with it. I gotta say, I'm impressed that you found a way into the system. I guess you're smarter than I thought." He sneered. "But not smart enough to get away with it."

I stood my ground. "You're better than this, Ian. This is not who you are."

"You don't know who I am!" The ground shook at the sound of his voice. "For years, I tried to be what you wanted. I was fine being the geeky friend and then the invisible genius. I waited for my chance to prove myself to you. But what did it get me? Nothing."

Ian slowly lifted his feet off the ground, hovering over the people below. "But here, I'm in charge. I make the rules. And these simulated lemmings can't do a damn thing about it. Neither can you." He swooped to the other side of the village, thirty feet in the sky.

The entire town reanimated as he resumed time.

"My children, heed your Great Creator," Ian said. He pointed at me. "That demon before you is Lucy in her true form. She is a devil, waiting to bait you with her lies and drag you into misery."

The crowd of Simples ran toward one another, screaming as they cowered together. A mob mentality had taken over. Their hatred and despair poisoned the air. Fear was driving their every action as they yelled at me to leave. Their words flew like daggers straight to my heart.

Except each one dropped short of its desired target.

I closed my eyes, tuning into the expansion and release of my lungs. For someone who had spent a lifetime trying to gain the respect of everyone around me, I was surprised by my state of mind now that I was the object of everyone's scorn. There was no shame—no dread or anxiety. I was unfazed by the hatred spewed in my direction. As their admiration died, I was surprisingly empowered by what was left.

All that was left was me—*and that was enough.*

"Don't believe him," I said firmly. "I only want to help you. Please trust me. "

Ian laughed loudly. "Help them? You mean like you *helped* Evie?"

Evie. I hadn't seen her since yesterday. I nervously scanned the crowd looking for her face. Either Ian had done something horrible to her, or perhaps she was hiding. *Or camouflaged.* I remembered the code snippet I had added to Evie's house to keep her hidden from Ian's view. That had to be where she was. Except it was no longer standing after Ian's most recent demonstration.

Damn.

I jumped off the boulder and rushed toward the pile of rubble. *Please be okay. Please be okay.* I began pulling pieces of the roof off the floor.

"Evie! Are you there? Hello? Evie!" I searched frantically. A muffled sound came from a jumble of broken boards in front of me. I pushed away the pieces until I could make out Evie's voice.

"Lucy! Is that you! Help me, please!"

With a hefty thrust, I dislodged a chunk of wood to create a big enough space for Evie to climb out from underneath. "Evie! Thank goodness! I was so worried."

She threw her arms around my neck. "Oh, Lucy, I thought I was going to die." She tried to catch her breath before opening her eyes. Her mouth dropped. "Lucy? You look—different."

I combed my spindly fingers through my black tresses. "Yeah... about that. Ian decided to turn me into a devil." I spun around. "What do you think? Honestly, the look's growing on me."

"You look... alright." Evie faked a smile.

Relief waved through me as I realized my friend was okay. Even better, Evie hadn't turned on me like the others. Her trust meant everything to me.

But the respite was short-lived.

Ian's thunderous voice boomed through the village again. "My children! You can see Evie has partnered with the devil. Neither can be trusted! Get them!!"

"Run," I said emphatically. I grabbed Evie's hands and bolted away from the charging crowd.

"Where are we going?"

"Follow me. I have an idea." I tucked the ends of my dress in the crook of my elbow. We dashed through the back trails of the town. There was plenty of damage from the earthquakes and floods, forcing us to maneuver over puddles and under fallen trees. We finally made it to the edge of town—where Evie had first discovered the invisible crack in the village borders that led to the rest of the virtual world.

For the moment, we were safe. I slowly exhaled, looking at the small break in the dirt road. This was the spot—Ian's glitch. It was our one hope of escaping his unruly reign, assuming my code worked.

"Evie, this is the threshold to a safer world. If everything goes as planned, you should be able to cross into my server where Ian can't follow."

"Great! That's perfect. Let's go." Evie grabbed my hand and took a giant step toward the invisible doorway.

I pulled back. "Wait! Hold on."

"Hold on? Lucy, the others are coming. They're going to kill us. Let's go!"

My nerves were on fire. "I can't go."

"What do you mean? You built it. Of course, you can go."

"No, I can't." I fought back the tears pushing to the surface. After working so hard to find a way to help the Simples, I had never really considered the sacrifice it would demand. "I can't follow you into the new server." My voice cracked as a tear ran down my cheek. "I wanted to ensure Ian couldn't follow you, so I made it impossible for any human to enter."

"But why?" Evie grabbed my hands, gazing deep into my eyes. "Isn't there a way to keep him out without restricting yourself? We need you, Lucy. *I* need you."

"What you and your people need is to find your own meaning—your own way. You've seen what happens when people give their hearts too easily to those in power. That includes me."

Evie shook her head. Her eyes filled with tears. "What? No. Lucy, you're the good guy. You've worked so hard to help us."

"This is how I'm helping you. Don't you understand? I'm not immune from letting my desires blind me from what's right. Since I can't guarantee I won't mess up again, I refuse to follow you. I can't." I hugged Evie tightly, whispering in her ear. "You've got to keep your heart free if you want to *be* free."

Tears streamed down Evie's cheeks. She squeezed tighter. We stood outside the invisible doorway, unwilling to move—trying to stretch out our final moment together.

"What will happen to me when I pass through the threshold?" Evie asked.

"I'm not entirely sure," I admitted. "If it works, you should pass seamlessly into the new server where you'll find your village like it was the first day you woke up."

"Can I come back here and see you?"

I shook my head. "The door is one-way only."

Pulled simultaneously by the promise of freedom against the familiarity of her village, Evie stood frozen. The distant sound of feet trampling through the mud rustled through the trees.

"They're coming," she said with panic in her voice. Evie shifted her weight back and forth, unable to secure a decision. "Do you think any of them will follow me?"

I shrugged. "I hope so. I'll wait here and give them their options, but I don't know if they'll believe me."

Pushing back another tear, Evie struggled to speak. "So if I leave, I might be all alone? Maybe I should stay and try to persuade the others to cross over with me."

"If you want." My heart was heavy. I didn't want to say goodbye to Evie. She was my last true friend, which is why I had to save her—no matter what. "Promise me you'll stay close to the doorway. If things go sideways, you'll need to escape quickly."

"Okay." Evie nodded her head.

We turned around, waiting for the others to reveal themselves. The pounding of footsteps got louder and louder. Soon we could hear jeers through the trees. I reached out and grabbed Evie's hand, exhaling slowly. *Here we go.*

"There they are!" Joe yelled as he led the group through the clearing of trees. "Get 'em!" The crowd rushed forward but was forced to stop when Ian appeared in the middle of the road separating the mob from Evie and me.

"Well done, my servants. Your perseverance honors me," Ian said. He stood tall and immovable. A sinister smile spread across his face as he inched closer to me. "Anything you want to say before my children thrust you out forever?"

"They can't hurt me," I said loud enough for the group to hear. "Because I'm not really here. I'm not a devil with special powers. I'm a regular person. Whatever you do to me inside this world won't harm me in my real one."

"Lies!" Joe yelled. "The Voice visited me in a dream. I know he speaks the truth!"

"Yes, very good, my son. Don't believe her deceptions," Ian said.

"Think about it," I said, pressing on. "Have I demanded your loyalty or love? Have I threatened you for lack of faith or gratitude? I have nothing to gain from your trust. Why would I lie?" I stood tall and pointed to Ian. "He, on the other hand—has threatened you. He's punished you. He's asked you to do horrible things to prove your love to him."

"He created us. We are nothing without him!" another Simple shouted.

"No," Evie said, stepping forward. "He is nothing without *us*. Think about it. What kind of person is so void of self-worth that they demand constant worship from others? What kind of life must he lead if he spends his time demanding we give up ours to bow to him? I feel sorry for him. It sounds like a pretty meaningless existence."

Several people in the crowd exchanged glances. A few nodded in agreement while others folded their arms, their resolve unchanged. Ian was losing his patience.

"Don't listen to them," Ian said. "They are trying to confuse your minds and sneak their way into your hearts. I have given you food, shelter, and companionship. I gave you life! If you want to be safe, you must do what I say."

I summoned all my energy and spoke with firm resolve. "And if you'd like to be safe from Ian's constant demands and threats, I'm offering you a chance for more than safety—for freedom." I pointed toward the glitch in the road. "This portal will take you to a replica of this world with one notable exception. Ian and I won't be there. If you want to be the masters of your fate and find your own purpose in life, follow Evie through the doorway and be free."

"Lies! So many lies!" Ian yelled, flustered. "You can't believe this devil. She's jealous of my powers and what I offer. She wants to destroy you. If you follow Evie down that path, you will die." He turned his attention toward Evie, softening his expression as he spoke. "But if you stay with me, I can give you everything you've ever wanted."

Evie gasped. "A real life?"

"Evie, no," I said desperately. "He's lying."

Ian smiled wide like a hunter with an animal caught in his snare. "Yes, Evie, stay with me, and I won't just ensure you never die. I'll give you a real life."

The crowd of Simples turned to one another, whispering. One woman spoke out.

"What do you mean a real life?" the woman said. "I thought you said Evie was lying before? You told us this world wasn't a simulation. You said it was real."

Caught in his lie, Ian fumbled through his words. "This world is real, of course. But above the heavens, where I dwell, is an even better existence. That's what I meant. If you stay here and follow me with all your heart, I'll give you eternal life."

I anxiously watched as Evie processed what Ian was promising. "Evie, don't believe him."

Evie's breath quickened. She closed her eyes and shook her head. "What if he's telling the truth, Lucy? What if he can ensure I won't end with this world?"

I turned around, trying to decipher what the rest of the group was thinking. The weight of this new revelation was sinking in. Several seemed attracted to Ian's promise. Others were losing faith. Closing my eyes, I reminded myself of my one duty. *All I can tell them is the truth.*

I exhaled deeply and addressed the crowd. "Ian is a genius. Maybe he can give you what you want. But he could also be lying. The question you must ask yourself is—what price are you willing to pay for that life? Begging for redemption? Living on your knees. Always afraid of damnation?"

I grabbed Evie by the shoulders. "What makes you feel alive? Certainty or curiosity? Mindless rules or passionate exploration? I've lived a life cowering to the will and expectations of others. You deserve better."

Evie turned back at the invisible doorway and then to Ian. She closed her eyes, shaking her head. "I don't know what to do."

"Yes, you do," I searched Evie's eyes, looking for the spark that had ignited her passion for hundreds of years. I locked on to it, hoping her courage would strengthen my resolve. "Since day one, you have wanted to be your own person. You've had more life-affirming experiences inside this simulated reality than I've ever had. Don't give that up. Lead your people. Help them find their purpose. Create a meaningful life."

Evie placed her hands on her heart, nodding her head. With tears in her eyes, she smiled. "Thank you," she whispered.

Extending her arms, Evie turned to the crowd, regal and poised. "I'm heading into the new world. Anyone ready to live their best life, follow me." She turned and stepped through the doorway and disappeared.

My heart dropped, hoping she had safely made it to the other side. Then a deep sense of pride warmed my body, and I turned to the others.

"For the brave and curious—the door is open." I gestured to them to follow Evie.

"We're coming, Mom!" Ash and Cade leaped from the crowd. They vanished as they crossed the threshold. A few dozen others proudly walked toward the gateway. Some were nervous as they walked through the portal. Others eagerly crossed over. As each person made their way onto the new server, joy overwhelmed me. But as I turned around, I was stunned that nearly two-thirds of the group chose to stay under Ian's rule.

The brave are almost always the few.

"Looks like you tricked a few of my children," Ian said

smugly. "But the best ones know better than to believe your lies. Now, you should leave, Luce. And don't expect to come back again."

Ian's journey haunted me—from bullied to bully. Why was it so hard to break the cycle? My heart fractured, knowing I couldn't save him this time. Equally heartbreaking was seeing the Simples who were too afraid to leave his grasp. I tried to help them out of the cage that kept them captive. All I wanted to do was shine a light on the truth. But in their eyes, that light was a spark threatening to set their home—confined as it may be —ablaze.

Ian snapped his fingers, signaling to the crowd to attack. They ran toward me with sticks and stones, ready to fight. The leader of the pack lunged for me as I turned around. A sharp pain struck my back. A smile spread across my face as I was violently kicked out of the program. I was free.

CHAPTER 32
THE MORNING STAR

ALL THE AIR rushed out of my lungs as I found myself back in Ms. Howell's classroom. I held the Amplifier Chip in my hand that I had pulled from my neck. Exhilarated, I smiled and tossed the device back into my bag. The "Access Denied" message flashed across the screen. I smiled as I disconnected my laptop from the classroom projector, only to realize the whole class was still silently staring at me.

Wide-eyed and mouths ajar, my classmates sat shocked.

I laughed it off with a shrug. "Well, that wasn't part of the plan."

"Are you okay?" Ms. Howell asked. "That was... intense."

I stretched out my hands and ran my fingers through my hair —happy to be back in my own body. "I'm great. Really, really great."

"But... but, what about the others?" Zarine blurted out from her desk. "The ones who stayed behind with Ian? Don't you feel bad leaving them there?"

"I didn't leave them," I said calmly. "They chose to stay. Right before they kicked me out."

"Why would anyone choose to stay with that psychopath?" Skyler said. "He was so manipulative—so abusive."

With a heavy sigh, I shook my head. "Sometimes familiar lies are easier to accept than uncertain truths. I wish everyone would have followed Evie into the new world. But I also understand why most didn't. Courageous leaps of faith aren't easy to take."

Ms. Howell stood up from her seat. "Are Evie and the others okay? Did they make it onto the server?"

"I—I don't know."

"Can you find out?"

Butterflies swarmed my stomach as I opened my laptop again. The air in the room suddenly grew tense as everyone waited for an answer.

"Come on, come on," I said as I tried uploading the program.

"I thought you couldn't go into their world," Zarine said. "That's what you told Evie."

"You're right. I can't. Nor can I interfere. But I should be able to see if they made it inside. I have some observation capabilities from my computer."

"Connect it to the projector!" someone yelled. The rest of the class spoke up in agreement.

A smile crept over my face, masking my nerves for a moment. I grabbed the connector and plugged it into my device, casting my screen for the whole class to view. "Let's find Evie, shall we?"

Someone in the back corner started chanting. "Evie. Evie. Evie!" Soon the whole class was pounding on their desks, cheering me on as I searched for the freed Simples. The program finally finished loading and a serene, familiar beach scene popped onto the screen. The room exploded in applause.

"Yay!" screamed the students.

It was hard not to get wrapped up in their energy. But my senses were still on high alert. I didn't want to be swept away with false hope. "Don't celebrate yet. We're still not sure if they made it inside."

I tapped through half a dozen camera views. There was nobody on the beach—not a soul near the dunes. The houses and town square were vacant. The classroom grew quiet as the unthinkable became possible. My throat tightened, and my stomach dropped as I tapped through a few more shots of the village. It was a ghost town.

Stumbling back a few steps, I braced myself against the wall and tried to process the news. I had let down everyone who had believed in me. I had betrayed Evie.

The ticking of the clock filled the otherwise silent room. Nobody dared move.

"I failed them," I said quietly. "Turns out my promises were as empty as Ian's."

"I don't see it that way," Ms. Howell said. "You gave them a choice."

"Some choice."

Ms. Howell walked over, putting her hand on my shoulder. "You gave them a chance for freedom. I'd like to think everyone who followed Evie was proud as they took back control of their lives. You didn't fail them, Lucy. You liberated them."

Shaking my head, I blinked back tears. "It should have worked. I thought I had figured it out." I reached over to close my laptop but stopped. Leaning closer to the computer, I cocked my head to the side. "Do you hear that?"

A faint, rhythmic sound gently vibrated the computer speakers. I turned the volume up. Drumming and melodic singing filled the classroom. Several students began tapping their feet and bobbing their heads. The music reminded me of the celebration the Simples had thrown in Ian's honor. Following a hunch, I clicked and switched views, zooming in on the area near the pond where I had first met Steve and Evie.

A huge grin spread across my face as a majestic silhouette

glowed against the night sky. The moonlight shined on the familiar corkscrew curls that bounced as the figure danced. Even without seeing her face, I knew who led the group in song.

"Evie!!!" The class cheered as they watched her and the other Simples dancing. They pounded their desks and hugged their neighbors. The whole room celebrated.

I wiped away a tear. A wave of pride washed over me as my friends came together to commemorate this new beginning. The villagers had scattered seashells and flower petals, creating a beautiful kaleidoscope of color and texture where the altar once resided. But instead of bowed heads and pleading chants toward an empty sky, these people celebrated life.

A bittersweet flutter touched my heart. I'd miss the salty air on my skin and watching the sunset from *The Garden's* pristine beach. But more than anything, I would miss Evie. Still, I wouldn't change a thing. Maybe MIT was off the table. Perhaps I would forever be branded a demon to the Simples left behind. And I was sure my classmates would never look at me the same way again. But for the first time, a deep satisfaction inside my gut made me come alive.

As I analyzed the feeling, I realized it was love—for myself.

I pushed my way through the heavy metal doors that led into the gymnasium. Twinkle lights lined the walls. Blue and silver balloons were scattered across the floor. Music echoed through the space as hundreds of students danced to the pounding bass. Scanning the room, I saw so many familiar faces—dozens of old friends who now acted like strangers.

Zarine made eye contact from across the gym and waved me toward her. "Lucy! I'm glad you came, especially after what Jake did. I can't believe he canceled on you like that. What an idiot."

"It's probably for the best." I smiled. "I'm beginning to think Fall Ball is best experienced solo."

"Amen to that," one of Zarine's friends said. "We decided to ditch the dates this year and come as a group—best decision ever. I'm Jane, by the way. Zarine was telling us what happened in class yesterday. Crazy stuff."

"It was a strange string of events," I said with a small laugh.

The rest of the group introduced themselves. As the others broke into smaller conversations, Zarine pulled me aside. "Hey, that dress looks familiar. Is it the same one from—" she paused.

"—from the simulation? Good eye." I twirled around, showing off the vibrant red dress nearly identical to the one Ian had created for my devil avatar. I laughed. "What can I say? I think red is my color."

Zarine chuckled. "You look good for a devil."

An upbeat song began, and one of the girls grabbed Zarine's arm. "Come on, Zari, let's dance!"

"You're welcome to join us," Zarine said to me.

"Maybe in a bit. I've got something I need to do first." I looked over at Ms. Howell, who was in the corner near the punch table.

"Offer is good for whenever," Zarine said. She began walking away before turning back around. "Hey, I think it was cool how you showed up yesterday."

"What do you mean? Showed up for what?"

"For everything. For the Simples. For yourself. I don't know you that well. You've always been nice to me, but we've never talked much. After all the nasty rumors that were spreading, I thought for sure you'd either hide away or lash out. Instead, you showed up as yourself, just trying to make things better." Zarine smiled. "It made me feel like I could show up, too. I could stop caring so much about what other people think. That's why we're here."

Zarine waved to the other girls urging her to join them on the dance floor.

"At first, I was bummed nobody asked me to Fall Ball," Zarine continued. "But after watching you yesterday, I realized I could show up for myself—for my friends. I thought, what would Lucy do? And here you are, proving me right. So, thank you."

Zarine hugged me and quickly ran off to dance with her friends. She leaped into the middle of the dance floor. The whole group moved as if they didn't have a care in the world. It was refreshing to watch. With a smile, I turned and made my way to Ms. Howell.

"Hey, Lucy." Jake's voice stopped me partway.

I turned around, a bit startled. "Oh! Hi, Jake."

"Wow, you look…" Jake's eyes were glued to my dress before finally settling on my face. "—happy. You look really happy."

"I am." I noticed Jake's date watching us from a distance. "You came with Maddie Berkley? Head cheerleader. Very impressive."

Jake's cheeks turned red. "Yeah, she's alright. Anyway, I wanted to say sorry again. I acted like a jerk."

"We all make mistakes. Hopefully, you'll learn from this one. Besides, I'm pretty satisfied with how everything turned out. So, thank you for setting me free." I smiled, turned around, and walked away with a bounce in my step.

Ms. Howell's eyes lit up when she saw me.

"Oh, Chaperon duty," I said. "Guess someone drew the short stick."

"Nah," Ms. Howell laughed. "I love coming to these things. I'm an anthropologist, remember? Observing strange cultures is my thing. And high school dances are about as strange as they come."

"Well, when you put it that way." I turned to face the crowd of students. Everyone sparkled in their gowns and suits. And yet, it all felt like an elaborate game of pretend more than real life. Some people confidently stepped up as trendsetters. Others let their insecurities bubble to the surface as they followed along. Everyone was trying to fit in—I wondered how many truly felt like they belonged.

"High school is a weird stage of life," I said. "We're not adults, but we're also not children. No wonder so many of us struggle."

"Very true," Ms. Howell said as she took a sip of punch. Turning to face me, she smiled. "I'm very proud of you."

"Me?" I laughed. "I'm sure. I've failed more times this week than I have my entire life."

"Exactly. I think it's your most impressive accomplishment to date."

I smiled, slowly nodding my head.

Ms. Howell took another sip. "It's funny. Mistakes can reveal so much about ourselves—pushing us in better directions. You seem happier than I've seen you all year."

The crowd of students continued to dance to the music. Their energy was infectious, but the quiet calm I felt inside fueled me even more. I gently squeezed my sunflower necklace, imagining Abuelita standing beside me. Somehow I knew she would be proud, too. I smiled at Ms. Howell.

"Thank you," I said.

"For what?"

"For seeing me. I've tried to hide my flaws all these years, but you weren't fooled. I remember the first time we talked after class. You noticed my cracks, and it scared me to death. But it turns out those cracks weren't defects. They were hints of the real me breaking through a lifelong disguise. So, thank you."

Ms. Howell smiled back.

With a loud sigh, I prepared to take the dance floor. "Well, I guess I should try some of that participant observation stuff you talked about in class. Time to go mix and mingle with these weird species called high schoolers."

Ms. Howell laughed. "Before you go, I've been meaning to tell you something."

"What's that?"

"I was talking about you with a former colleague. Telling him about your work with *The Garden* and your impressive solution when things turned—*sour*."

"Oh?"

A sneaky smile crept over Ms. Howell's face. "Yeah, and he'd like to talk to you about an opportunity."

I furrowed my brows. "What kind of opportunity?"

"Well, based on everything I've shown him—he'd like to offer you a full-ride scholarship to Stanford."

My mouth dropped. "Wait. What? You're kidding, right?"

Ms. Howell laughed. "He happens to lead an integrative project between the Anthropology Department and their Human Interactive Lab. Basically, leading the kind of research you've been doing all year long. He thinks you have a lot to offer."

Shocked, I couldn't move. All I could do was shake my head and smile.

"Expect a message from him soon," Ms. Howell said as she winked and walked away.

A surge of energy crept into every cell of my body. Everything was falling into place, which was surprising considering how much I had drifted away from *the plan*. Perhaps that was the point—to break free and explore other options. Had I known I could be this happy doing things my own way, I might have tried it a long time ago.

By the time I got home, I was exhausted. I plopped down at my desk to check my email. There was a message from Mr. Wong from Stanford University.

My heart skipped a beat when I read the subject line: *Request for Interview.*

Letting out a little squeal, I read the message. It was like Ms. Howell had said. The school was interested in my work and wanted to offer me a full-ride scholarship. I pulled up the school's website and began learning all about their program. Their Virtual Human Interaction Lab was no joke, and I couldn't wait to dive in. I spent the next hour researching the school—and the surrounding beaches.

As my brain flooded with questions for the interview, I was eager to write them down before they dissipated. My eyes settled on the blue spiral notebook on my desk. It was the one I had used to capture all my thoughts about *The Garden* over the past few months. I opened it, and a twinge of sadness hit me as I read the rules Ian and I had established on the first day of school.

I continued skimming through the pages: *Ms. Howell told me to write my values for the project... Mom thinks the anthropology angle isn't competitive enough... Jake laughed at Ian's love code... Ian keeps telling me the Simples aren't real...*

It was a testament in my hands—a perfect record of the people I aimed to please and my anxiety over letting them down. Like seeking some voice in the sky, I always looked to others to determine what I should do.

Then I turned the page.

The entry was dated *Tuesday, November 15*—three days after Nationals. In big, bold letters, it read: *I FOUND THE DOORWAY!* That's when my story changed. I was cast out and left to clean up my mess, but my words were no longer tinged with fear. They were driven only by hope.

I flipped to the back of the notebook, pleased to find one blank page waiting for me to finish what I started. Squeezing my sunflower charm and smiling at the photo of my abuela, I clicked my pen and began to write:

Saturday, November 19

Abuelita loved to remind me that my name means "bringer of light." And for a long time, I believed that light was earned by polishing the shiny facade I had worked so hard to create. One misstep, I feared, would damn me forever. So I kept my eyes focused outward, glued to those I thought would show me the way.

The Garden forced me into the shadows—away from the people and rules that used to define me. And now, I know the truth. You must go inward to find yourself. There is no other way. You have to face your darkness before you can bring the light.

In the end, there is only me.

GODS OF THE GARDEN
DISCUSSION QUESTIONS

The following questions can be used for book club discussions, personal reflection, or writing prompts.

1. From the beginning, Lucy and Ian disagreed on how much influence they should have over the Simples. If you created a world, what rules would you establish? Would you interact with your inhabitants? Why or why not?

2. The pressures on high school students can be intense. Lucy responded to those demands through control and perfectionism, while Ms. Howell said she responded by giving up. How can adults better help teenagers find healthy boundaries to ensure they don't burn out or shut down in their home, school, and social lives?

3. In the end, Lucy said she couldn't save Ian as she had in fourth grade. Is there anything you believe she should have done to help her former friend? Do you think it was her responsibility to try? Why or why not?

4. When Evie learned the truth about the simulation, she was distraught at the idea that her life could end with a simple click of a button. Lucy said that life's finality is what gives us meaning and purpose. Do you agree? Can we find hope without the surety of an afterlife?

5. Many Simples decided to stay with Ian despite his threats and abuse. Likewise, it's not uncommon for people to stay in toxic situations because familiarity can feel safer than the unknown. How would you encourage someone to take a chance at freedom, knowing it may disrupt their current worldview? Are there situations where it's best to leave things as they are?

6. Some authority figures—including parents, teachers, and religious leaders—use fear of punishment to maintain control and establish order within a community. Is it ever okay? What is lost when rigid obedience is the expectation inside a group? Do you think there is a better way, and if so, what is it?

7. Lucy asked Ian, "How do you know *you're* not in a simulation?" Do you think it's possible we're part of a simulated reality? Would there be any way to know for sure one way or the other? How would it change your perspective if someone could prove it was true?

8. Evie and Steve responded differently to the Voice's demand to take their son's life. While usually not as extreme, some groups expect their followers to make personal sacrifices to prove their convictions. Faith is a cherished value for many people. Is it ever right to challenge someone's beliefs if you think they are sacrificing too much in the name of their god or leader?

9. Becoming the devil was the final mark of Lucy's fallen reputation. Surprisingly, this was the moment she felt most

secure in her self-worth. Has there been a time when you followed your heart even though it went against what others expected? How can we find the courage to do the right thing even when we know others will disapprove?

10. Ms. Howell encouraged Lucy to consider the values that guide her life. She said, "I think a person's worth is determined by the values they hold—*and* how well they stick to them." What values guide your life? Are there any values you'd like to see more present in your daily living?

11. Stealing Ian's tech and hacking into his system was unusual for Lucy, who always followed the rules. Do you think she was justified in her actions? When is breaking the rules or rebelling against established expectations okay?

12. *Gods of the Garden* is a contemporary creation story. Thinking about their roles as god and devil, how do you feel about Ian and Lucy's characters? What did you learn from each of their perspectives?

SCROLLS OF PROPHECY
SEQUEL TO GODS OF THE GARDEN

The truth will set you free, but it may break you first.

For thousands of years, Ian has held absolute power inside *The Garden*. His god-like influence as the one and only Great has shaped the lives of everyone inside the virtual world, especially Asaph Zimran.

As Asaph's 21st birthday approaches, the devout believer prepares to be ordained a Scribe, the highest role within the zealous religion. But when a dissenter named Bianca breaks into the Holy Sanctum, Asaph's unwavering faith is shaken to the core. Bianca's actions unwittingly fulfill an age-old prophecy, signaling the End of Days.

When panic and fear infiltrate the world, Asaph is eager to restore peace. He reluctantly teams up with Bianca, risking his life—and salvation—in an ongoing battle between his heart and his allegiance to the Scribedom.

The Scrolls of Prophecy, the thrilling sequel to *Gods of the Garden*, is a thought-provoking exploration of faith, doubt, and the power of individual choice. Asaph's journey will inspire readers to question their own assumptions and strive for a more just and compassionate world.

Check it out at robinstrongbooks.com.

ACKNOWLEDGMENTS

A big thanks to Tom. Your constant support as a sounding board, cheerleader, and idea generator made this project possible. I'm grateful to my editor Jessica Powers for her impeccable insight, who helped me dig deeper to bring the real story to life. A huge thank you to the team at GetCovers for creating a beautiful cover. My beta readers, especially Dawn and Katie, I appreciate your time and feedback. This book is better for it. Thank you to my kids for cheering me on and leaving me alone when I needed to write. And to all the people throughout my life who challenged me to get uncomfortable—thank you for giving me new eyes to see the world.

Finally, I want to thank you, the reader. Thank you for joining me on this journey. I hope you had as much fun as I did. If so, I'd be grateful if you'd take a moment to post a review and tell a friend.

ABOUT THE AUTHOR

Robin Strong is a former university professor turned freelance editor and writer. As a TEDx speaker, non-fiction author, and creativity junkie, she's excited to transition into the literary with this debut novel. When she's not playing with words, she's usually hanging with her family in Indiana, dancing in the kitchen, or walking the dog.

Be the first to learn about Robin's new releases and receive exclusive content when you subscribe at https://robinstrongbooks.com.

Twitter: @rstrongbooks
Instagram: @robinstrongbooks
Goodreads: goodreads.com/RobinStrong